THORNTON BROTHERS

BOOK THREE

Taken

SABRE ROSE

ISBN: 1718654553
ISBN-13: 978-1718654556

1

TYLER

The numbers on the speedometer crept higher. I knew I needed to back off, reduce my speed, but there was an urgency in my chest that made my foot heavy. Screw the speedometer. Screw the pelting rain.

I needed to see her.

She had left the hotel abruptly. One minute she was standing in the middle of the room, her gaze caught between my brother and me, and the next she fled the room like she was fucking Cinderella.

I started after her, but I was met by Gabe's fist. I should have seen it coming. The wild, drunk look in his eyes was a dead giveaway, but I was too busy worrying about Lauren to notice as he stormed across the room. His first blow smacked into my cheekbone, but the next I caught easily, thanks to the amount of alcohol in his system, and twisted his fist behind his back, bending him to his knees in the middle of the room. My intention was to keep it quiet, guide him away from prying eyes, but Gabe had other ideas. He let out a gush of expletives, calling me every name under the sun. His free fist flayed through the air, trying to connect with any part of my body he could, but I held him down, waiting until

Jake approached and helped me lead him from the room. The look of disdain on Dad's face was palpable, but he hid it behind a clenched jaw as he strode across the room and dragged me away to talk business with some guy with skin tanned by money, laughing it off as sibling rivalry. Right then, I didn't care what Mr Atterton thought of the casino, or whether he was interested in investing, I only wanted to go after her. But Dad relied on my forced charm to win people like Mr Atterton over. Charm. It was a curse and a blessing. And it was all fake. I could turn it on like a switch. There one minute. Gone the next. I learned from the best.

While I was stuck stroking the ego of the over-tanned and under-wrinkled Mr Atterton, Gabe walked out the door after her. I wanted to tear after him. I wanted to yell at him that she was mine now and he needed to leave well enough alone. But duty called.

When the last of the guests dripped out the door in the early hours of the morning, I immediately called, but her phone was off. I didn't leave any messages. I didn't know what to say. How did you ask the woman you loved to choose you over your own brother in a voicemail?

The next flight I could book wouldn't land me in her hometown for another ten hours, so I threw off my jacket and tie, hopped into the car and drove. The GPS told me it would take six hours to get there. The speed I was driving, I would have probably done it in five. That was until lights flashed behind me.

Cursing, I pulled over to the side of the road, smoothing my hair and plastering on a smile that could convince people to sell their souls.

"Officer." I nodded as the window rolled into the door frame.

"Do you know what speed you were doing?" The policeman peered through the window, ignoring the rain soaking his uniform and trying to make out my features in the dim morning light. I was hoping for some sort of recognition, but he just stared at me blankly. He wasn't from the city. He didn't have a clue who I was. This was going to be harder than I thought. I considered my options. I could try to charm my way out of it, or go with the truth. Tell him I was on my way to see a woman, the only woman who had piqued my interest in years, and I was afraid she was lying in my brother's arms right now. But instead, I simply grunted at him to hurry up. I didn't want to waste my time.

I didn't even glance at the ticket when he handed it through the car window. I tossed it onto the backseat and pulled back onto the road, eager to be on my way.

The first time I was introduced to Lauren Greer, her hand was firmly clasped in Gabe's, a wild and carefree smile danced across her face, and her cheeks were flushed with passion. When her eyes locked with mine, insane jealousy bolted through my system like a shock wave. It was purely physical and I'm still not sure what elicited such a strong and immediate reaction. It had never happened before. Ever. I wanted to rip her away from Gabe. I wanted to throw her over my shoulder like some fucking caveman. Instead, I stood mute and watched the colour creep up her cheeks. She stood on the second step of the stairs, her body positioned slightly behind Gabe's, staring back at me like a frightened deer from a tumble of divinely messy hair. Well, that's what I thought until I stepped forward and shook her hand. She met my gaze almost defiantly, chin slightly raised, eyes challenging.

And that's when I knew I was done for. By the tilt of her chin and the fire in her eyes, she would be forever stuck in my mind. Trapped there like the lyrics to a song I couldn't forget.

Suddenly, it didn't matter that her hand was in my brother's. I wanted it to be in mine. As she moved past me, the flash of her pale skin caught my eye. Her back was completely exposed, the zip of her dress resting on the curve of her backside. It both excited and pained me. Excited by the sight, pained by the reason it was there. Before I could stop myself, I reached out and took her hand. She froze. Electricity bolted through that touch and I wanted to run my fingers up her arm, wind my hand around the back of her neck and pull her to me, crushing her mouth against mine. But I contented myself by moving behind her, taking in the flush of her bare skin, the gentle swell of her hips, the dimples that peeked through the split in the dark fabric of her dress, the careless hair that fell in a cascade down her back.

It was a cruel and unusual punishment watching them together. At first, I tried to resist, but I was a moth drawn to the flame even while knowing it would burn. I tried to extinguish it with alcohol, tried to wash away the thoughts of her with whiskey, but she found me and I couldn't look away. I couldn't stop the thoughts that tumbled through my head. Confusing thoughts. Conflicting thoughts. Thoughts of our bodies tangled together on dark sheets. Thoughts of her lips on mine, even as she pressed them to Gabe's.

It was sickening.

Still, when Dad asked about a photographer, I basically leapt at the chance to spend time with her, even though it was torture. Even the way she staged her photos drew me to her. The splash of mess she inserted was like a splatter of colour on a black and white image. Poised and staged, but hinting at an untamed wildness that I was desperate to explore.

I wanted to look away when Gabe, drunk and stupid, carelessly fumbled, groping and pawing at her as she tried to push away. Even though he was my brother, I wanted to throttle him. I wanted to gather her in my arms and take her away. But I had to placate myself with simply stopping him. Every muscle in my body twitched to do more. I couldn't understand what she saw in him.

She was blinded by his angelic smile and failed to see him for the irresponsible idiot he was.

I battled with myself over the next few months. She wasn't mine. She was loyal to Gabe. I should have left her alone, but I couldn't. I was inexplicably drawn to her. I wanted her. I needed her. And the thing that got me the most was I knew she wanted me too. Every time our eyes met, I could see it. The way she glanced at me when she thought no one was looking. The way her body froze at my slightest touch. The way she melted when our lips finally met. I had to have her.

Then I did and it was heaven.

It was pain and pleasure. And now she was probably with him again and the thought of it was driving me insane.

When I finally neared the outskirts of her town, I spoke to my phone, telling it to call my assistant, Sadie. Her voice was croaky and blurred with sleep when she answered.

"I need you to get an address for me," I said.

"Tyler?" There was rummaging in the background and I imagined her searching for her glasses, pushing them up the bridge of her nose, staring at the numbers on the screen. "What the fuck are you doing calling me at this time? It's fucking seven o'clock in the fucking morning. You know I like to sleep in over the weekend."

"Sadie," I said gruffly, though too amused by her colourful language to be properly annoyed. "I need this address."

"Alright, alright, keep your knickers on. Whose address do you need?"

"Lauren Greer's."

"The photographer's?"

"Yes," I replied tersely.

"The photographer who's dating your brother?"

"Are you going to get me the address or not? It should be on her employment record."

"It's company policy not to give—"

My patience was wearing thin. "Sadie!"

"Okay, okay." A muffled scuffle sounded in my ear and then the clicking of keys on a keyboard.

"The street is called—"

"I know the street," I said impatiently. "I just need the number."

The line fell silent and I wondered if I had pushed Sadie too far. We had known each other for years. Sadie knew my moods, she knew me, and she was one of the few people I counted as a friend. Finally, I heard her sigh. "There is none."

"None?" I repeated.

"None."

"How can there be no street number on her address?"

"I don't fucking know, Ty. It's just not here."

"Fuck," I cursed.

"Ty?" Sadie said hesitantly. "Do you really think you should be doing this?"

"It's too late not to."

"Just remember the meeting—"

I ended the call and turned onto Lauren's street. The street lights were still on, their timers adjusted for the winter, and pools of light cut the wet road into patches. I didn't even know what sort of car she drove and the only person who I knew that could tell me where she lived was Gabe. That was not happening.

Barely able to see through the rain falling in sheets, I pulled over to the side of the road and started to walk up and down the footpath, scanning each house for any sign of her. As the rain soaked my shirt, it struck me how ridiculous this was. I was wandering the streets like a discarded lover, desperate for a glimpse of the woman he loved. But flashes of the night before kept running through my mind.

Her warm eyes gazing at me with a mix of desire and guilt. The feel of her legs wrapped around my waist as I carried her to the bedroom. Her silky flesh under my tongue. Her breasts, round and full, spilling between my fingers. The taste of her. The smell of her. The feel of her.

Her.

I wanted to do everything and nothing. I wanted to devour her, yet leave her untouched. She made me forget everything yet remember it all. She was purity and sin. Both Eve and Lilith.

And then I saw her. It was just a glimpse, a flash through a rain-streaked kitchen window. Her hair was piled messily on the top of her head. She wore a loose t-shirt and baggy sweatpants, but she had never looked so beautiful. I stopped and just watched for a moment. She didn't notice me as she walked to the sink and filled the kettle, her lip caught between her teeth. It was such an exquisitely simple action, but it was one I wanted to watch over and over, simply because it was her performing it.

And she was alone. There was no Gabe lurking in the background, no arms clamped around her waist. My body slumped with relief.

Despite my reputation, most of which was carefully crafted, I hadn't properly dated since university. I took dates to functions. I occasionally slept with said dates, but ultimately I was a loner, attached only to my work. I relished routine and order. I thrived on independence and freedom.

But I was about to change all that for her.

2

LAUREN

"Can I come in?"

Tyler stood at the door as a wet dream. His white shirt clung deliciously to his toned body, his wet and mussed hair hung in threads over his eyes and trails of rain weaved through his stubble.

"Please?" he asked when I didn't answer. I stepped away from the door, allowing him inside. Puddles of moisture formed under his feet as he scanned the lounge. "I thought he might be here."

"Who?"

"Gabe."

"He's not. I haven't seen him since last night."

"He didn't follow you?"

I shook my head, restraining myself from reaching out to touch him, from feeling his stubble under my fingers, from pressing my lips to his and licking away the droplets of rain. As if sensing my thoughts, Tyler ran his tongue over his lip, catching the drips that I desperately wanted to. But instead of reaching out to touch him, I crossed my arms over my chest, holding them in place, telling myself I needed to resist the urge before I embarrassed myself.

"What are you doing here?"

Tyler's eyes dropped to the floor. "Have you got a towel or something?"

As soon as I walked into the hall, I leaned against the wall, allowing myself a few deep breaths before facing him again. What was he doing here? Did he regret last night already? Had he come to tell me it was a one-time thing and he couldn't do this to Gabe after all? Part of me regretted falling into bed with him so easily. I never intended to. I intended on completing the work I was contracted to do and then walking away from the Thornton brothers and never looking back. But then last night happened and I found myself in Tyler's arms, his mouth on my skin, and I wished I could stay there.

Pulling myself from the wall, I grabbed a towel from the cupboard, tossing it to Tyler as I passed him and walked into the kitchen. He followed, running the towel through his hair, the result ending up haphazardly wild and undeniably sexy. He ran the towel over himself, causing the blush of his flesh to seep through the transparent material. I tried not to watch. I tried not to lock my eyes on the way his shoulders dipped, the way his chest swelled, but it was near on impossible.

Tyler shifted uncomfortably. He was nervous. I had never seen Tyler Thornton nervous before. I thought it an impossibility. But he stood before me, shifting his weight uneasily, glancing up at me hesitantly.

I leaned back against the kitchen counter and reached across to flick on the kettle again. "Do you want a coffee?"

Tyler's cell phone rang and he fished it out of his pocket, looked at the screen and then silenced it. "Coffee would be great. Black. Straight."

As I turned to reach for the plunger, I could feel Tyler's eyes on me and I regretted my fashion choice. Sweatpants and a t-shirt was hardly the most flattering of outfits.

Tyler cleared his throat, started to speak, stopped, and then started again. "I need to know what you are thinking."

His nervousness empowered me. I leaned against the counter again, crossing my arms back over my chest, aware of the way it emphasised my breasts, aware of the way Tyler's gaze slipped and his Adam's apple bobbed up and down.

"About what?" I asked.

Tyler ran his hand through his hair, flattening some of the strands that were poking into the air. I enjoyed seeing him like this. He was usually so calm, so controlled, but now, standing in my kitchen, his eyes held a desperation and uncertainty I was unfamiliar with.

"About us. About you and me. Do you regret it?" He took a step towards me, reached out, then thought the better of it and stepped back. His motions were fluid but undecided.

Thoughts of Gabe, of the look of horror on Billie's face when she realised what was happening, rushed through my mind. I didn't know how to answer. Did I regret the way he made me feel? No. Did I regret the pain I saw in Gabe's eyes? Yes.

"I don't know. Maybe?" I offered finally.

Tyler ran his hand over his face as though trying to scrub away the worry plastered there. "I can't do maybe," he said.

The kettle whistled and I filled the plunger, watching the grinds of coffee float until they stained the water.

"I'm not that sort of a guy. I'm all or nothing, Lauren. You're all mine or not at all."

I tried to deny the thrill that shuddered through me at those words. Tyler was too intoxicating. He addled my brain. I needed distance to think. I pushed the plunger down and stood with my back to him. Footfall sounded across the wooden floor. Tyler's hand brushed my hair to the side, leaving my neck exposed and vulnerable. His lips were hot and soft when they pressed into the tender flesh. I closed my eyes, breathing in deeply as the sensation of his mouth on my skin sent tendrils of desire to the parts of me I wanted to ignore.

I stepped away. "Tyler."

The hesitation of his gaze was gone, replaced with scorching hunger. He stepped forward, caging me against the counter. "Lauren," he growled.

I moved, sidestepping his advance. "I can't think when you're this close."

Indecision danced in his eyes. He adjusted the visible bulge in his pants. "What do you need from me?"

I laughed. "Not to be Gabe's brother."

"And that's your only hesitation? Gabe?"

"Yes." I shook my head. "No. Maybe. I don't know, Tyler. I feel like I barely know you. My brain is scattered when I'm around you. I don't think clearly. I don't think about what happens next. I only think of now. That's not who I am. It's not who I want to be."

"But do you want to know me?" He smirked then, the old Tyler, the confident Tyler returning with force. "I mean in more than just the carnal sense. Because that's what I want too, Lauren. I don't want to sneak about behind my family's back to see you. I want you on my arm for all the world to see, and I want to be on yours and for you not to be ashamed that I'm there."

I pushed the plunger down, forcing the grinds of coffee into submission. Ashamed is not a word I could use in relation to Tyler. No one would be ashamed to have him at their side. I poured the thick liquid into a mug and held it out to Tyler as though it were a shield between us.

He placed it on the counter, removing the barrier, and stepped close to me once again. "Do you want me, Lauren?"

"Wanting something and knowing what is good for you aren't always the same thing."

Tyler leaned back, resting against the bench and picked up the mug of coffee, bringing it to his lips. "Ask me something," he said. "Ask me anything. I will answer anything you want to know. I'm an open book. Get to know me."

"It's not that simple."

"Why can't it be?"

"It's—" I struggled to find the right words. How could I explain to this man that I wanted him more than I had ever wanted a man in my entire life? My insides were literally quivering as he stood there, dark eyes locked on mine with a lust I desperately wanted to quench, but, at the same time, I was scared. I was scared of hurting Gabe. Scared of the intensity of my feelings. Scared I would get lost in him. "It's just that Gabe—"

Tyler let out a frustrated gush of air. "Stop thinking about him. Stop thinking about how it will affect my family or how it will look to others. Just tell me how you feel. I can see it in your eyes, Lauren. We are meant to be together and I am damned if I'm going to let my little brother ruin that." He reached out and took my hand, tugging on it gently. "Come," he said. "Sit."

I sat beside him on the couch, knees pressed together and tentative as he relaxed beside me, his ankle hooked over the opposite knee.

"Let's start with something easy. Cats or dogs?" he asked.

"Excuse me?"

Tyler shrugged and took a sip of his coffee, running his tongue over his lips once he had swallowed. The sight was enough for me to squeeze my knees closer together. Tyler noticed and ran a finger over his bottom lip, rubbing it roughly, toying with my hormones. It was cruel the way he played with me.

"Are you a cat person or a dog person?"

Smudge entered my mind and I wondered where he was. It wasn't like him not to greet the stranger in his house. "Dog," I said firmly.

"See?" Tyler sat forward. "That wasn't so hard, was it? Now I know something about you that I didn't know before. I also prefer dogs over cats. Your turn."

I scooted back on the couch a little, adjusting myself, hooking my feet under my knees and twisting to face him a little more. "What's your favourite flavour of ice-cream?"

"Straight to the tough questions, huh?" Tyler rubbed his chin, feigning the thought-provoking nature of the question. "Cookies and Cream. You?"

"Vanilla."

"Plain old vanilla? I see I need to broaden your horizons." Tyler's voice was peppered with amusement. "Right. Next question. Would you rather be poor and happy or rich and miserable?"

"Can't I be rich and happy?"

Tyler shook his head. "That's not the question."

"It's a stupid question."

"Why?"

"Who would choose to be miserable?"

"Ask all the miserable rich people."

"Are you miserable?" I asked.

"Sometimes," he admitted. "It has nothing to do with wealth though, and you didn't answer the question."

"Happy," I said. "I would choose to be happy."

Tyler raised his coffee mug. "To happiness," he said. He took a large gulp, draining the contents and inched forward, resting his elbows on his knees. "You're not asking any questions."

"What do you do for fun?"

"For fun? I don't really do fun. I work. That's about it. Rather boring."

"I would hardly call that an answer. Surely there is something you enjoy doing in your downtime."

"Does working out count?"

"No."

"Playing cards? I host a monthly game of cards with some of the staff at the company. Does that count?"

"It will do."

Tyler's cell phone rang again. He sighed and looked at the screen, swiping to accept the call. "What?" he demanded, somewhat abruptly. "Yes, yes, I know. Cancel it. Yes. I know. Tomorrow. Reschedule for tomorrow. I'm a little caught up right now." He paused for a while, turning away slightly. "I know," he said forcefully. "Goodbye."

"What were you like as a child?" I asked.

"It was my turn," he insisted.

"I didn't know there were rules."

"There are always rules."

"Answer anyway."

Tyler smiled. "As you know, I am the eldest. Let's just say it held a certain level of responsibility that the others never knew. My father had high expectations of the firstborn."

"Do you regret it? Following in his footsteps."

Tyler shook his head, his knee jiggling. "I love my work. I love the challenge it brings. I wouldn't change it for anything. The expectations of my father I might change, but not my career."

"He certainly seems like he knows what he wants," I said.

"We Thornton men usually do."

I laughed. "I love how you talk about yourselves like that. Like you are a certain breed."

Tyler shrugged. "In a way, we are. Dad made certain of that. He was…" Tyler paused, searching for the right word. "Very demanding. Very sure of what he wanted and he went after it. He required the same of his children. I was the only one who took up the challenge. Jake pretty much ran away from it. And Clark—" He stopped abruptly, falling away to nothingness. "He was the best of us. The only one of us not plagued with darkness. The only one not obsessed with drink, pain, or work."

"I'm sorry." I reached over and placed my hand on his knee, stilling the jiggling that started the moment his father came into the conversation. Tyler's eyes locked on my hand.

"My turn now." He cleared his throat, his voice deepening. "Do you still love him?"

I removed my hand. "Tyler."

"It's a legitimate question. Do you still love Gabe?"

"In a way," I admitted.

"In what way?"

"In the way that I feel bad that I've hurt him. That I don't want to hurt him any more than I already have." I hooked my feet out from under me and pulled my knees to my chest. Tyler reached over and pushed away a strand of hair that was hanging over my face. Tears sprung to my eyes.

"My god, Lauren," he said hoarsely. "What are you doing to me?" He moved along the couch and pulled me close. I collapsed against his chest, breathing in the scent of him. I wasn't sure why I was crying. I wasn't sure if it was for myself, or for Gabe, or for the ache of longing that felt like a chasm in my chest. Tyler's hands feathered over my hair, running over the messy strands that had fallen from my hair tie. He shushed me, telling me he was sorry over and over, as though all of this was his fault and not mine. I knew better though. I knew this was all my doing.

"I will make you forget him, Lauren. I will do everything I can to make you forget him."

Pressed into his chest, his hands running over my hair, his breath brushing against my scalp, I knew my tears were because of the things that were to come, because I couldn't resist this man.

I tilted my head until my lips found his, fumbling and hesitant at first until he took control, our lips moving in unison, his hands roaming over my shoulders, down my back, crushing me against him. The gentle groans that escaped him only served to fuel the urgency of my desire. His lips were instruments of wonder. I threaded my fingers through his hair, twisting into the dark strands as he shifted back on the couch, creating room for me to climb onto his lap, our lips still locked. I didn't notice as the dampness from his clothes seeped into mine. I was desperate for him. I needed him.

Tyler's hands fluttered down my side and slipped under the material of my t-shirt. He fumbled with the clasp of my bra, moaning contentedly into my mouth when the latch released and his hands engulfed my breasts. We were passion and urgency, burning with desire, our brains flooded with the rush of blood.

I needed to see him. I needed to feel his flesh under my fingers, so I tore at his shirt, not caring as the buttons flew off in the rush.

Tyler sat up a little, mouth still devouring mine as he wrestled out of the damp shirt. As soon as he was free, he tore himself away from our kiss and grabbed the hem of my t-shirt, ripping it over my head and tossing it to the ground alongside my discarded bra. Taking both my breasts in his hands, Tyler studied them for a moment, his eyes dark and intense, before slowly lowering his mouth to my nipple and swirling his tongue over the stiffness. Between the thin material of his dress pants and my sweatpants, his hardness pushed against me like a rod of steel and I ground against it.

"My god, Lauren," Tyler panted. "I want to taste you. I want to be inside you."

Movement flickered in the corner of my vision. A car out the window.

"Shit!" I exclaimed, bending down to hide.

"What?" Tyler sat up to peer out the window.

"Who's that?"

"Peta."

"Peter? Doesn't look like a Peter to me."

3

LAUREN

Tyler laughed as I scrambled from his lap and fell to the floor, hiding under the sill of the window as Peta walked past. Thankfully, the net curtains hid us from view. I pulled my t-shirt over my head and hid my bra under the couch.

"Peta," I said, throwing Tyler's shirt at him, "is my best friend and also my boss."

"At the coffee shop?"

I nodded as Tyler threaded his arms through his shirt sleeves and adjusted the collar around his neck. It was only as he started to do up the buttons that he looked back at me, eyebrows raised. There were no buttons.

Peta knocked on the door. "I've brought you coffee and food for your hangover," she shouted, and banged some more. "How's that knocking working on your head?"

Smoothing the hair from my face, I pulled open the door with a ready smile plastered on my face. "Hi," I greeted chirpily.

Peta frowned. "That does not sound like the voice of someone who is hungover." She barged past me and walked towards the lounge where I knew she would find Tyler. "So?" she threw over her shoulder, "Did you hear from—Oh."

Stopping in the middle of the room, Peta's eyes canvased Tyler, the corners of her mouth turning upwards, her gaze shifting from his exposed chest to the cushion carefully positioned over his lap, then to the sprinkling of little white buttons on the carpet and finally to my dishevelled appearance. I crossed my arms, attempting to cover myself.

"Oh," Peta said again, smirking. She moved across the room, tucking the paper bag of food under her arm and holding out her hand. "You must be Tyler. I'm Peta."

Tyler moved uncomfortably, getting to his feet, the cushion from the couch still firmly held in place, while holding out his free hand. "Yes. Tyler Thornton. Nice to meet you, Peta." His smile lit up the room, despite the comical placement of the cushion.

Peta shook his hand and then dumped herself on the couch, patting the space Tyler just left and indicating for him to sit back down. "Did I interrupt something?"

"Not at all," I replied at the same time as Tyler said, "You could say that."

I glared at Peta, trying to telepathically send her the signal to leave. She got it but chose to ignore, her eyes glinting with mirth as she angled herself towards Tyler. "So, Tyler Thornton." She said his name slowly. "Tell me about yourself."

"What do you want to know?" he asked, raising that one eyebrow that mimicked Gabe's so convincingly.

Peta turned to me slowly, her eyes wide, and smiling mischievously before turning back to Tyler. "Everything. You can start with everything."

"From the looks you and Lauren are sharing, I'm gathering that you may already know something of me."

"You could say that."

"Why don't you start with what you know and I can fill in any gaps."

"I know you have a younger brother."

"Peta, please!" I scolded.

"What? It's true," she said, laughing.

"I think you should go." I walked over to the couch and tugged Peta up. "I'm sure you have lots to do at the café."

Peta resisted the pulling on her arm. "I'm sure it's fine for a few more minutes. I'm interested in getting to know Mr Thornton here a little better." Peta flicked her hair over her shoulder and battered her eyelashes until Tyler laughed.

I tugged at her arm again.

"Okay, okay," she said, letting me drag her to her feet. "I will go. But you had better call me later, Lauren Greer." I pulled her towards the door. "My husband is rather good at sewing," she shouted back to Tyler. "He'll be able to sort that shirt out."

I shoved Peta outside and pulled the door shut behind us.

Peta grinned. "He's even better looking in real life," she said. "No wonder you couldn't resist. If I had that hitting on me I'm not sure I would be able to resist either. My goodness!" She shook her whole body, as though trying to rid herself of the thoughts running through her head. "I think I'm going to need a cold shower."

"Peta," I hissed. "He could hear you."

She slapped my arm. "Let him. I'm sure it's nothing he hasn't heard before." We started walking towards her car. "So I guess you've made up your mind then?"

My whole body sunk. "I can't seem to resist him, Peta."

"It's probably because you have eyes."

I whacked her arm again.

"Okay, serious now." She wiped the grin from her face. "Perhaps you should just stop trying to. You tried to resist Gabe and you made yourself miserable. Finally, you gave in but tried to keep it quiet, which made both you and Gabe miserable. Then you were with Gabe while being attracted to his brother, which, no surprise, made you miserable. Maybe it's time you just let yourself be happy."

"You really think?"

Peta took my shoulders in her hands and held my gaze firmly. "Yes, Lauren Greer. That is what I think. I think you should march back in there and fuck the brains out of that man sitting waiting for you and not feel a wisp of guilt about it. You are not with Gabe anymore. Just let yourself be with Tyler." She let go of me. "Either that, or just don't be with anyone."

"That's probably the best idea you've had yet."

"It's an awfully boring one though." Peta grinned.

I rolled my eyes and pulled her in for an embrace. "See you tomorrow," I muttered into her ear.

Peta opened the door to her car and sat half in half out. "I expect a full report. I take it 'hot lips' in there will take you to collect your car?"

I nodded, rolling my eyes again.

Tyler was sitting on the couch, one ankle hooked over his knee, his open shirt exposing the tanned muscles underneath. "I like her," he said. He held his hand out and I walked closer. "She gives good advice."

I stopped, looking at him questioningly. "I believe she said something about fucking my brains out?" He grabbed my hand and tugged me onto him. "I liked the sound of that. Now, where were we?" he asked, his lips moving to my mouth, his erection already hard and pressing into me as he pulled me onto his lap.

"No you don't," I said, pulling myself away. "I can't think that close to you."

"You don't need to think." He pulled me back again but I stood firm.

"Will you give me a ride to the airport to collect my car?"

Tyler pouted. "I've driven all this way and you want to use me as a taxi?"

"No," I said slyly. "That's not what I want to use you for. But it's what we are going to do."

"As you wish." Tyler stood. "But I really wish you had told me this before ripping all the buttons from my shirt." His phone rang. Tyler looked down from where he had discarded it on the coffee table and scowled. "I've got to take this." He picked up the phone and swiped accept as he walked into the other room.

His answers were short and direct. "Yes. No. I understand. Yes. I know that. I'm taking care of it now. Yes. Yes. You've said that twice now. Of course I know how it affects—" He sighed deeply and ran his hand over his face. "Yes. I know." His voice was getting more strained and impatient. "Tomorrow. I know but—"

Grabbing my bag from where it lay on the kitchen counter, I searched through it in an effort to locate the keys I couldn't find the night before. They were there, lying in the bottom of the side pocket, right where they should be. I walked past Tyler so I could go and get changed but he reached out and caught my hand, holding me in place with his finger and thumb wrapped around the tender flesh of my wrist. What was it about that spot that was so erotic? When he touched me there I froze and melted all at once.

Tyler locked eyes with me. "No," he said down the phone. "Tomorrow. Yes, first thing. I understand. Bye." He placed the phone into his pocket, sliding closer to me, the serious expression from his phone call melting into something different, something warmer. "And where do you think you're going?"

"To get changed."

Tyler shook his head. "I don't think so. If I have to drive to collect your car in a shirt with no buttons you can certainly go in sweatpants and a t-shirt."

He tugged me closer, pushing his lips onto mine. Immediately, heat burned between my legs and I scolded myself internally for the response that came so quickly. "But I've got no bra on," I murmured into his lips.

"I know." I felt the corners of his mouth turn upwards as his hands travelled down to capture my breasts. They felt heavy and full in his caress and I leaned into him, losing myself in the moment for a few seconds before pulling away. Tyler groaned in frustration, letting his head drop to my shoulder. "You're killing me here."

I slid out from under him, letting his head fall. "Come on." I walked towards the door, holding it open. "This car won't wait all day."

Tyler walked out the door. "I'm pretty sure you'd find it would."

As I climbed into the passenger's seat, Tyler popped the boot and got something out of the back. When he sat behind the wheel, he had a new shirt on. One with buttons.

"Hey," I said. "No fair."

"Always be prepared." Tyler started the car. "That's my motto."

"I'm pretty sure that's the Scout's motto."

"I could have been one," he replied.

"Were you?"

He shook his head and tapped the airport into his GPS. "Nope."

"It's not a big town. I can show you the way to the airport."

"I like to be prepared," he said again and smirked. Through the speakers of the sound system, Tyler's phone began to ring. 'Sadie' was the name displayed on the screen. Tyler swiped reject.

"Is that who you were talking to before?"

Tyler shook his head. "Sadie's my assistant. I was supposed to be playing golf with some of the investors today."

"I'm sorry," I replied.

He glanced over at me. "It's not your fault. I'm the one who chose to come down here. Besides, I hate golf. I only ever play to keep the old money happy."

"So who were you talking to before?"

Tyler narrowed his eyes. "Why are you so interested?"

I mimicked holding a phone to my ear, deepening my voice. "I'm taking care of it now."

"You heard that?"

"I was in the next room. It was hard not to hear."

"I would tell you it wasn't about you, but that would be a lie. It was my father. He wanted to know what happened last night." Tyler cleared his throat. "Let's just say things got a little messier after you left."

"With Gabe?"

Tyler nodded. "When Clark died and Dad found out what Gabe had done to him, he was furious. Dad never had any brothers or sisters and he hates seeing us fight. He thought what Gabe did was unforgivable, but losing his son for years cured him of that. Because of you, Gabe had come back into his life and he was rather fond of the little shit. But now, that's threatened again."

"Because of me," I said quietly.

"No." Tyler shook his head and reached over to pull my fingers to his lips. "Because of me."

I sunk into the seat, letting the weight of what he just said crush me. "Your family is going to hate me."

"No, they aren't."

"I'm the girl who has torn you guys apart."

"Our family was torn apart long before you came into the picture."

"But this isn't going to help."

"Nothing about this was ever going to be simple, Lauren, but I want this to happen. I want you. Gabe will get over it."

Tyler's phone rang again, this time with just 'HE WHO MUST BE OBEYED' written all in caps across the screen. Throwing a sideways glance my way, he swiped ignore before pulling his phone out of his pocket and turning it off. "I'll deal with him later."

4

LAUREN

"What time do you have to leave?" I asked, popping a piece of chicken into my mouth, and looking at him with what I hoped was an innocent expression on my face.

We had picked up my car, collected some food from a drive-thru and now sat casually eating it on the couch, pretending to be interested in the late night news.

Despite my attempt at resistance, climbing into bed with Tyler was foremost on my mind. Everything about him was driving me insane with desire. The glimpse of flesh that peeked between the buttonholes of his shirt when he leaned forward to grab more food from the coffee table. His mouth. Whether it be while talking, while eating, or rubbing his lips with the back of his hand, my mind was stuck on the way his mouth felt on mine. The urgent softness of his lips. Had Peta not interrupted us earlier, I'm sure I would have spent the entire time in bed with him, but now there was a certain nervousness in my chest.

Tyler casually slung his wrist over and studied the time. "Soon," was all he said.

"How soon?" I asked.

"Is there something you had in mind that you wanted to do?" Tyler sat back on the couch, his head resting in his hands.

Colour crept up my cheeks even as I willed it away. "I just—"

He slid across the couch. "I hope you don't think I came here for only one reason. Well," he said, inching closer. "I did come here for one thing but it's not what you are thinking."

"And what am I thinking?"

"That I wanted to get you into bed."

"And you don't?"

He leaned forward, tilting his head so it angled into the crook of my neck. He was close enough that I could feel the heat of his breath, but not close enough to touch. "I do," he said with a growl. "But that's not the reason I came."

My heart beat in my chest heavily. His lips brushed my skin with the lightest of touches and I shuddered, wanting to melt into him, press him against me and feel his body over mine. "Why did you?"

"Because I wanted to make sure you didn't regret it."

"What?" I said dreamily. All I could think about was getting closer to him. I inched forward and he kissed the smooth skin of my neck, causing waves of desire to ignite.

"That you didn't regret me."

"You?" I asked as his lips travelled up my neck. Never had anyone's lips affected me so much. Never had I melted so quickly, so intensely.

His kisses trailed along my jawline. "Are you expecting anyone else?"

I shook my head, words having fled my mind.

"You sure?" His hand snaked around my waist and up my back as he leaned over me, guiding me back onto the couch and climbing on top.

I nodded and a gasp stuck in my throat as he caught my lip between his teeth. Claiming my mouth hungrily, his lips were urgent and rough as he dragged them over my skin. Moving down my neck, he nestled his head between my breasts, breathing deeply before searching out the fullness of them. The friction created by the softness of his mouth and the roughness of the material over my tender skin arched my back. He took his time, taking one nipple then the other in his mouth. The sounds he made tore at my emotions, tossing me between slow-burning desire and urgency. Moving further down my body, he lifted the hem of my t-shirt and stuck his head under it, kissing his way up my stomach until he settled back on my breasts, a sigh of contentment escaping before he took as much of the fullness into his mouth as he could. I sat up a little, fumbling with the material of his shirt until Tyler popped his head back up.

"Let me," he said, undoing each of his buttons hurriedly and tossing his shirt to the floor. "I might get a few dodgy looks if I send two shirts to the tailor in that state." He leaned over and hooked his fingers at the hem of my shirt, pulling it over my head and groaning when my breasts were free beneath him.

"I need to see you. All of you," he said, toying with the waistband of my pants. He dragged them down my legs, taking my underwear with them as I twisted to free myself, then he nestled himself between my knees, his eyes dark and hungry as he took in my nakedness. "You are divine," he said reverently.

There was a voice in my head that wanted to protest, but the look in his eyes stopped me. There was hunger and desire, tenderness and need. I didn't need to hide from him. He saw all of me and he didn't look away. Lifting myself to a sitting position, I ran my fingers along his shoulders and down his chest, resting them on the broad expanse of his pecs and pushing him back onto his knees. Tyler closed his eyes, taking in deep breaths as I marvelled at the way he was cut. The dark spattering of hair that dipped under his belt caught my attention and I pressed my lips to it. A sharp breath inflated his chest. I fumbled with his belt buckle, ripping it through the loops of his pants when I finally got it undone and tossing it to the floor to join his shirt. Tyler watched with heat in his eyes as I pushed his pants over his hips, moving side to side to assist me. And then he was free.

Shuffling back along the couch, I angled myself so his erection, hard and ready, was close to my mouth. Tyler pushed my hair to the side so he could see as my mouth hovered dangerously close to his hardness. I didn't touch him, just held myself at a distance so he could feel the heat of my breath. He twitched beneath me and wrapped his hand through my hair, gathering it where it was messily piled on the top of my head, and holding it firmly. I held my mouth open, staring up at him and willing him to direct me. He did not disappoint. His fingers tightened on my hair, the pressure of it making my scalp sting as he guided my mouth. As I wrapped my lips around him, the hardness of him caused burning between my legs. Even though I had only felt him inside me once, my thighs clenched in anticipation of what was to come. Tyler's grip on my hair loosened as I worked my mouth up and down his shaft. No other parts of me were touching him, only my mouth. I moved slowly, my lips and my tongue moving up and down as he groaned. The sounds of his pleasure only increased my desire to please him and I took more of him into my mouth, gagging slightly when he hit the back of my throat. Tyler twisted his fingers in my hair and pushed my head down a fraction further. I gagged again, surprised by the wetness that oozed between my legs as he encouraged me to take more. He moved me up and down, working himself into my mouth more and more until I reeled back, gasping for air. He pulled me up then, pressing his mouth to mine, no doubt tasting the lingering scent of him.

His mouth found its way down to my jawline, following the line of it until his lips pressed against my ear. "I want to taste you," he said, his voice urgent and deep. "Can we take this to the bedroom?"

Removing myself from the couch, I stood naked in front of him and took his hand. We walked across the lounge and had just about reached the hallway when there was a knock at the door.

Tyler slumped, his head falling to my shoulder. "You've got to be fucking kidding," he moaned. "How many visitors do you get?"

I laughed and pressed him against the wall, reaching down to take him in hand, and stroked him carefully. "It's probably just Peta looking for an update. Just ignore it and she'll go away."

He devoured me hungrily, sinking down so his lips trailed between my breasts and over the soft flesh of my stomach. Stopping when he was between my thighs, he inhaled deeply.

Peta knocked again. Angrily.

Tyler dragged himself back up and placed a gentle kiss on my nose. "Maybe you should get it before she tears the door down."

"Lauren?" a hesitant voice called through the door.

Tyler looked at me, one eyebrow lifted in a question. "Who's that?" he mouthed.

"Lauren, it's Drew."

"Shit," I said under my breath.

"I know you're in there. Your car is up the driveway. Can we talk?"

"Just a minute," I called out, sliding away from Tyler who banged his head repeatedly against the wall.

"Who the fuck is Drew?" he asked.

"Gabe's flatmate," I replied, running into my bedroom and grabbing my dressing gown. Tyler followed and I pushed him onto the bed, tossing a towel at him. "You stay here." I pressed a kiss to his lips and avoided his hands as he groped. "Behave," I whispered.

Tyler merely saluted and fell back onto the covers, the towel still in his hands and his erection protruding into the air.

"Hi!" I smiled brightly as I opened the door.

Gabe pushed past me. "Where is he?" he yelled, dishevelled and wild.

"Sorry." Drew stood in the driveway, looking up at me sheepishly. "He saw his car outside. I couldn't stop him."

"Tyler!" Gabe's voice boomed through the house. "Where the fuck are you?"

I ran to follow Gabe down the hall, grabbing his arm just before he reached the bedroom. "Gabe, don't," I pleaded. His eyes rested on me for the first time. They travelled over my body, taking in the loose-fitting gown and the flash of my breasts between the silky material. I jerked it tighter with one hand as Gabe half groaned, half cried.

"Fuck," he said. "Fuck, fuck, fuck."

"Gabe, please," I said, trying to pull him away from the bedroom door. "You're drunk. Now's not the time."

"Thanks to you, I'm always fucking drunk!" he roared. He lifted his fist and banged on the door. "Tyler!"

Just as he was about to bang again the door flew open and Tyler stood before him, only the towel wrapped around his waist hiding his nakedness.

"I would suggest you leave, little brother," Tyler said darkly.

Gabe didn't reply with words. Quicker than his drunken state implied, he lifted his fist and punched Tyler in the jaw. Tyler's head flung back before he regained control, rocking his jaw between his finger and thumb before gritting his teeth.

"I will give you that one, little brother. But don't think that—"

Gabe's fist wound back for another punch but this time Tyler stopped him. "You should know better than to attack me when you're drunk, Gable. It's an unfair fight. One I believe we've had before. Many times."

Gabe threw his weight at Tyler, knocking him to the ground. "Don't you fucking even talk to me you useless fucking—" The rest of his words were lost in a mumble of fists and grunts, curse words and sweat.

Drew ran down the hallway and we both watched on in horror as the two brothers rolled around the floor, Tyler dodging Gabe's flailing fists until he finally had him pinned down.

Gabe bucked underneath Tyler's knee. "Get the fuck off me!" He strained against Tyler who held him until finally, the fight left Gabe.

"You going to behave?" Tyler asked, adjusting the towel around his waist.

Gabe nodded and then jumped to his feet somewhat shakily when Tyler released him. His eyes darted between Tyler and me.

"How could you?" he said, tears welling in his eyes. "How could you do this to me, Lauren? You know how I feel about you. You know how I feel about him." He jerked his chin in Tyler's direction. "You're nothing but a fucking—"

Tyler moved towards him. "I wouldn't finish that sentence if I were you," he growled.

"I shouldn't?" Gabe scoffed. "We've barely broken up and she's already jumped into bed with you. How many times does this make? How many times did you fuck her behind my—"

"Enough!" Tyler roared. He advanced on Gabe, the height difference suddenly becoming very clear. "You will not speak to her like that. And for you to do so is highly hypocritical. How many girls have you found solace in since you two broke up? And never once did she 'fuck me' as you so eloquently put it, behind your back."

Drew placed a hand on Gabe's shoulder. "Come on, let's just go."

Gabe shoved off his touch, glaring at Tyler. "This isn't over," he hissed.

"As long as you keep it between you and me and leave Lauren out of it, I'm fine with that," Tyler replied.

Gabe held Tyler's glare a little longer, the threads of his neck bulging, before turning to me, the anger slumping out of his muscles. "Lauren," he said, his voice broken. "Please?"

I swallowed the thick ball of guilt in the back of my throat and lifted my hand to his cheek. Tyler tensed. "I'm so sorry," I started to say, but Gabe turned and strode away, not wanting to hear the words I couldn't find.

"Sorry," Drew offered. "I didn't know what to do. He's been so dark since you two broke up. I thought that maybe—"

"It's okay," I said to Drew, following him down the hall. "None of this is your fault. It's all mine."

Gabe was already in the car when we reached the door. Tyler stuck his hand out to Drew. "Thanks for looking after him," he said. "For what it's worth, I never set out to hurt him."

Drew looked over at Tyler but didn't smile, or take his hand. "I think you would have chosen someone different if you really meant that."

I closed the door behind him and fell heavily against it, pulling my gown tight and covering my face with my hands.

"You okay?" Tyler asked, his voice low.

I nodded. But I wasn't. I was exhausted and confused. I was wracked with guilt but at the same time, I knew I didn't want to give him up. I wanted Tyler. There was a part of me that somehow knew we were meant to be together.

"I should probably leave," he said after silence filled the room.

I nodded again and drew in a shaky breath. "I'm sorry that happened."

Tyler let the corners of his mouth turn up a little. "Believe me, not as sorry as I am." He pressed his forehead to mine. "When can I see you again?" He pressed a kiss to my nose.

"I'm coming up next week to take the next lot of photos."

"Can you stay?" he asked.

"I'm not sure."

"Ask Peta for time off. Come stay with me. A month. A week. A day. I'll take whatever I can get."

I nodded against his forehead and then crumpled into his chest, breathing in the scent of musk and mint that clung to his skin.

"I'm sorry," I said again.

"You have nothing to be sorry for. You need to stop saying that."

But if I had nothing to be sorry for, why did I feel so bad?

5

LAUREN

Peta pulled me away from the coffee machine as soon as the customers at the café dwindled enough that we could sit in a secluded corner.

"I'm dying," she said, tossing her blonde hair over her shoulder and leaning over the table eagerly. "Spill everything. Now."

"It was horrible."

"Horrible? I find that difficult to imagine. And I have imagined it a few times now."

I looked at her lopsidedly.

"Not you," she assured me. "Not that I wouldn't go there. I'm sure that we could make some sweet, sweet love together, but this particular imagining was strictly a Tyler thing. I mean, that man is to die for. Have you looked at him? I mean really looked at him? I showed Shrek his photo and I swear he got a hard-on."

"Gabe showed up."

"Shit."

I nodded glumly and chased the straw of my iced-coffee around the glass with my mouth. "Right in the middle."

"In the middle of what?"

I looked at her over the edge of my drink, eyebrows raised.

"Oh," she said. "In the middle."

"He was drunk. Drunk and angry. He threw a punch at Tyler."

Peta's hand flew to her chest and her eyes widened. "What I wouldn't give to be you just for one day."

"Peta," I groaned.

"What?" she said. "Yes, I know it's old-fashioned and whatever to want two men fighting over you and all, but please, show me a girl who wouldn't?"

"Sure, sure," I said, rolling my eyes exaggeratedly. "The thought of it is romantic, but the reality of it isn't. Well, maybe it could be if I didn't care for them both, but I do. I never wanted to hurt Gabe. He looked so sad."

"And how do you feel about Tyler?"

I couldn't help the smile that covered my face. "I like him." I toyed with my straw. "I like him a lot."

"Is that all you're going to give me?" Peta complained.

"For now."

"When are you seeing him again?"

"That's what I wanted to talk to you about."

Peta sighed. "You want time off for when you go up to do the photos, don't you?"

I nodded and screwed my nose up hopefully.

"It's a good thing you are best friends with the boss, you know. Otherwise, you would have lost your job ages ago."

I leaned across the table and hugged her. "Thank you. I'll owe you. I'll work double shifts up until then. No, I won't leave. I'll eat, breathe and sleep this place. I'll—"

"Okay, okay," Peta said, detangling herself from my embrace. "But you have to promise me one thing."

"Anything."

"You will bring him for dinner when he's down next."

"We've only just—"

Peta held up her hand. "No debate."

I grinned. "Deal."

"Shake on it," Peta ordered, sticking out her hand.

I shook it, laughing. "What about you, anyway?"

"What about me?"

"I've been so caught up in my man dramas over the last few months, I feel like we've neglected yours."

"I have no drama," Peta replied.

"None?"

She held up empty hands and looked at them as if the drama might be hiding there. "No drama. Things are almost dangerously boring. Work is work. The kids are the kids. Shrek is Shrek. The in-laws are still the in-laws." She shrugged again. "It's all rather boring compared to your life."

"Peta, you own your own café, you have three children and one sexy husband. I can't see how you would find the time to be bored."

"Maybe bored is the wrong word. I'm not bored as in nothing-to-do bored, I'm bored in the sense that I have too much to do and it's the same thing over and over. Rinse and repeat." She took a gulp of her coffee and then her eyes widened and sparkled. "So, your mother will be pleased that you and Gabe are no longer together."

I slumped back in my seat. "I haven't told her."

"She still thinks you're with him?"

I nodded, picking up the straw and dragging it between my teeth. "They all do. It took enough guts to pluck up the courage to tell them I was with him in the first place, I don't want to see

Mother's smirking face when I tell her it didn't last. She'll be thrilled."

"So they don't know about Tyler?"

I shook my head. "Not even Morgan."

"Your sister is not going to be happy when she finds out. She expects you to tell her everything."

"Little does she know how little she knows."

Peta frowned, replaying my words over in her head until she smiled and nodded. Reaching under the table, she patted my knee. "Right. Back to work, it is."

"But we've only just sat down," I said, pouting and looking at my not even half finished iced-coffee.

Peta shrugged. "Next time, bring me more details."

* * *

Tyler called three times before I saw him again. The first was while I was at work the day after he left.

I was getting a bag of coffee down from the high shelf in the storeroom and trying not to think of Gabe. The storeroom brought back memories I was trying to forget. Ones where he pressed me against the wall. Ones where his smile was seductive. Then, ones from the night before when he looked at me with so much anger.

Mark, having noticed me struggling to reach the top shelf, leaned against the wall, popping crumbs of lemon slice into his mouth as I balanced precociously on a wobbly stepladder.

"So?" he drawled in the way only Mark could drawl. "What is this new one like? The 'older' brother." Mark placed air quotations around the word older, then crossed his arms again and cocked his head to the side. "Peta says he's a handsome buck."

Finally having tugged the bag of beans down, I placed it at my feet and stepped off the ladder. "She said that? A handsome buck."

Mark nodded. The corners of his mouth twitched as he picked off some more of the lemon slice. "She may have used different words, but I'm sure that was what she was implying."

I hoisted the bag on my shoulder. Mark followed me back into the kitchen, wiping his hands on his apron.

"So?" he demanded.

"So what?"

Mark rolled his eyes as I flopped the bag of beans onto the counter and pulled the lid off the grinder. He did some sort of gesture with his hands, body, and feet. I wasn't sure if it was supposed to represent the antlers of said 'buck', or if he was mimicking some strange 'buck-like' mating ritual and he was about to start pawing at the ground and snorting. "The handsome buck?" he said again.

I stood watching as the imitation continued and pondered the answer I should give. "Yes?" I cautiously decided on.

Mark stopped his antics and reached across to rip the top of the bag before letting the beans flow into the grinder. He raised his voice and stuck out his lower lip. "Poor Gabe."

The guilt was instant. "Have you seen him?"

Mark put the lid on and leaned against the counter, adjusting the tea towel casually thrown over his shoulder. "Just the once. He came in one night while I was closing up, drunk as a skunk, arm around some floozy."

I laughed. "Floozy?"

"Yup," Mark confirmed. "Floozy. He looked pretty dark too. Not happy drunk. Dark drunk." Mark sighed and heaved himself from his leaning post. "Typical Gabe," he said. "You would think he would have learned by now not to throw tantrums when he doesn't get what he wants." Mark paused in the doorway between the kitchen and the café. "Still…" He left the word hanging while he lifted his brows. "His brother?"

My head dropped involuntarily. "I know."

It was then that my phone rang and I pulled it out of my apron pocket to find Tyler's image lighting up the screen. It was the profile picture linked to his social media accounts, him leaning against a concrete wall, dressed in a suit, one hand in his pocket, and one ankle hooked over the other. Poser.

Mark peered over my shoulder. "Well, well, well," he said. "He is a handsome buck."

* * *

The second call came while I was already on the phone. I was driving back from a whinge session at Peta's when Billie's number flashed onto the screen. It was not long ago that I was avoiding her calls, but now I pulled over to the side of the road, eager, and a little nervous, to answer. I hadn't spoken to her since the investors' party and I didn't know what she thought of the recent developments in my relationship status with her step-sons.

"Hi," I answered, trying to keep my tone neutral from emotion.

"I've decided to forgive you," Billie said without preamble.

I was momentarily puzzled. "Thanks?" I offered.

"I mean, I'm sure you didn't intentionally set out to break poor Gabe's heart and in the process tear my family apart."

"Billie," I started. "I never—"

"It doesn't matter now anyway," she interrupted. "I've decided to forgive you. Not because you deserve it. Hamish is livid, you know. He finally had his boys back together. He finally thought Gabe was getting his act together. He was so happy you brought Gabe back into the family, so to speak, but now, well—" She paused, something knocking around her mouth noisily. "Well, now he's not so happy. But I've decided to forgive you because I'm desperate for some female company in my testosterone-filled world. Tyler said you would be in the city next week."

"I'm coming up on—"

Billie talked over me. "Meet me for lunch on Friday?"

It was posed as a question but I knew it wasn't. "Sure."

"Great," she said quickly and abruptly. "I'll message you the details."

It was then that the call came through from Tyler. I had Billie on speaker so I stared at his image glowing in front of me as I listened to her.

"And Lauren?" she added.

"Yes?" Tyler's image faded as the call drifted to voicemail.

"Don't mess with my men, okay?"

I didn't know whether to fold into laughter or tears. "I never—"

"Tut, tut, tut," Billie scolded. "Excuses, excuses. It's about what you are going to do from here, not what you've already done. I never thought of you as someone to do this. You were always so nice at school. So don't mess with Tyler, leave Gabe alone and I'll see you Friday." And then the phone went dark.

I sat on the side of the road, the sun setting over the peaks of the houses, one street light flickering erratically, and returned Tyler's call. He didn't answer.

* * *

The third call was the night before my flight. I had a shift at the café the following day, and then I would leave to spend three days with Tyler. I wasn't exactly sure how to feel about it. I was nervous. I was excited. Our calls so far had been brief and slightly awkward, wanting to talk but not completely sure what to talk about. This time it was different.

I was sitting in my pyjamas, slouched on the couch, binge-watching re-runs of a reality cooking show while drinking from a bottle of wine. I didn't bother with a glass. No one was there to witness my uncouth behaviour. When my phone flashed to life, I muted the TV.

"Sorry I didn't get the chance to call you back earlier," Tyler said. "I've been in meetings all day." The background noise drifting through the phone was loud. Clinking glasses and laughter.

"Where are you?"

"Hold on." The screen changed and asked me to accept a video call. "There," he said. "That's better. I can see you now."

He was standing on a balcony of some sort, the lights of the city twinkling behind him, whiskey glass in hand. His smile was happy and lazy. "I'm at some function for—" He looked away from the screen. "What is this for, Sadie?" He took a sip of whiskey while a faint voice replied, then turned back to me. "I can't make out what she's saying," he said. "I'm at a function for something." He shrugged and leaned closer, swaying slightly with the movement. "I'm desperate to see you."

I laughed and, noticing the way his pupils widened, I wished I was wearing something other than flannelette pyjamas. Tyler was typically dashing in his suit. Groomed to perfection, though a strand of his hair had fallen out of place and hung over his eye.

"Tyler Thornton," I jokingly scolded. "Are you drunk?"

"Me?" He grinned and pressed one finger to his chest, the others wrapped securely around his glass. "I don't get drunk," he said. "But I might be slightly inebriated."

"Just slightly?"

"I'm here on a professional basis." He winked. "Of course it's slightly." He drained the contents of the glass. "I can't stop thinking about you. It's like you're stuck in my head and no matter what I try to distract myself with, you worm your way back in. I'm sure it's some sort of witchcraft."

"Don't let my mother hear you say that. She'll have me booked for an exorcism."

"I want to meet her."

"No." I shook my head. "You don't."

"I do," he insisted. "I want to meet all your family. Tell me about them."

"Now?" I asked.

Tyler moved from his position against the railing of the balcony and sat at a table, motioning for the waiter to bring him another drink.

"Why not?" he said. Then he was blocked by a flash of green. His laughter floated through the speaker, followed by exclamations of surprise and comments that were lost to the music of the background. "Lauren," he said, leaning around one of the people blocking my view. He reached for the phone and I saw a flash of the night sky, the glow of lanterns, and the side of his whiskey glass before I saw his face again. "I've got to go. I'll see you tomorrow."

"Who's Lauren?" I heard someone ask before the screen went blank.

6

LAUREN

During the flight, I fidgeted with my headphones, trying to concentrate on the words of the audio book playing in my ears, but after pressing the button to skip back ten seconds at least five times in a row, I gave up, and rested my head against the seat, closing my eyes to the patchwork of green beneath me. It had been exactly eleven days since I had last seen him. Eleven days since his lips had been on mine. Eleven days for me to stress over what he wanted from me. Over what I wanted from him.

He told me he would meet me at the airport, so I walked cautiously, looking out for him as I weaved my way through the crowd of people waiting to collect their luggage. Tyler was leaning against a wall, phone in his hand, eyes glued to the screen, a deep red flower casually stuffed into his shirt pocket. I stopped for a moment and just watched him. His eyebrows were furrowed, his bottom lip caught between his teeth as his jaw worked back and forth. He typed furiously.

I didn't know how to approach him. Should I hug him? Kiss him? Did I walk up and shake his hand? And then he looked up and the most delicious smile broke over his features and I no longer had to figure out what I'd do because he did.

"Hey you," he strolled up to me, took my face in his hands and planted a full and sensual kiss on my lips. My breath fled the moment our lips touched and returned violently when he broke away, still holding my cheeks between his palms.

"Here." Plucking the flower from his shirt pocket, he held it out to me. "It's all they had." He looked down at the bag in my hand. I had only packed two. Most of my camera gear was in the pack with a few of my clothes. My toiletries were stuffed into my oversized handbag that Peta insisted I needed to upgrade.

"Is that it?" he asked.

I nodded, bringing the flower to my nose and inhaling its scent while Tyler took my pack, slinging it over his shoulder. "You didn't bring a lot."

I shrugged. "Figured I wouldn't need much."

Tyler took my hand, a smirk covering his face. "I like the way you think."

Realisation dawned. "Oh! I didn't mean it like that." Colour crept up my cheeks.

"Like what?" he teased as we started walking towards the exit.

"Like, like—"

He leaned close, so his lips brushed against my ear. "Like you are going to spend all your time naked in my bed? Because that was what I was hoping you meant."

I whacked his arm playfully. "Behave yourself, Tyler Thornton."

"I can assure you I have no intention of behaving. I finally get you all to myself. There will be very little behaving going on."

The lights of Tyler's car flashed when he pressed the key and the boot popped open. He placed my pack carefully in the boot.

"Jimmy told me you'd bite my head off if I wasn't careful with your camera gear."

Once inside the car and on the way to his loft, the awkwardness that I had been worried about earlier, descended over the car.

Tyler cleared his throat. "How was the flight?"

"Good." I flashed him a smile. "Uneventful."

"Just the way you want them." Tyler laughed nervously and wiped one of his hands down his pants before wrapping it tightly around the steering wheel again.

"How's the casino?" I asked.

"Coming along nicely. You'll see big changes since last time you were up. Some of the inside décor is being installed on the lower levels." Tyler cleared his throat. "I thought we could go back to Maria's for dinner tomorrow night."

"Sounds wonderful."

"And on Saturday night, I've got to attend an art gallery opening. You don't mind, do you? The opening exhibition is some photographer who's supposed to be the next big thing in the art scene. Could be interesting for you."

I smiled across at him, pressing my hands between my legs. "Sounds wonderful." I had said it twice now.

We fell into silence. Tyler twisted his hands around the steering wheel. I think we were both grateful when the car filled with the sound of his phone ringing, even if the screen read in bold, 'HE WHO MUST BE OBEYED'.

"You're on speaker phone," Tyler greeted his father.

"Well take me off it," was Hamish's reply.

Tyler's voice was cold. "I'm driving."

"Who's listening?"

Tyler cleared his throat again and tilted his head from side to side as though trying to relieve an ache in his neck. "Lauren."

"Call me later," Hamish ordered and then the sound of the radio filled the car again.

Tyler smiled nervously. "He's still a little sore from what went down at the investors' party with Gabe."

"So Billie said."

"You called her?"

"She called me. I'm meeting her for lunch on Friday."

"I've got meetings tomorrow so that works out well."

By this stage, we had arrived at the building that housed his loft. Tyler parked the car under cover on the lowest level. The sound of the car doors closing echoed loudly around the space. He reached for my hand as the elevator travelled through the levels, clanking and groaning loudly.

"Jake home?" I asked as it jerked to a stop.

Tyler shook his head and pulled aside the heavy door. Everything was neat and tidy. Everything in its place. Black and white images dominated the large space. The only thing that was different from last time was Jake's bed was missing.

Tyler placed my bag on the floor as I wandered over to the fireplace. Flames licked up the chimney. A rug lay where Jake's bed had been. Footsteps padded over the concrete floor and then his hands were on me, his mouth was on me and all the nervousness of before vanished.

"I've been waiting for this." Tyler's lips urgently burned across my flesh until he pressed into the nape of my neck, breathing in deeply. "You smell of everything good." He pressed against me, walking me backwards, mouth pressed into the tender, soft skin of my neck, heat burning between my legs until I was against the wall. I wound my hands into his hair, mussing up the slickness of it and fisting the strands between my fingers.

"I promised myself I wouldn't do this." Tyler toyed with the buttons of my shirt, plucking the seams apart and sliding it over my shoulders. "I promised myself I'd wait. We'd wait. I'd take you out to dinner." His mouth found its way over my collarbone, down to the bulge of my breasts. "We'd talk. Do something, anything but tear your clothes off and dive into you, but I can't."

His hand reached behind as I arched my back away from the wall and he flicked the clasps of my bra apart in one swift movement. He pulled the straps over my shoulders as I fumbled with the buttons on his shirt, frustrated that they suddenly seemed more difficult than they needed to be. As he took my breasts in his hands, waves of pleasure washed over me and I bit my lip in anticipation as I removed his shirt. Winding my hands back into his hair, I pulled him towards my chest. He took me hungrily, desperately, groans coming from him that only fed my desire. Falling to his knees, Tyler pressed his face into the soft flesh of my stomach. He wrapped his hands around my middle before letting them fall to grip the cheeks of my backside, massaging the backs of my thighs, urging me to open for him.

He was slow at first, teasing at what was to come. But as the pressure of his hands gripped my thighs, encouraging them apart, his head buried against me, his tongue working furiously at my sex. I gasped. My hands, no longer tugging at his hair, were flattened against the wall behind me.

Tyler paused for breath, steel eyes moving up my body until they met mine. "My god, you taste good," he muttered before lowering his head again.

My chest heaved. My legs weakened. "Tyler," I moaned.

His mumbled reply vibrated against me.

"Tyler," I said again. "You need to stop before I come."

Tyler moaned against me again and it was just about my undoing. He removed his tongue from my wetness and rocked back from his knees to his heels, his erection straining against his pants. Dark hunger flashed through his eyes as he stared at me exposed before him. His hands fell from my thighs and we locked eyes as he ran a single finger down my slit and inserted it. His cock twitched, and his eyes half closed as if in a trance as he drew in a breath.

"I need to be inside you." He got to his feet, ripping his belt from his pants and then letting them fall to the floor. "Come," he ordered and took my hand, leading me to the bedroom and laying me down on the large bed.

Crawling between my legs, he slid his way up my body until his lips met mine and we writhed together. He tasted of fire. Holding his weight above me, Tyler placed just enough of himself against my body to drive me wild. His erection pressed against my wetness, sliding over me, sending shockwaves of pleasure rippling through every inch. His lips were still glued to mine when he guided himself inside, breaking away enough so he could watch my expression as he filled me. He was slow. He was gentle. He pushed an inch at a time, pausing to pepper my neck with kisses as I arched against the mattress, both excited and scared to take him fully.

"You're so wet." He pressed a kiss to my chest. "You're so tight." He took my nipple between his lips and swirled it about his mouth. His hands moved down my sides and hooked under my legs, opening me and pulling me further to him. I widened myself and Tyler surged inside, causing moans of satisfaction to slip from my lips. Lifting himself onto his elbows, he moved, pushing in and out, his thick hardness filling me with each thrust. I hooked my legs around his, both trapping him and pulling him closer. Tyler thrust harder. My skin gripped against the covers as he shoved me across the bed until my head knocked against the headboard. Tyler twisted his hand into my hair, shielding me from the headboard at the same time as the tightness of his grasp intensified the sensation of his body inside mine. His movements became more urgent and small gasps and moans filled the air as I began to lose control. It built slowly and extended out to every inch of my body. I ached for release. Balancing on the edge, caught between ecstasy and torment, Tyler fucked me mercilessly until I cried out, exploding into a million shards of satisfaction.

"Lauren," he moaned, twisting his hand tighter into my hair. He moved faster and harder as I lay spent and undone beneath him, until he too cried out, the muscles of his body straining as he pulsed inside me.

Untangling himself from my body, Tyler rolled to the side but kept his head pressed to my chest, his ear pressed to the erratic thud of my heartbeat. The hotness from his breath danced over my nipples.

Threading my hand into his hair, I played with the dark strands. Tyler's head tilted until his mouth found my flesh and he pressed a kiss against the side of my breast, causing it to ripple with the movement. Running his hand across my stomach, he rested it over my breast protectively as he let out a contented sigh. I squirmed beneath him, needing to freshen myself in the bathroom.

Tyler shook his head against me. "You're not going anywhere. I'm not done with you yet." He moved lazily against me until his mouth found my nipple. Adjusting his position, he slipped it into his mouth, his tongue flicking over the peak until it hardened in response. "See?" he said, the word muffled by my flesh. "You aren't done with me either."

I laughed and moved his head until it flopped down on the mattress and I was able to walk to the bathroom. "I'm pretty sure we can spend some time recovering."

Tyler flopped onto his back and placed his hands behind his head. "Food?" he asked.

I shook my head and closed the bathroom door. After refreshing myself, I walked across the polished concrete floor and stood in front of the mirror. My body was shiny with sweat and smudged with red marks where Tyler had gripped onto me. My lips had that crushed look about them and my hair was mussed, strands falling around my face. My eyes were glazed as though I were drunk. I leaned closer to the mirror, studying the afterglow of sex with Tyler.

He knocked and I called out, giving him permission to enter. The door swung open slowly and Tyler walked in, still naked, and wrapped his arms around my waist from behind, pressing a kiss into my shoulder.

"I hope you're not considering getting dressed," he pressed against me, swaying our reflections in the mirror. "Fuck, you're gorgeous."

The desire to cover myself, my scars and my faults, rose as uncertainty. I swallowed as Tyler covered my breasts in his hands, the fullness spilling between his fingers.

"Look at you," he said.

I laughed. It was weak. "I could probably do with there being a little less of me."

Tyler stood back and slapped my backside, causing me to jump with surprise more than from pain. It was sharp but playful.

"I would never want there to be less of you." He moved towards me and pressed against my back. Once again, his hands wrapped around to cover my breasts and his mouth moved to my neck.

I melted.

It was as though there was something in his touch that was my undoing. I couldn't resist even if I wanted.

Tyler's hardness pressed into my backside.

"Already?" I said, reaching behind to take him in my hands.

Tyler grinned wickedly into the mirror. "I told you I was desperate to see you. I need to work you out of my system, though I'm not sure if that's entirely possible. But I do plan on fucking you at least twice more tonight. Maybe more." His eyes closed as I stroked him. He sucked on my neck, delicious moans falling between his kisses. One of his hands drifted down and over my belly, his fingers slipping inside me as his moans intensified. As my head fell back onto his shoulder, my hands twisted behind my back, sliding up and down his rock-hard shaft.

Tyler's hand roamed across my chest while the other dove between my thighs, slick with moisture. His hips ground against me as he moved a hand to my back, pushing me forward, bending me over the bathroom sink until my backside rose to meet him. He removed my hands from his cock and placed them on the edge of the sink before parting my cheeks so he could slide into me once again.

It was a different sensation this time. I had been introduced to his length, his girth, his hardness, but the intensity of our previous encounter added a tenderness that wasn't there before. Tyler held onto my hips as he watched himself slide in and out in the reflection of the mirror. His breathing deepened and he caught his bottom lip between his teeth as his eyes darkened. I felt every inch. He moved slowly and repeatedly until I clenched around him.

Then, he withdrew quickly, turning me around and pressing my backside against the counter. Propping me up until I was sitting, Tyler pried my legs open, dropping down until his mouth was on me. It didn't take long, just a few masterful strokes of his tongue and I came, my fingernails leaving white marks on his shoulders.

Giving me little time to recover after coming down from the dizzying effects of my orgasm, Tyler turned me back around and, using the grip on my hips to pull me against him, our bodies met with a thud. He didn't hesitate. He didn't stop. He rammed into me until he shuddered and released.

7

LAUREN

Midnight had passed and it was the early hours of the morning when we lay on the couch, my back between his legs and my head resting on his bare chest. Tyler twisted and picked up his laptop from the floor. "I want to show you something." He reached behind him, his body growing taut with the movement, and grabbed his glasses from the table, sliding them over his nose. Resting the computer on my lap, he reached around me, his fingers dancing over the keyboard. His desktop was as organised as the loft. Clearly labelled folders in the corner, symbols neatly stacked in rows. Screens appeared and died until a neat row of logos appeared, all sporting my name.

"What do you think?"

I sat up a little so I could get a better view. "Where did you get these?"

"I designed them."

"You?"

"Yes, me." He laughed. "No need to sound so surprised."

"I'm not. I mean, I am. I didn't think graphic design was in your wheelhouse."

"There are a lot of things in my wheelhouse that you don't know about, Lauren Greer. I've spent time in almost every department within the company and picked up a few skills along the way. Design has always appealed to me." He straightened the angle of the screen. "Do you like them?"

I pulled the laptop closer, examining the images. There were a couple in a flourished font, a few with focus-styled crosshairs, but the one that I liked the most was plain and simple. Just my name scrawled across the page, the finest line beneath it and the word 'photographer' spaced out evenly in small print below.

"I can change anything about them." His hands floated over the screen. "The name, if you want to go by something else. The font. Graphics. Mix and match."

"They're great," I said. "But I'm not sure I really need a logo."

"Of course you do. You need to go into business for yourself."

I laughed. "I don't think I'm ready for that."

"Why not?" he asked. "You've got talent, especially with architecture. And this city would be the perfect place to drum up more business."

"I don't live here though."

Tyler shrugged, his chin hooking over my shoulder. "You could."

"Well, aren't you the fast mover?"

"I know what I want."

It was as though those words flicked a switch. Suddenly, I was aware of his scent, the fresh, soapy smell of his still wet hair, the smoothness of his chest, the feel of his thighs pressed against my hips. Lowering the laptop to the ground, I twisted around until I was kneeling between his legs, facing him. He looked glorious with his mussed hair, black-rimmed glasses, bare chest and loose-fitting pants. My hunger to please him scared me. I removed his glasses, folding the arms over on themselves and placing them on the table beside the couch.

"So what other skills do you have in your wheelhouse that I don't know about?"

Tyler smiled slowly, his legs sliding together as I lifted to straddle him. "All of them," he said.

"All of them?" I asked, wrapping my arms around his neck.

He nodded, tipping his chin so his mouth met mine. "All of them," he repeated, our lips scraping against each other.

I hovered over him, teasing him with the closeness of our bodies, pressing my backside into him and moving seductively until he breathed in deeply and cursed.

"What about construction? Have you got skills in construction?" I asked.

"Yes," he murmured, pressing his mouth to mine and taking what was his. "Even construction." He smiled against my mouth and the movement caused my own lips to curve with his. "I know how to hammer a nail."

"You do?"

Tyler slid his hands up my back and around my sides until they reached the neckline of my t-shirt which he tugged down until my breasts were full and free.

"I do," he whispered and then he took my nipple into his mouth, sliding further down the couch until I was bent over him, my breasts pressed to his face as he assaulted them with his tongue. The hardness of his cock pressed against me as I ground into him, moving my hips in a circular motion as his attention to my chest intensified. His mouth moved back up my body and he toyed with the hem of my shirt, this time lifting it over my head before crushing his lips back to mine. Squirming beneath me, Tyler lifted his hips until he was able to slide his pants down his legs enough to free himself. Reaching between our bodies, he guided himself into me, groaning with pleasure as I slowly sunk onto him. As I lifted up and down, he simply lay on the couch and watched, hands hovering lightly on my hips. His eyes darkened with desire as they roamed between catching my gaze, falling to my lips, then down to my breasts. His hands moved up the side of my waist, detouring to fondle my breasts before applying pressure to my chest, pushing me, arching me backwards over his beautiful body. He was so large and strong between my legs. His length slipped further inside each time he pushed me back. I braced myself against his legs as his hand travelled down my body, twisting over my flesh until it found the soft wetness between my legs. He massaged me with his thumb as I continued to ride him. The sensation of his fingers at my clit, his cock like steel inside me, and the intensity of his glare as he watched me writhe on top of him built until moans slipped from my lips uncontrollably. Tyler's fingers moved faster and his other hand snaked up my body, grabbing onto my chin and tilting it downwards.

"Look at me," he growled.

My eyes fluttered open, but with the sensations floating about my body ready to explode into tiny pieces, my head rolled back and my eyes closed. Tyler jerked my chin towards him again, sitting up so he could watch me closer.

"Look at me," he said again, his voice filled with a deep rasp.

My eyes locked with his as my breathing increased. Tyler's hips rocked back and forth, matching my rhythm. Intensity built. Pleasure rose until wave after wave washed over me. I cried out and my body went limp, collapsing from my arched position. The motion of Tyler's body stopped and he stayed still and hard inside me as I convulsed around him. His bottom lip was caught between his teeth, concentration displayed on his features as he struggled not to come. His arms twisted around my back, supporting me as he sat up, still impaled inside. Getting to his knees, he lay me back on the couch and adjusted himself so he was hunched over me. He froze against my entrance, the tip of him teasing.

"Look at me," he said again, and I lifted my gaze from where I had been watching him, roaming over his toned stomach and chest until I met his eyes. They were dark and hungry. I was tight and tender. He kept his gaze fixed on me as he pushed inside, inch by inch, allowing me to feel the fullness, the hardness of him again. I cried out, gasping when he roughly plunged in the remaining few inches. Then he just lay there, against me, inside me, his forehead pressed to mine, his eyes blurred and dizzying with their closeness.

"I like watching you come," he whispered. "Your cheeks flame red, your eyes glaze over and your mouth—" He claimed mine hungrily, then tore away. "Words cannot explain what your mouth does to me."

And then he kissed me gently, grazing my lips with his teeth, teasing my tongue with his own. The tenderness and tightness of my recent release began to relax and I squirmed beneath him, begging for him to move instead of trapping my body with his own. He chuckled at my eagerness and relaxed, pushing me deeper into the couch, allowing his hardness further inside but still not giving me the friction I now ached for. After a few more moments of this tender torture, he rose to his knees, lifting my legs into the air and hooking them over his shoulders. This allowed him deeper access and I gasped once again as he plunged inside, giving me no warning of the power of his thrust. He rocked in and out, slowly at first so I could feel the ridges of his girth, the fullness of his length before he slipped from me, leaving just the tip hovering. Then he began the gentle assault again, sliding himself in slowly before powerfully plunging the last few inches. He repeated this over and over until he unhooked my legs from his shoulders and slid his hands down to the back of my thighs, pressing them wide to my stomach, giving him unfettered access.

His eyes were no longer locked on mine. They were stuck where our bodies joined. And then he slammed into me, his grunts in time with my muffled moans. I tightened. Pleasure built once again.

In feeling me wrap tighter around him, Tyler withdrew himself and bent down to put his mouth where his cock had just been. He lapped at me hungrily and I struggled to breathe as the sensation to come conflicted with the pressure of my thighs pressed roughly to my chest. I bucked, but Tyler held me firmly in place, his tongue teasing and lapping. I strained, my back arching as I exploded once again, flopping back onto the couch as Tyler continued his assault until I went limp. When he rose, he wiped his hand across his mouth, before plunging his hard cock back inside. My limbs were jelly. My body rippled as he pounded into me. His gaze locked on my heaving breasts which jerked with each thrust until he tensed and pushed harder, causing me to whimper as he exploded, the spurts of his come coming out in pulses.

***

I'm not sure how I got from the couch to the bed, but I woke the next morning with the sun streaming in the window dotted with leftover rain, and alone. I expected to turn over and find Tyler beside me, his glorious body stretched between the dark sheets. I wanted the opportunity to study him without his knowledge, but he wasn't there. I was naked, so I slipped on the t-shirt I wore the night before and headed out to the kitchen, giving a cursory glance around the loft to check for occupants. But neither Tyler nor Jake were there. Gentle jazz music drifted from the sound system and a freshly brewed pot of coffee sat on the thick marble benchtop. Sauntering over to the sound system, I turned the music up louder, searched the fridge for some bacon and eggs, the pantry for some tomatoes and grabbed a frying pan out of the cupboard. I was in the middle of frying the bacon, careful not to let the splatters of fat hit my bare thighs when the elevator groaned and the door opened. I thought it would be Tyler.

It wasn't.

She had her back to me as she walked in, dry cleaning draped in a clear bag over one shoulder, an oversized gym bag slung over the other. "No need to thank me," she said, dumping the suit over the edge of the couch. "I'm more than happy to stop mid-workout just to collect your dry-cleaning. No need to thank me at all." She bent down and started rifling through her gym bag, pulling out clothing and tossing it over her shoulder. She was dressed in yoga pants, a crop top, and a light rain jacket. Her hair was piled into a messy bun on her head, strands falling out to frame her face. She looked like a sports model. Tall. Blonde. Tanned. Undeniably beautiful. She also seemed strangely at home in Tyler's loft.

"I've shifted a few things around for this weekend like you asked, but you're still going to have to have that meeting with your father and Wilson. They are quite insistent." High heeled shoes fell to the floor. "Shit. I forgot a towel. Oh, and I'm using your shower."

She stopped talking and got to her feet, finally turning to face me. She blinked a few times, her eyebrows furrowing together before a brilliant smile spread over her face.

"You must be Lauren." She walked towards me, hand extended, the wide smile still plastered on her face. I didn't smile back and shook her hand hesitantly. Her eyes suddenly grew wide. "Oh!" she exclaimed. "This is not what it looks like, I promise."

"And what does this look like?" I asked, withdrawing my hand from her tight grasp and pulling the hem of my t-shirt down further.

"Like I'm fucking Tyler."

I blinked at her bluntness.

"I'm not," she assured me. "I'm his assistant, Sadie."

8

LAUREN

Tyler had only mentioned Sadie a few times in passing and, because of the way he spoke about her, her mothering tendencies, her bossiness, her strict attention to the job, I had wrongly pictured an older woman. Someone motherly. Grandmotherly perhaps. Sadie was anything but.

She stuck her hand out again. "Sadie Anderson. I've heard so much about you."

My gaze flicked down to her extended hand but I didn't take it. Sadie laughed. "I guess we've already done the handshake thing, huh. My bad. It probably doesn't help that I'm all sweaty and I've hardly got any clothes on." Her eyes fell to my naked legs and I tugged my shirt down further. "Mind you, you're not doing much better."

"I wasn't expecting visitors."

"Didn't Tyler tell you I was coming over?" Her eyes travelled from my legs back to my face as I shook my head. "Arsehole. He asked me to pick up his dry cleaning. I don't know why it was so urgent. I mean, he has, like, hundreds of suits. I don't know why he needed this one so urgently." She sighed, leaning against the kitchen bench, watching as the bacon crisped in the pan. "But I guess that's my job, isn't it? Fetch. Do as I'm told. Yes, sir. No, sir. Three bags full, sir." She plucked a piece of bacon from the pan and popped it straight into her mouth, not even blinking at the scalding heat. "Where is he, anyway? He's usually done by now."

Done with what? I wanted to ask, but that would have been admitting I had no idea where he was. Sadie walked back to where her bag was dumped on the floor, picking up the clothes she had discarded to greet me. "Tell him I'm here." And then she sauntered into the bathroom as though she owned the place. Or, at least as though she had done it many times before.

When Tyler finally walked in the door, the bacon, eggs, and tomatoes were ready and sitting on a plate and I had pants on. Dressed in shorts and a t-shirt, he was covered in sweat, a towel slung around his neck.

"Morning," he greeted as he walked across the floor. He took my cheeks between his hands and pressed a firm kiss to my lips, a smacking sound filling the air. "I'll just have a shower and then we'll eat, okay? Feel free to have yours though. No need to wait for me."

I looked down at the plates, no longer caring whether the food was hot or not, as Tyler walked towards the bedroom. Catching the dry cleaning out of the corner of his eye, he changed direction to collect it.

"Sadie came, I take it?"

"You could say that," I replied, dragging a stool out from the bench and plonking myself onto it. "She's in the shower."

"Huh." Tyler hung his suit on the back of the bedroom door. "I guess I will be eating first, after all." He sat beside me and plucked some bacon from his plate, tearing a piece off with his teeth. "I was going to cook. I didn't expect you to."

"Good," I replied. "Because I'm not that good at it."

Tyler shrugged. "Tastes great to me."

He clearly thought nothing odd about another woman using his shower. He sat beside me, chewing each mouthful, oblivious to the thoughts that were stampeding through my mind.

"Where were you?" I asked.

Tyler glanced at me sideways. "Sorry, I should have left a note or something. I've got a gym of sorts on one of the lower levels. I work out most mornings, though I was running a little late this morning." He grinned. "Might have had something to do with the late night workout I had." Reaching out, he took my hand, tugging me so I slid off the stool and stood between his legs. "You okay?" he asked. "You're awfully quiet."

I shook my head and plastered on a smile. "I'm fine."

Tyler frowned. "Fine? That bad, huh?" The way he said 'huh' sounded just like the way Sadie had said it and my stomach twisted. "I'm no expert, but as far as I'm aware, when someone says fine they never mean fine."

The bathroom door opened and Sadie walked out, looking impeccably groomed for someone who had spent so little time in front of the mirror. Her hair was deadly straight, flowing down either side of her face, high-heeled shoes were now covering her feet, and she was wearing a black one-piece pantsuit with a short, crisp white jacket over the top. Any makeup she had on was flawless, giving off an appearance of unaffected and natural beauty.

"Hey Sades," Tyler greeted her, his gaze barely flicking over her.

She rolled her eyes, bunching her workout gear into a ball and shoving it into her bag. "You could have let Lauren know I was coming."

He looked between us. "Sorry," he said again. "I guess I'm not used to having someone else around."

And yet, Sadie was clearly used to being there.

Tyler pushed the remains of his breakfast towards Sadie. "Want some?"

She shook her head, leaning over to peck a kiss on his cheek. "I'm going to get a head start. See you at the office."

She was just about at the door when Tyler turned. "Have you—"

"Yes," she yelled over her shoulder.

"But what about—"

"Goodbye, Tyler," she called out and threw a wink in my direction. "It was a pleasure to meet you, Lauren. I hope I'll see a lot more of you."

As soon as the door slid shut and I heard the grinding of the elevator, I twisted to face Tyler. "That is your assistant?"

Tyler looked up, startled. He could hear the accusation in my tone. Before answering, he cleared his throat. "I told you about Sadie."

"You didn't tell me she looked like that."

"Like what? Like a woman?"

"Like an extremely attractive woman." I moved away from the space between his legs and sat back on the stool to finish my breakfast.

Tyler lifted a single brow, leaning over to place his elbow on the bench, his head in his hand. "You find her attractive?"

"Of course I find her attractive," I said a little more forcefully than I intended. "Anyone would find her attractive."

"I guess she is."

"You guess?"

Tyler frowned. "I feel like I'm being led into some sort of trap here. Am I supposed to find her attractive?"

I pushed my plate away, no longer wanting to finish the last strips of bacon.

"Are you jealous?" he asked, the slightest hint of mirth playing in the corners of his mouth.

I deliberated in my head. Truthfully, I was feeling jealous. This woman just sauntered into his apartment as though she had done it a million times before, thought nothing of using his shower, and then proceeded to kiss him before leaving. Even if it was just a peck on the cheek, it still made my heart beat erratically and uncertainty settle in my gut.

Tyler got up from the stool, walking behind me to wrap his arms around my waist. The scent of him was intensified from his work out and I inhaled unintentionally, cursing myself as a tingling sensation prickled between my legs.

"You have nothing to be jealous of," he said into my ear, his lips brushing over my skin until he sucked the drop of my earlobe into his mouth, teeth grazing the tender flesh. I squirmed on the stool, clenching my thighs together, determined not to succumb. It both annoyed and excited me how easily I was turned on by him.

When I didn't turn, didn't melt to his kiss, he dragged my stool with me on it, backwards, creating room for him to stand in front of me.

"Sadie and I have been friends for years. She's been my assistant for years, though I doubt she will be for much longer. We have never been, and never will be together. You have nothing to worry about. I'm all yours."

He looked straight into my eyes as he said it and, as each word fell from his mouth, my annoyance dissipated to be replaced with a touch of guilt. There was nothing either Tyler or Sadie did that I should be annoyed about. And yet, it was still there niggling at the back of my mind, her familiarity with him, her knowledge of his life, his whereabouts. I was new in his life and she had been there for years. I had everything and nothing to be jealous of.

I sighed. "I'm not jealous."

"You're not?"

"No."

"Well, I guess I have nothing to worry about then."

"Nope, guess not." I shook my head.

Tyler leaned over and hooked his finger on the neckline of my t-shirt, his eyes darting downwards. "Care to join me for a shower?"

* * *

Emerging from the shower clean and satisfied, if not a little tender, I gathered my gear and collected what I would need for the day into my pack. Tyler stood at the mirror, twisting the loops of his tie.

"I've organised Jimmy to come and collect you." He adjusted the knot until it sat evenly at the base of his throat. "I've given him strict instructions to keep his hands to himself."

"Tyler!" I exclaimed.

Tyler grinned. "Kidding," he said. "Though I did inform him of the change in our relationship, just in case he had any ideas."

I laughed and was about to say that Jimmy was too young for my tastes, before remembering that Gabe was probably younger. My laughter died away and I cleared my throat, watching as Tyler took the suit jacket from its hanger and shrugged it over his broad shoulders. He was so gorgeous it made my heart ache.

"Did Jimmy really need to know?" I asked cautiously. "Don't you think that maybe we should wait a little before announcing to everyone that we are together?"

"Why?"

"Because of…" I didn't say his name. It still hurt. The guilt.

He walked over and placed a kiss on my nose. "No," he said simply.

"No?"

He shook his head, hands resting on each of my shoulders, and peered down to look into my eyes. "No." Releasing me, he turned to collect his keys. "We'll go to Maria's for dinner tonight. I'll pick you up from the site around six. Will you have enough to do to keep yourself busy until then?"

Having gathered my gear, I followed him into the elevator. "Billie's picking me up for lunch. No doubt that will take a while."

Jimmy was waiting beside the car, hands stuffed into the pockets of worn jeans and squishing a discarded cigarette butt under the toe of his boot. He smiled nervously when I approached and held the door open.

"Why thank you," I said, smiling at him mischievously. "Such a gentleman."

"Ma'am," he replied seriously. He looked over to Tyler and nodded, a look passing between them I didn't understand.

Jimmy was quiet in the car, fiddling with the radio, adjusting the angle of his seat, the distance between his feet and the pedals, anything but acknowledging my presence.

"Is everything okay?" I asked when I couldn't stand it any longer.

He looked up sharply. "Everything is fine, thank you."

"You're very serious, and not one swear word has been said."

A small smile crept over his face, but he wiped it away quickly. "You're with the boss now."

"And that changes me?"

Jimmy shook his head, eyes set firmly on the road. "Not you. Me."

"Why?"

"Why?" he repeated. "Because you're with the boss now and Mr Thornton is not someone I want to mess with."

"And being relaxed, talking to me and being friendly, that is messing with Tyler?"

Jimmy looked across and narrowed his eyes, unsure how to answer.

"I believe that what I say should be the gauge of how you treat me, not Tyler."

He swallowed, his Adam's apple bobbing up and down. "Mr Thornton said some strong words."

"Like what?"

The smile that was threatening before slowly crept across his face. "I'm not telling you."

I crossed my arms, feigning annoyance and looking at Jimmy sideways.

His usual cheek-splitting grin overcame his face. "Fuck it."

He didn't shut up after that, telling me of all the recent developments at the site. How the interior of the lower level was being done, and the interior designers strutted around in high heels and refused to wear the correct footwear on the site. How the construction on the upper levels had hit a snag due to the roofing contractors not doing what they were contracted to do, so all work had been halted on the top floor. And how he was ever so slowly getting over his fear of heights by making himself crawl out on the scaffolding each lunch break.

* * *

When Billie arrived to collect me at lunchtime, I had completed all the shots to showcase the development of the exterior and I only had the interior of the lower level to go. She had sent a text to let me know she'd arrived, and when I walked outside she was waiting in the car, phone stuck to the side of her face. She pointed to it and rolled her eyes when I sat in the passenger's seat.

"It will have to be another time," she said to the person on the phone. She rolled her eyes again and put the car into gear, flicking a glance over her shoulder before pulling out. A vehicle braked behind us as she cut it off, horn blasting to show its frustration. Billie adjusted her chin, wedging the phone between it and her shoulder and held her hand out the window, pulling the finger at the driver behind us before joining the flow of traffic.

"No. It doesn't suit. I need a different appointment time." She looked over at me, motioning a flapping mouth movement with the hand that wasn't on the steering wheel. "Fine. That will have to do."

She threw the phone into the holder between the seats before plastering a smile on her face and performing another award-winning eye roll. "Doctors," she said. "They think that everyone should change their schedule to suit them. Does it not occur to them that other people have lives too and can't just drop everything because they have an 'opening'?" She put air quotes around the word, causing the car to swerve slightly. My fingers curled around the seat belt, and I sent up a prayer that it would do the job it was intended for if needed.

The café that Billie chose was modern, minimalistic and trendy. The dishes that came out of the servery were pretty but the size of them looked more suitable for a sparrow than a human. Billie couldn't decide what to have and none of the options sounded appealing to me. The vegetables were all fermented, and everything was organic, but the menu spoke more about the process to create each dish than what it actually consisted of. Even the coffee tasted weird.

I heard about every doctor's appointment and every bout of morning sickness, which, she informed me, did not stick exclusively to mornings. I even heard about Hamish's hesitation to have sex in case he hurt the baby. I did my best to forget that little piece of information.

After we were done eating, Billie reached over the table and took my hand in hers, tears glistening. "I don't care what Hamish says." She blinked and the tears lessened. "I want you at the birth."

To say I was shocked was an understatement. I choked a little on the carrot, beetroot and wheatgrass juice that Billie had ordered for me—because it would change my life—and had to thump my chest, coughing to recover.

"You want me at the birth?"

"Of course I do," Billie said, taking my choking for emotion rather than shock. "In case you hadn't noticed, I am surrounded by testosterone. There are zero females in this family and I need another female around. You're the first girl any of the boys have brought home. Like, seriously. Maybe they brought the odd girl home when they were back in high school or something, to like, 'hang'." Again, the air quotes. "Well, I imagine anyway. I wasn't there. Obviously. I've decided I like having you around. I told him that too."

"Told who?"

"Hamish." She winked mischievously. "Whether you're dating Gabe or Tyler, I like you." She threw the remainder of her juice down her throat. "And if you get tired of Tyler you can always move onto Jake."

"Billie!"

"What?" she said. "You might like that caveman thing." She screwed up her face, making it clear she did not. "Just stay away from Hamish."

I didn't know whether to protest or laugh. I went with laughter.

Billie cleared the smile from her face. "I mean it."

9

LAUREN

Due to my less than appetising lunch, I was starving when Tyler's car finally pulled into the carpark. But when the tinted window rolled down, it wasn't Tyler's face who smiled back at me. It was Sadie's.

"Hey," she greeted happily. "Tyler's stuck at work. He won't be too much longer but he couldn't get away on time so he sent me instead. He'll meet us at Maria's."

"Oh," was all I managed to say. I put my pack in the backseat and climbed into the car.

"Good day?" Sadie asked.

I nodded, choosing to keep my eyes fixed on the blur of buildings out the window. The car fell into silence. Sadie kept glancing over at me, but I didn't know what to say to her. It was best to say nothing.

"Sorry about this morning," Sadie said finally. "It was never my intention to make you feel uncomfortable. Ty should have told you I was there. He should have told you I was coming over."

"Have you worked with him long?"

"About seven years now. We met at uni when he was an overzealous student with no friends. I taught him how to have fun." Her face twisted into a comical smile. "Well, I did. I'm not so sure he's capable of it anymore." She smiled, trying to get one out of me, but I still wasn't sure what to make of this woman who was such a big part of Tyler's life. A big, beautiful part.

"There's nothing between us," she added.

"So you keep saying."

Maria greeted us enthusiastically, throwing her arms around us both when we were seated at the same table Tyler and I had sat at a few months ago.

Sadie ordered a drink and kept checking her phone, silence sitting between us awkwardly. When her gin and tonic arrived, she threw it back in one mouthful, wiping her mouth afterwards but still, somehow, managing to look together and glamorous. "He's so used to getting me to fill in for him at work, meetings he's running late for, conference calls he can no longer attend, so I guess it just never occurred to him that it wasn't a good idea in his personal life."

Tyler appeared behind her and she got up from her seat quickly. "Oh good, you're here," she said.

He grinned and walked over to plant a kiss on my forehead. "I am."

"Well, that's my cue." Sadie gathered her jacket from where she had hung it over the back of her seat and slipped it over her shoulders. "Don't forget about tomorrow night," she warned Tyler.

"What's happening tomorrow night?"

Tyler waved aside my question. "How was your day?"

I slunk back onto my seat and folded my arms. "Next time you're running late, a simple text message will do. I don't need a babysitter."

"You're annoyed," Tyler said. I wasn't sure if it was a question or a statement, but either way, it was correct. Tyler sat back in his seat, crossing his arms, mimicking my pose. "Because of Sadie."

"As I said, I don't need a babysitter."

"Lauren." Tyler leaned forward again, reaching out, urging me to take his hand but I kept mine folded across my chest. "Sadie is a big part of my life."

"So she said."

He ignored my comment and continued. "We went to University together. We kept in contact as she travelled the world and when she came back, I offered her a job as my assistant until she found something better. She has been with me ever since and is brilliant at her job. We have never been together. Ever. Never even shared a kiss, nothing more than a peck on the cheek. Any problem you have with her is purely in your head. You need to get over it." He spoke so plainly and bluntly, annoyance crept up my spine.

"Get over it?" I repeated. I was annoyed but knew there was truth in his words.

"I give you my word that I am only interested in you. So unless you don't trust me, you are going to have to learn to get along with Sadie."

My skin prickled. Although I agreed with his words, the way he expressed himself, the way he told me what to do, how to feel, sat uneasily with me. Tyler shuffled his seat around the circular table until he was beside me. His hand stretched out under the table and rested on my knee. "I swear to you that Sadie is nothing but a friend. A good friend. An old friend. But just a friend, nonetheless."

"So next time I come across Gabe, you wouldn't have a problem if I'm friends with him?"

Tyler tensed. His hand fell from my knee. "That is a completely different situation."

"How?"

He took a sip of the whiskey the waiter placed in front of him. "Because," he leaned closer, his voice dropping low. "You haven't had to see a freshly fucked look on Sadie's face when she appeared with me. You haven't had to watch her grope me while drunk, or watch my lips on hers as I stared at you over her shoulder. You haven't had to see those things because they never happened. If they had, I would understand your feelings, but given the circumstances of the relationship you had with Gabe were very different from the one I have with Sadie, I don't think I'm the one being unreasonable here." He turned to the waiter and pointed to the now empty whiskey glass. "Another, please."

The rest of the conversation during dinner was polite but strained. Suddenly I felt as though I were back in the car when I first arrived, though instead of butterflies flitting around my stomach, it was dread. I didn't want him to look at me with hesitation in his eyes. I wanted him to look at me with affection, with desire, but I didn't know how to get back there. Our conversation about Gabe and Sadie weighed heavily between us.

* * *

Once we arrived back at the loft and the elevator groaned to a stop, Tyler walked into the bedroom, removing his tie and jacket. He returned moments later wearing a plain shirt and ripped jeans that hung so wonderfully off his hips.

"Want a coffee?" he asked, as he moved to the kitchen, his bare feet padding softly across the polished concrete floor.

"I'll never sleep if I have one this late."

"I never do, anyway." He flicked the kettle on and moved to the pantry to get more beans for the grinder.

I looked over the kitchen bench, noting a lack of a coffee maker. "No fancy coffee machine?"

"I like plunger coffee best. Dark and strong."

He barely looked at me. Instead, he rifled through the cupboards, searching for something he never found. I missed the way he looked at me. I wanted to see desire, and know that it was me who had put it there.

With trembling fingers, I began to undo the buttons of my shirt, quietly and slowly, so not to catch his attention. Buttons released, I let the shirt slip over my shoulders to the floor before reaching behind my back to unclasp the hook of my bra and letting it follow. Tyler leaned against the bench with his back to me, staring out at the lights of the city while he waited for the coffee. I undid the buttons of my jeans and wiggled out of them, discarding them along with my shoes and underwear. The movement caught Tyler's attention and our eyes met in the reflection of the window.

I stood naked and vulnerable in the middle of the room, my heart pounding in my chest, my nipples hardening with anticipation.

Tyler turned slowly, his steel-coloured eyes dark and stormy. They travelled over my body slowly, slipping down my neck and over my chest. I almost could feel it when they fell to the patch of hair between my legs, and my breath hitched.

"Come here," he commanded.

I trembled. But it wasn't with fear. There was nothing he could do, nothing he would do, that would make me fearful of him. I knew I could walk away from anything he might ask of me. The reason I trembled was because I didn't want to. I wanted to do whatever made him happy. And that scared me.

I walked across the floor as Tyler's jaw tightened, working back and forth the closer I got. When I was only inches from him, I stopped. He didn't touch me. His hand didn't reach out and stroke my flesh like I wanted, like I was aching for. He adjusted himself, his arousal now obvious and then started undoing the buttons on his shirt. One by one they fell, exposing the tanned and muscled skin beneath. I longed to lean forward and run my tongue over the smooth plane of his chest. But Tyler was still undressing, his eyes locked on mine, dark and hungry. His shirt fell to the floor. His shoes got tossed to the side. His jeans pooled in a black puddle at his feet. But still, he did not touch me.

"Kneel."

My heart leapt at his command. There was something undeniably sexy in the way he spoke. Something that had me aching to obey. I dropped to my knees, keeping my eyes firmly fixed on his and knelt in front of him. Reaching down he ran his fingers over my lips roughly, his thumb dipping inside my mouth.

"Open."

I opened my mouth and he closed his eyes, taking a deep breath before gripping onto himself and stroking his hardness. Reaching down once again, he gripped my chin, pulling it down to open my mouth further and then guided himself in, groaning as my lips wrapped around his cock. I sucked him hungrily and eagerly, moving closer to place my hands on the backs of his thighs, running them up his flesh until I felt the roundness of his backside. His fingers threaded through my hair, gathering the strands and piling them between his fingers in a fountain on the top of my head. His hands rested there, gripped in my hair as I moved back and forth over the length of him, his hardness growing to steel every time the tip of him brushed against the back of my throat.

The tightness of his grip increased. I could feel the wetness creeping between my legs, the ache of my breasts as they longed for his mouth. Tyler grunted and my scalp tingled as he used the grip on my hair to control the motion of my mouth. I convulsed when he pushed deeply, confused by the strange waves of desire that pulsed through me. I drew back, gasping for air before Tyler pulled me towards him again and I took him in my mouth, hungry for more. Holding my head still, he pushed into me. I struggled to breathe for the briefest of moments before he released, pulling me to my feet and taking my mouth roughly. He pressed his body against mine, pushing until my backside hit the lip of the bench and he wrapped his arm under me, lifting me onto the cold marble. Scooting me forward so I was balanced on the edge of the bench, Tyler pushed my legs apart, fell to his knees and inserted a single finger into my glistening sex.

"My god, you're wet," he said as he worked his finger in and out. Dipping his head, he ran his tongue along the full length of my slit, before sitting back and sliding his finger inside once again. A second finger, and then a third. The desire I wanted to see earlier screamed in his eyes. Removing his fingers, he licked off my juices before closing his mouth over me again. His dark head bobbed between my thighs and the familiar feeling of wanting to dissolve began to creep through my limbs. No longer able to control it, I lay back on the bench, surrendering to his affection. I was so close when he stood up and pushed my legs further apart before standing between them, the tip of him resting against my entrance.

"I need to fuck you before you come," he said, and the gravel of his voice throbbed and pulsed through me.

He was gentle at first, rocking back and forth, his hand spread across my stomach. "I love your breasts." His hands moved upwards, massaging the flesh between his fingers as his intensity increased and he rammed into me. He pulled out, leaving me feeling empty while he bent and pressed his mouth to the crease of my thigh. "And this little part right here." I squirmed as he ran his tongue along the sensitive flesh, before moving to the other side. "I find this part of you very, very sexy."

Again I squirmed and tried to adjust the position of him, letting him know I wanted—no—I needed him inside me again.

"What do you want, Lauren?" he asked, holding my legs firmly apart but not giving me the attention I desired.

I moaned, writhing against the cool marble. My hand moved down to touch myself but Tyler caught it in his. "No," he said, pulling my hand away and brushing his mouth over the knuckles. "What do you want?" he asked again.

"You," I panted.

He thrust inside. And, as I was wrenched across the bench, the skin of my back gripped to the marble painfully.

His fingers dug into the flesh of my hips. "And what do you want me to do to you?"

I whimpered, grinding my hips against his, but he held me tightly and firmly, not letting me rock against him.

"What do you want me to do to you?" He was hard and big and I felt incredibly tight wrapped around him. Letting go of one side of my hips, he gripped onto my chin, directing my gaze to his. "Tell me."

"I want you to fuck me," I whispered breathlessly.

His hand gripped back to my side and he began to move inside me forcefully. With each thrust, my skin pinched beneath me and I was jolted across the bench. Tyler held my thighs and pulled me back against the bench towards him, slamming into me with a slap, his cock ramming further than it had before. Time and time again, he thrust until the ripples of desire began to pulsate through me and I cried out. Pulling me closer, his rhythm did not stop as I dissolved, my body turning to jelly beneath him.

"Look at me," he growled.

My eyes fluttered open and Tyler leaned over, his mouth fumbling over mine, our breath mingling as he released.

10

LAUREN

"You sure you don't want some?"

Tyler sat on the couch, chest bare, hair mussed from our recent encounter, glasses perched on his nose, and a cold cup of coffee at his lips.

I shook my head, stifling a yawn, huddled on the recliner chair, trying to keep my eyes open. The hours Tyler appeared to keep were a lot later than I was used to. It was the wee hours of the morning before I fell asleep the night before, and it was already approaching midnight.

"Where's Jake?" I asked sleepily.

Tyler looked around the room, as though surprised not to find him there.

"Last time I was here, Jake's bed was over there in front of the fireplace," I explained.

"He's on the second floor. He's converting it like I did this one. Gives him something to keep his hands busy."

"He's adjusting to life back here okay?"

Tyler shook his head, running his hands through his hair, making it stand up at odd angles. "Not really. He won't talk about it, his time over there, I mean. He says he's not allowed to, but there's a part of me that thinks he just really doesn't want to. I don't think he wants us knowing who he was over there."

"What did he do? I mean, what was his position?" I didn't know much about the army, but I knew there were differences in the roles and positions.

"Something confidential. All I know is that at one stage he was in the Special Forces."

"He's told you nothing else?"

"Nothing." Tyler reached forward, grabbed his laptop off the coffee table and pulled it onto his lap. "I've just got to do a couple of things before work tomorrow."

"Tomorrow? I thought you said you took the day off."

"I did." He glanced up from the screen. "But that was before Dad changed my plans. I'm sorry. I know you've come all this way to spend time with me and I'm running off to work, but I promise I'll make it up to you."

"Why don't I come with you?"

"To the office?"

I nodded, stifling yet another yawn.

He laughed. "I don't think it's bring your girlfriend to work day until next month."

"But can't you do whatever you want? Aren't you the boss?"

Tyler tapped the keys of his laptop. "Far from it."

I pouted. "I really don't want to be left alone all day. I didn't even bring a good book."

"I could call Sadie to keep you company." Tyler smirked.

Grabbing the cushion, I threw it at him. "Why don't I pretend I'm a reporter from a magazine or something? We could say I'm shadowing you for a day for some exposé on the dashing younger generation of the Thornton Empire."

"Hamish would love to hear you call it an empire."

The words he had uttered before rolled through my mind. "Did you just call me your girlfriend?"

"Well, you are, aren't you?" Lines of confusion creased between his brows. "We're together, aren't we?" He placed the laptop beside him and leaned forward. "I just assumed you felt the same as I did. I never thought to ask." He inched forward on the seat. "I need to know if you feel the same. I'm not here for some casual fling. I'm here for you, Lauren."

Unfurling from my huddled position, I padded across the floor to take his face between my hands, squishing his lips together in a pucker before kissing them loudly. "That depends."

"On what?"

"On whether I get to come to the office with you tomorrow." I ran my hands through his hair as he rested his head against my stomach. Bending over him, I whispered into his ear, "Think of the fun we could have when no one is looking."

Tyler's hands snaked around my waist before cupping the cheeks of my backside, his fingers digging into the flesh, his mouth moving its way up the fabric of my t-shirt, searching for my breast.

"Hey, hey, hey," I said, stepping away from him. "I'm much too tired for you to start anything."

Tyler sat back. "Are you sure?"

As if to emphasise my words, I was overtaken with a yawn. "Yes," I said. "Very sure. Goodnight," I called over my shoulder as I walked to the bedroom.

"Are you sure, you're sure?" he called out again.

I shut the door, chuckling to myself and climbed into the large bed, turning onto my side and pulling the sheet tight to my chin.

* * *

"Morning."

The word was too loud. It was too early. I jostled in the bed, trying to ignore the gentle shaking of my shoulder.

"What time is it?" I half mumbled, half moaned.

"I've got to be at work in an hour. I didn't know how long you'd take to get ready."

I opened my eyes, peering over the edge of the sheet. Tyler was dressed and ready. The scent of soap clung to his body. "How long does it take to drive there?"

"Twenty minutes."

I groaned and tossed the sheet away, flopping onto my back. Tyler pressed his head between my breasts, his lips nipping at the soft flesh. "Believe me, I would be staying right here in bed with you if I could." He took hold of my hands and dragged me upwards.

I reluctantly got out of bed, bending down to pull some clothes from my bag. When I turned, Tyler's head was tilted to the side, his eyes plastered on my backside.

"Do you need some help in the shower?" he asked.

"I thought you said you had to be there soon."

Tyler walked behind me, his hands reaching around to cup my breasts, his mouth falling to the curve of my neck. Immediately my nipples hardened, and they drew his attention. Turning me around, he bent his head to kiss the hardened nubs. I drew in a breath, my back arching as the roughness of the fabric conflicted with the softness of his mouth. But before I melted completely, I pulled away and Tyler whimpered, his eyes stuck on the wet stain left on my t-shirt.

"Behave," I said, smirking as I walked towards the bathroom.

"Can I at least watch?" he called out.

I shut the door.

Twenty minutes later I was dressed and ready. I had opted for something a little more business-like than I usually chose to wear. It was an office, not a construction site, after all. I dressed simply in a pale blue shirt and paired it with a black pencil skirt. Slipping on heels completed the outfit.

Tyler was on his phone when I emerged. His eyes lighted on me and he dismissed the caller telling him he would call him back once he was at the office. "Fuck me," he said with a low whistle.

"I believe I already have," I replied.

"Fuck me again?" he offered.

* * *

Watching Tyler through the lens of the camera only made me fall for him more. I wondered what the photos would turn out like, and was worried that they would somehow end up with an overly sensual tone. Not that it mattered. They were for my eyes only.

When he spoke to one of his co-workers, discussing the problems he had with the roofing contractors, I found myself focussing on his mouth and the way it moved. I took photos purely of his lips, once catching an image when his bottom lip was caught between his teeth. When he spoke on the phone, I took images of his hands resting on the desk or running through his hair when he got frustrated. From behind, I captured the brace of his shoulders, the flex of his muscles beneath the dark fabric, and the freckle that sat just below his hairline.

He hardly spoke business to any of the people on the phone. He consulted his computer then asked about the health of their children, their current golf handicap, how their holiday went. It wasn't until the end of the conversation that he would bring up some sort of paperwork, some sort of deal they were working through.

People came and went in his office, asking questions or providing reports he needed before his next phone call.

"I'm afraid my job is rather boring," Tyler said after hanging up from yet another phone conversation. "It would be far more interesting if we visited some sites, maybe a few of the hotels, but I don't actually leave the office all that often. Well, not unless there's an attractive photographer on the scene." He pushed his chair back from the desk. "You can leave if you want."

I shook my head, closing the gap between us and hoisting my skirt up my thighs so I could climb onto his lap, my legs wrapping around his hips.

"Or you can stay," he said.

I lowered my mouth to his and kissed him deeply, like I'd been dying to for what seemed like an eternity. The chair tilted back, causing me to fall into him heavier. His hands feathered up and down the exposed skin of my thighs.

"Do you want to have a quickie?" I asked, finding myself incredibly turned on, making out in his office, knowing people were walking past the frosted glass walls behind us.

"A quickie?" Tyler shook his head. "I don't do quickies."

I lifted one eyebrow, smiling seductively. "The thought kind of arouses me."

Tyler matched my expression, one brow lifting into the air as though pondering my suggestion. He tilted the chair forward again and reached for a button on the phone. "What time is my next call?" he asked the black box.

A voice came back over the line. Not Sadie's, she didn't work weekends. "Ten minutes, Mr Thornton."

Tyler pushed me from his lap, walking over to twist the lock. Grabbing my hand, he pushed me against the door, his hands against the wood, trapping me. He moved in slowly, teasing my mouth with his own, nipping the sag of my bottom lip. His hands moved to my breast and he crushed it under his fingers, plucking the buttons of my shirt apart until he found skin against skin. Then his hand slid down to the waistband of my skirt, slipping beneath, and moving the material of my underwear aside until his fingers brushed against my sex.

"You're wet." His fingers moved in a slow circular motion.

"Ah, huh," I moaned.

"Shhh," he hushed, and slipped a finger inside me, his eyes following the shadow of someone walking past the frosted window. He spoke quietly into my ear, his voice deep with desire. "I can't tell you how much it turns me on to have my fingers inside you while people are walking around on the other side of this door. They have no idea what I'm doing to you." His mouth brushed over my jawline. "No idea that my fingers are inside you." He pushed deeper and I rose up the door, my breath caught in my throat, my heart pounding erratically.

The desire to come welled inside me and I reached forward, toying with his belt, eager to feel him between my hands. But Tyler pulled back, shaking his head. When he was assured I wasn't going to touch him, he leaned back into me, pushing his fingers in and out until I panted with expectation. Then, he removed them and sucked the stickiness off before tucking my shirt back into my waistband. Cloud fogged my brain. I wanted to come. I needed to come. I wanted to get to my knees and suck until he came, but he walked away from me, returning to sit at his desk, hiding his erection under the mahogany top. Still leaning against the door, breath and breasts heaving, I looked at him questioningly.

"I told you I don't do quickies," he said. "But believe me, I'm not done with you yet." And then he picked up the phone and told the person on the other end to dial the number, leaving me breathless and wanting and burning. Tyler appeared to be able to switch it on and off, leaving me wet and weak as he spoke on the phone, no hint that he had just had me pressed against the door, fingers inside me. Only his eyes gave his desire away. They watched me hungrily as words, straight and plain, slipped from his mouth. I remained pressed against the door, slowly doing up the buttons of my shirt, making sure he was watching and waiting for each glimpse of flesh that peeked through the material. I left upper buttons undone, allowing the crease of my cleavage to show between the strips of blue and then sat opposite him, sliding my skirt higher up my thighs and crossing my legs.

The inflection in Tyler's tone did not waver, but his eyes roamed over me with such intensity it was as though I could feel them. He was so controlled. And all I wanted was to see him undone. I wanted to see him trembling with lust and desire.

I shimmied the edge of my skirt higher up my thighs until a flash of red lace could be seen. Tyler sat up, phone still pressed to his ear, all the right words still coming from his mouth, but eyes firmly fixed at where I slowly slid my underwear down my legs. He stood when they fell to the floor, taking a deep breath, his chest rising and falling heavily. I slouched a little on the chair, opening my legs and moving a hand closer to myself, arching my back and biting my bottom lip. Excitement trilled deliciously as Tyler's erection strained against its material cage. He cleared his throat, steel-coloured eyes glued to where I was pleasuring myself, and ended the call abruptly, telling the other person, "Something has come up."

The phone was slammed into the receiver and Tyler stalked around the desk, hands fumbling with the buckle of his belt until his hardness unfurled and he began to stroke himself roughly as he leaned against the edge of the desk, watching. I let a small moan escape my lips and groaned as an echo.

"I need to be inside you," he said hoarsely.

I rolled my head back seductively. "But," I panted. "But you don't do quickies and your next appointment could walk in here at any moment." Biting my bottom lip, I closed my eyes and breathed in deeply. "We haven't got enough time."

Tyler released himself and stalked over to me, pulling my fingers away and wrapping his lips around them. Then he roughly pulled me to my feet, jerking me over to the desk and bending me at the waist. His hands pushed the material of my skirt higher up my thighs until my backside was displayed, bent over the edge of his desk, ready and exposed for him.

While one hand braced my back heavily against the desk, the other played with the cheeks of my backside, massaging, his fingers digging into the flesh, pulling them apart. He groaned when he slipped his finger into my wet folds.

"My god, you're wet," he said for the second time that day. The hand pressed to my back was removed and he parted the cheeks of my backside further, allowing the hardness of his cock to press against my opening.

The door handle twisted and someone pounded against the door.

"Tyler?" Hamish's voice was cold.

"Fuck," Tyler cursed, the tip of him disappearing from my entrance. "One minute," he called out, pulling his pants up. Lifting me from the desk, he slid my skirt back down my thighs and helped me to hurriedly do up the buttons of my shirt. I took a seat as he opened the door to his father then hurried to sit behind his desk.

11

LAUREN

Hamish stormed in just as I noticed the splash of red lace lying on the carpeted floor. I shoved it under the desk with the toe of my shoe, hoping Hamish didn't notice.

"Why was the door locked?" Hamish said gruffly.

"Good afternoon to you too," Tyler said, his eyes lazy, his tone impatient. He sat back in his chair, cupping his hands behind his head. "What can I do for you? I thought the whole reason I had to come in today was because you couldn't. And now you're here."

Hamish noticed me for the first time and his eyes narrowed. "Lauren." He nodded in greeting, but there was no warmth to it. His eyes drifted over me and I desperately wanted to shrivel into the chair and disappear. I felt like he noticed every wayward ruffle of my clothing, every flush to my cheeks, and every strand of disarrayed hair.

"Mr Thornton." I nodded in return and hoped more colour didn't flame my cheeks.

Tyler, having recovered enough, got up from his chair and walked between his father and me, blocking the line of vision. "What can I do for you?"

"I need you in a meeting with me this afternoon."

"I was planning on leaving shortly. Lauren and I have plans."

"You will need to cancel them. Something has come up and I require your presence. It's non-negotiable. Lauren will just have to wait."

The set of Tyler's shoulders twitched imperceptibly and he took a protective step towards me. "Can't it wait?" he asked Hamish, his voice tight.

"If it could wait, do you think I'd be in your office right now, demanding that you attend the meeting?"

Tyler's shoulders slumped. "What time?"

"The meeting starts in half an hour."

With a firm nod, Tyler moved back behind his desk. "I will be there."

"Good. Now, do you mind stepping out for a moment? There is something I wish to discuss with Lauren."

"Do I mind stepping out of my own office so you can speak to Lauren? Yes, I do mind. There is nothing you need to say to her that you cannot say in front of me."

"It's not something that concerns you, and you don't mind, do you, Lauren?"

There was little more I could do other than shrug and agree. Tyler ran his hands through his hair, giving me an apologetic smile, and then walked out the door, closing it loudly behind him.

Hamish walked around the office, staring out the window in painful silence before taking a seat at Tyler's desk and swivelling the chair around to face me.

"Lauren," he said.

"Mr Thornton," I replied, matching his tone.

"It would serve you well not to mess with my family."

A cough of surprise caught in my throat but Hamish continued, barely looking at me, choosing instead to focus on the pen hovering between his fingers.

"There is nothing to be done about Gabe now. I have lost him once again, thanks to you. But I will not have you ruining Tyler. That boy has a future as the head of this company and I do not see it happening with his younger brother's ex-lover at his side. But there has been enough turmoil for now. Just keep Tyler happy and stay away from Jake."

"From Jake?" I repeated. Somehow, it was funny when Billie said it but infuriating when Hamish did.

"Who's to say you won't go after him next? For all I know, you might be trying to bed all the Thornton men. Soon, I could be the only one left who you haven't fucked, literally and figuratively."

Anger lifted me to my feet. "Excuse me?" I said, levelling my gaze.

"You heard me." Hamish tossed the pen onto the desk before getting to his feet. "Keep Tyler happy until he tires of you. You know he will tire of you, don't you?"

Tyler chose that moment to stride back through the door, holding two coffees in his hands. He held one out to me, a question hovering in his eyes.

"Everything okay in here?" He pushed past his father to sit at the desk.

Hamish waved aside his question, a smile appearing on his face. "Everything is fine and dandy. I just had some business to discuss with Lauren and her role during the casino build." He kept his voice steady and even, without a hint of the lie that was hidden in it. "I think we understand where things stand, don't we, Lauren?"

I managed a smile. "I think we do." I lowered myself back to the seat and begged the seething anger to subside.

Hamish walked out the door. "Fifteen minutes," he called out to Tyler.

The moment his father was out of earshot, Tyler turned to me. "What did he say?"

I shrugged. I didn't know whether to tell Tyler or not. Telling would enrage him and only strain things further between him and Hamish and, no doubt, in Hamish's eyes that would end up to be my fault. In the end, I plastered a smile on my face and decided dismissing the comments was the only action to take. "Wouldn't you like to know?"

"Yes," Tyler said seriously. "I would."

I shook my head, trying to downplay the effect his father's words had. "It was nothing. Just the usual. Don't hurt my boy and all that."

Tyler's eyes hardened. "He didn't."

I shrugged again and took a sip of the coffee he had brought me. "Good coffee."

"Don't change the subject."

I sighed, letting him think I was impatient with his line of questioning. "It's fine, Tyler. Go to your meeting. I will wait for you here." Getting to my feet, I walked around the desk to sit in Tyler's lap and wrap my arms around his neck. Hamish's words floated through my head as I pressed my lips to his, draining away the pleasure that usually rippled through me. *Just keep him happy until he tires of you.* Pulling away from Tyler's returned embrace, I adjusted the tilt of the image on his wall. "Why don't I go get us some dinner while you're at the meeting? Anything you feel like?"

Tyler fished into the top drawer of his desk and threw me some keys. "Here, take my car. I'll meet you back at the loft as soon as I'm done. Get anything you feel like. I'm easy. And Lauren?" He waited until I looked at him. "I'm sorry. This is not how I intended our first weekend together to be. You are leaving tomorrow and I feel like I've only just got you. I don't want to let go again just yet."

I bent down to retrieve my underwear from under the desk, but Tyler, seeing what I was doing, plucked them from my fingers and shoved them into his pocket, smiling wickedly. "I don't think you need those," he said, coming closer. "I'm not done with you yet." He turned back to his desk. "And remember we've got to attend that art gallery opening tonight."

"What art gallery opening?"

Tyler shuffled through some papers on his desk. "Did I not tell you?" I shook my head. "I thought I told you. I've got to attend an art gallery opening. I only have to pop in and make an appearance. We don't need to stay long. Sadie's arranged a car to come and collect us at eight. That way we can have a few drinks without worrying about driving." He stopped rifling through the papers and looked up at me. "That okay? If you'd prefer not to come, you could stay back at the loft, but I've promised a brief appearance."

"I'll come. What sort of art?"

Tyler smiled and winked. "Photography."

* * *

I decided on Thai food, knowing Tyler had an affinity for it, and returned to the loft. I couldn't get the television to work, well, I could get the picture or the sound, just not at the same time. I wandered around the loft, flicking through the shelf upon shelf of records, the names of Etta James, Nina Simone, Miles Davis, Ray Charles and Louis Armstrong repeating on the covers frequently. Pulling one of the records out of its cover, I toyed with the idea of placing it on the vintage turntable sitting in pride of place in the centre of the shelving, but I was too afraid of accidentally damaging it. I looked for something to read, but most of the books that were lined neatly in alphabetical order were non-fiction with only a few of the classics appearing sporadically. In the end, I gave up and flopped back onto the couch, plugging earphones into my phone and listening to the audio book I had started on the plane. It was over two hours before Tyler returned. The food had gone cold and we only had an hour before we were to be collected to attend the art gallery opening. Tyler reheated the food and we ate hurriedly before getting dressed for the occasion. Once again my lack of formal dress wear became evident as I donned on the black dress with the zipper down the full length of the back. I walked over to Tyler, swiping my hair over my shoulder and asking him to pull up the zipper. His eyes burned into my exposed skin.

"I still find it difficult thinking of the first time I did up this zipper," he murmured into my ear. "It's torture mixed with pleasure. Pleasure because of the way you felt under my fingers, pleasure because of the flash of skin I saw and those delightful dimples that grace your lower back. Torture because it was when you were with Gabe. Torture because I knew what he had done to you moments before." His lips pressed against the flesh of my shoulder. "I want to devour you until there is nothing of him left. You've always been mine, I knew it from the moment I saw you. It just took you a little longer to realise it."

Heat flamed between my thighs at his words, at the pressure of his mouth, but then his father's words entered my head again. *Just keep him happy until he tires of you.* I tried to banish them, but they haunted me, dissolving the desire that had so quickly flamed.

"We're going to be late," I said, moving away from him and clasping a necklace around my neck.

Once I was done, Tyler caught my wrist between his fingers. "Are you sure you're okay?"

I pulled my hand away and said those fateful words. "I'm fine."

Sadie was waiting outside the entrance when we pulled up. Once again she was dressed from the pages of a magazine and part of me wanted to shrink back into the car and tell Tyler I would see him once he was done, but I pulled myself together and climbed out of the backseat to be greeted by her embrace.

"How was the office?" she asked.

I tossed answers around in my head and finally decided on, "Interesting."

Sadie briefed Tyler on the artwork of the exhibitioner, showing him images and titbits from his portfolio. Tyler nodded, taking in the information and then offered one arm to me, the other to Sadie and we walked through the doors. The room was dimly lit, the only lighting coming from the spotlights on the images gracing the walls. Tyler knew almost everyone that approached him, only once having to bend to hear Sadie's hushed explanation of the person approaching. He introduced me proudly, saying I was a talented, up-and-coming photographer. I blushed at his embellishments, but he looked at me with such pride, sliding his hand over the small of my back protectively, letting people know without words what I meant to him.

The 'artwork' was horrible. Each image was up-close and blurred, making the subject matter undetectable. I had no idea what half of them were, but I smiled and murmured words that I hoped sounded like approval, and prayed my lack of knowledge about the art world didn't come across as too evident. My eyes followed the nibbles of food floating on trays around the room but I didn't partake. My dress was already feeling too tight.

Tyler discussed the photography as though he had been a fan of the artist for years instead of only just being introduced to his work.

"It's very subjective," a man in a black and white suit with a protruding stomach said. He rested his hands on his belly protectively, reminding me of Billie.

Tyler nodded in agreement. "I'm sure to some it speaks to the obscurity of life, the 'out of focus' viewpoint of modern society."

"Is that what you see?" the man asked.

Tyler shook his head and took a sip of his whiskey. "No. No, I do not see that at all."

The suited man frowned. "Well, what do you see?"

Tyler stroked his chin as if pondering his words. I was momentarily distracted by the darkening stubble and the way his fingers brushed against it. The roughness of it against my cheek, my thighs. I tried to shake the thought from my mind as Tyler studied the image again. It was of stairs, or maybe a ladder, I wasn't sure. He tilted his head to the side. "In that question lies the answer."

The man's brows furrowed further. "The answer?"

"Yes," Tyler continued. "Only I can see what I can see, and that's what this image is saying, don't you think?"

The man nodded thoughtfully as Tyler excused himself from the conversation, drawing me away to a secluded part of the gallery, tossing the remainder of his drink down his throat. "I can't wait to get away from here."

"I thought you were enjoying yourself?"

"Enjoying myself?" Tyler laughed. "All this is for show, nothing more. I can't even understand how this can be called art. It's nothing but out of focus, blurred photography. I'm not sure why Sadie insisted I attend."

At the sound of her name, she appeared at his side. "At least pretend to look like you aren't bored to death," she hissed, smiling at a person as they walked by, nodding in Tyler's direction.

"Do you like this?" Tyler waved his hand in the direction of the illuminated images.

Sadie scoffed. "Fuck no."

"Why are we even here?"

"Because some of the people who do like the artwork have a lot of money lying around just waiting for someone to convince them of the next best thing to invest in. You—" Sadie stuck her finger in Tyler's chest, "are that person."

Tyler sighed and ran his hand through his hair, messing up the perfectly groomed style. "Lauren's photography is much better than this."

"It's not like this," I said, looking around the room. "This is art. My photography is more commercial."

Sadie frowned, a small single line forming between her brows. "Yes and no. Your images have an art to them. You bring a humanity to your photos despite the lack of people." Sadie ran her finger around the edge of her wine glass as she spoke. "I noticed it first with the images of the retirement home, and again now with the construction site. In most of the images, excluding maybe a few of the exterior, there is always something in them that speaks to the people responsible for the building. Whether it's a footprint in the dust, a helmet lying discarded on the floor or, even when it was early on and there was only the steel framework, there was this one image that was black and white, lines and light, and lying on one of the beams was a glove, the tips of the fingers hanging over the edge. That image convinced me there was an art to your work. I've sent it to the printer actually. It's getting enlarged to be placed on Tyler's office wall."

"I've told her she needs to go into business for herself. Stop mucking around at the coffee place," Tyler told Sadie.

"Totally!" She gripped my arm. "You must do it. You would be a hit. People would be lining up to get you to take images for them. Actually…" She pondered for a moment. "I might know of a place that is looking—"

Tyler grabbed my hand, bringing it to his lips and brushing them gently over my knuckles. "You can't take her away yet. She's still working on the casino."

"She can do both if she wants to."

I listened as Tyler and Sadie bantered back and forth over the future of my imagined career until a woman approached, her hand resting gently on Sadie's arm until Sadie stopped talking and excused herself, following the woman across the room to a group of people.

"You don't like the idea of going into business for yourself?" Tyler asked.

"I think you have a lot more confidence in my abilities than I do," I replied.

"You've barely said a word tonight. Are you sure you're okay?"

I nodded and smiled tightly before tipping my glass to my lips.

Tyler's eyes narrowed. "Why don't I believe you?" He stepped closer, blocking me from the gathering of people. "Is it because Sadie is here?"

I shook my head, letting my eyes grow wide. "No! Not at all. I heard what you said the other night. I admit I find it a little difficult to see how a woman can be your best friend for all these years and not fall in love with you, but I believe you when you say you're just friends."

"So what is it then? Something has upset you ever since—" Tyler stopped, biting on his bottom lip. "Hamish," he said bluntly. "Ever since you spoke with Hamish. What did he say?"

"Nothing." I shrugged, hoping to appear nonchalant. "It was nothing."

"Don't lie."

"I'm not lying."

Tyler took another step forward and I took one back, bumping into the wall. "Don't lie," he repeated gruffly.

I swallowed the knot in the back of my throat. "It was nothing," I said again. "Hamish just told me to keep you happy and stay away from Jake."

Tyler's brows shot skywards. "Jake? What's he got to do with anything?"

I lowered my head, mumbling my words. "He said for all he knew, I could be working my way through the Thornton men. He said there was nothing to be done about Gabe, and I should just keep you happy until you tire of me."

Tyler tilted my chin towards him, the beginning flashes of anger flickering through his steel-coloured eyes. "He said what?"

I repeated it again, this time more clearly and the tension rose through Tyler's body. "That fucking bastard," he hissed, pulling his cell phone out of his pocket. "Wait here."

I stepped after him, grabbing his arm. "Tyler, no."

He pulled away, holding the phone to his ear. I could hear the ring tone in the background.

"Please, don't make it worse."

"Worse? He's the one who—"

"Please?" I said again, gripping onto him. Words scrambled through my mind. "I think what upset me most was that's exactly what I want to do."

Tyler placed the phone back in his pocket. "What?"

"Make you happy. That's why it annoyed me so much. I want to make you happy. Every part of me wants to make you happy, but somehow, by him saying it to me like an order, I'm left feeling like—"

Tyler's hand hovered over my arm, his fingers like feathers. "In what way do you want to make me happy?" He looked down at me with such heat in his eyes, I felt myself melting into the floor as if I could dissolve right there and then.

"All the ways," I whispered below my breath.

Tyler smiled slowly. "All the ways?"

"Yes."

"And did he say anything about me making you happy?"

I shook my head, unable to look away. Trapped in his gaze, his fingers burned trails where they fluttered across the bare skin of my arm. His fingers slipped down until he threaded them through mine. "Come with me."

I stumbled after him, still a little uncertain on the height of my heels. "Where are we going?" Tyler wove through the people stroking their chins and studying the fuzzy images, pulling me after him. "What are you doing?" I asked in a lowered voice.

Sadie looked over questioningly, but Tyler either didn't notice or didn't care. He pulled me into the bathroom and pushed me against the wall. Kissing me, he crushed his lips against mine, mumbling into my mouth, "I'm going to make you happy."

"Tyler." It started as a protest but ended in a moan as his mouth travelled across my skin, settling on the sensitive spot on the curve of my neck. My head fell to the side, allowing him better access.

"But," I panted. "But what if someone…" Once again, my protest faded as he turned me around, pulling on the zipper and letting my dress fall to the white tiled floor. His hands cupped my backside before snaking around my waist and gripping onto my hips, drawing me back into him and grinding his hardness against my backside. I braced myself against the wall as his hands roamed over my body, clutching at my breasts which felt like they were straining against my bra, begging to be released. He turned me to face him and slipped his hand under the lace to rub his thumb over my now taut nipple.

"Lauren." He breathed my name as a sigh, then, pulling my flesh from its confines, he dropped down my body, taking as much of my breast into his mouth as he could, while his hand slid over my belly and slipped past the lace until he brushed against my clit. He moaned and the sound vibrated across the flesh of my breast.

I was almost lost to desire when the door started to open. Tyler slammed it shut. "Busy," he growled.

"Tyler," I breathed, but he hushed me, his fingers sliding into my mouth where I sucked them hungrily as he dropped to his knees and let out the most delightful of sighs, his breath hot and warm against the apex of my thighs.

"Remove your underwear."

"But what—"

The rumble that came from Tyler's throat stopped my words. "Remove your underwear," he said again, firmly, his voice like gravel.

For some reason, my fingers trembled as they took hold of the sides of lace and lowered them down my legs. They fell most of the way and I stepped out, Tyler collecting them from the ground and placing them in the inside pocket of his jacket, before shrugging it off his shoulders and hanging it over the hand-dryer.

"Open your legs."

I moved them apart.

"Further," he instructed. He applied pressure with his hands to the inside of my thighs, pushing until he was content with the distance that separated them. His eyes darkened as he dipped his head, looking up to watch my expression as he went down on me.

His tongue was like velvet. Hot velvet. Velvet fire. He teased at first, running over my flesh light as a feather, before flattening his tongue and diving between the folds. My head fell back to the wall, barely noticing when another person tried to enter. Tyler slammed his foot against the door, denying any further attempts. There was a soft exclamation of surprise as the door shut in the woman's face.

With one knee on the floor, his foot jammed against the door, and his head buried between my thighs, I tilted my head to the side so I could see the bulge of his hardness.

"I want you inside me."

Tyler's hands wrapped around my legs and his fingers dug into my backside almost painfully, drawing me closer, giving him further access.

"Please," I panted. It was an ache, a need I had been denied all day. The feel of him inside me. His steel-like hardness filling me, stretching me, ramming into me.

But Tyler shook his head, removing his tongue and replacing it with his finger. He pushed inside and I rose up the wall, drawing in a deep breath and letting it out slowly as his finger moved in and out.

"Not now," he said, looking up at me.

The need to feel him inside me had reached an intensity I wasn't sure I could deny. Wrapping my hands into his hair, fistfuls between my fingers, I tried to pull him to his feet in order to get him to fuck me. But Tyler resisted. With my hands still wound in his hair, his head dipped between my legs, his hand moved to pull me towards him again. The feverish passion of his mouth drove me over the edge and I exploded, my clit throbbing as he sucked until there was nothing left to give and I was left as a quivering puddle of satisfaction against the wall.

Tyler got to his feet slowly. He kissed me and I tasted myself. "To be continued," he said.

12

LAUREN

Helping me back into my dress, Tyler made sure the path was clear before opening the door, adjusting himself until his hardness subdued enough not to be noticeable.

"Underwear?" I asked before he could step into the hallway.

Tyler smiled wickedly and shook his head. "No."

"I can't go out there with nothing underneath." I meant it as a protest, but my voice was lazy and satisfied and Tyler knew it.

"No one will know. No one except me." Tyler patted his pocket. "I will know, and it will be all I think about until we leave."

Taking my hand, he guided me across the floor to where Sadie was entertaining a group of people with a story about Tyler at some work function.

"What happened?" I asked Tyler as the people laughed.

"It's entirely untrue," he said. "Sadie likes to make things up to entertain. You wouldn't believe some of the rumours floating around about me. They make me sound a lot more interesting than I really am."

Every chance Tyler got, his hand slid to my backside and caressed my cheeks. His thumb rubbed over where the line of my underwear should be and his entire body tensed, almost as though the thought was too much for him.

As soon as the clock struck ten, Tyler excused himself, stating he needed to go, and leaving Sadie slightly bemused in the middle of the circle. A car was ready and waiting and Tyler held the door open as I slid inside. We sat side by side and Tyler rested his hand on my leg, moving his fingers back and forth to work the hem of the fabric up my thigh. He looked out the window as he lifted the material higher and higher, as though, if he couldn't see it, then neither could the driver who was happily chatting in the front seat. When his fingers finally brushed against bare skin, Tyler sighed visibly, and shuffled closer, shifting the placement of his hand to run up the inside of my thigh. When his finger fluttered over my nakedness, he gripped onto his groin, groaning as if in pain.

The driver's eyes flicked to the rear-vision mirror and I smiled, giving my best silent assurance that everything was fine. While asking the driver a question, I slid my hand across Tyler's lap and wrapped it around his hard cock. He took in a sharp breath as I worked the zipper of his pants, lowering it enough to slip my hand inside and find the opening of his boxers. Desire trembled through me as I closed my hand. He was rock hard and I stroked his length, longing to free him, longing to climb on top and sink onto him. I squeezed my thighs closer together as wetness warmed me. Tyler's fingers, trapped between the muscles of my thighs, pushed further up, pressing between the folds before finding the hardness of my clit and rubbing over it. I stroked his cock in time to his attention until the driver announced we had arrived. We let go of each other hastily, grateful for the dim light.

Tyler thanked the man and paid him before we exited the car. Feverish with anticipation, we ran to the elevator. As the doors shut, Tyler tore the zipper down the length of my dress, pulling it from my shoulders and tossing it over his shoulder, leaving me standing in nothing but my bra and high heels. He urgently fumbled with his belt, pushing me to the bars of the walls, before plunging deeply, his breath coming out in a grunt.

He froze once he was inside, pinning me against the bars with the hardness of his cock and the pressure of his clothed body against my naked one.

"I have been waiting for this all day," he said.

I moaned and ground against him, trying to urge him to move, start rocking inside me and give me the friction I craved. But Tyler held steady, swiping my hair across my back and over my shoulder, giving free reign for his mouth to fall to my neck. "I have imagined doing so many bad things to you today. I imagined you beneath my desk, mouth open, sucking on my cock." He moaned again and withdrew himself before slamming back into me forcefully. The coldness of the bars tingled across my skin. The hardness of his cock stretched me.

"I imagined you naked on my desk, slamming into you until the desk shook." He moved his hips in a circular motion, allowing me to feel every inch of him. I dipped my hand between my thighs but he caught it and held it away. "No." He pushed in deeper. My skin gripped against the bars. "I imagined what it would have been like to press your naked body against the frosted windows. The curve of your breasts thrust to the glass. The redness of your arse as I pounded you."

The elevator halted but Tyler still held me firmly, his cock deep inside me. "When I open this door, and once I remove myself from inside you, I want you to walk across to the bedroom, remove your bra and stand with your hands on the glass window overlooking the city."

My insides clenched.

"You like the sound of that, don't you?" he whispered hoarsely.

Again, I involuntarily clenched around him.

"This will be the last night we have together for a while, and I want you to remember it. I want you to feel me inside you even when I'm not there." His breath was hot on my ear. "I want you to be sore and know that it was me who made you feel like that. I want you to know that no other man will make you feel like I do." He moved his mouth closer so it brushed over my ear as he spoke. "I want you to touch yourself when you think of me. Will you do that for me?"

I no longer knew what I was agreeing to. I no longer cared. I nodded and moaned, grinding my hips into him. He moved out and back in with one swift moment. "I love how eagerly you respond to me."

"Please fuck me," I whimpered.

"Fuck," Tyler cursed. I could feel him wrestling with the temptation, which was exactly what I wanted, but instead, he swelled without movement. "You can wait."

I shook my head. "Fuck me."

Bracing himself with his forearm pressed to my shoulder blades, pressing me harder into the cold bars, Tyler withdrew himself and I thought he was going to open the doors, but instead, he gave me what I longed for and slammed into me. My jaw hit one of the bars. My cheek caught between my teeth. I whimpered from pain and pleasure, and Tyler withdrew again before slamming back into me. He increased his tempo, fucking me with abandon until he withdrew and fell against the opposite wall of the elevator, reeling back as though I contained some power over him that he was trying to resist. "I told you to wait," he panted.

I turned around to face him, unhooking the clasps of my bra and slipping the straps over my shoulders. His eyes locked onto my breasts, full and heavy and red from being rubbed against iron.

"My god, you've got glorious breasts." His tongue ran over his bottom lip and he stepped forward, reaching out to cup my left breast in his hand. "You're turning me into some sex-crazed maniac," he said, feeling the fullness. "All I think about are the things I want to do to you. The things I want you to do to me. You're going to be the undoing of me, Lauren Greer." Tyler's hand hovered over the button which would open the door. "Are you going to do as I've instructed?"

I nodded.

The elevator door opened and I stepped out, only to turn and hurry back to the safety of the dark compartment, my heart pounding in embarrassment.

"I told you to—"

I pressed against Tyler and whispered urgently. "Jake's out there."

"Sorry," Jake called out. "I just popped up to do some laundry. I wasn't expecting you to be out of clothes too." I could hear the amusement in his voice and I felt mortified, cowering into Tyler who merely chuckled.

My head shot up and I glared at him. "He saw me naked!" I hissed.

"I don't think he'll complain," Tyler replied.

"Definitely no complaints," Jake echoed.

Tyler wrapped my dress over my shoulders. The straps of my bra hung from his pockets. "Come on," he said, taking my hand and tugging me towards the door.

"I'm not going out there."

"I promise not to bite," Jake called out. "Lick maybe, but I'll only bite if you ask me to."

Tyler rolled his eyes. "Okay, that's getting a little too close for comfort. Enough."

Jake laughed as Tyler stepped out of the elevator. He poked his head back around. "If you want him to leave, you might need to get out of there."

I stepped out of the elevator cautiously, holding the back of my dress together where the zipper had got caught in my haste in attempting to close it.

Jake stood from where he had been perched on the couch, guitar across his chest, long hair falling over his shoulders. "Lauren, so good to see you again. I see you and Tyler are getting well acquainted."

I crept across the room and slipped into the bedroom.

"Goodbye! We'll catch up next time, will we?" Jake called out as I closed the door.

There was laughter and scuffling and finally silence. I sat on the bed, unsure whether to poke my head outside, or just remain hiding in shame.

"He's gone now." The door crept open and Tyler filled the space.

I stood from the bed and walked toward the door, but Tyler shook his head. "You've got clothes on."

"You're not still thinking…" My voice fell away, feeling like there was a possibility Jake could still hear.

Tyler shrugged his jacket from his shoulders, hanging it on the hook behind the door, and started pulling at the knot in his tie. "That's exactly what I'm thinking. Remove the dress and stand with your hands pressed to the window." He undid the buttons of his shirt and tossed it aside. My eyes roamed the dips of his body and the heat between my legs came back as though there had been no interruption.

Tyler nodded towards the darkened window. The lights of the city blurred in the background. "Now," he ordered.

I stood, my dress falling to the floor and padded across the carpet to stand in front of the window, hands pressed against the glass. In the reflection from the light, I watched as Tyler undressed. He methodically removed every item of clothing and hung them neatly on the back of the door. Pairing his shoes together, he bent down to place them tidily at the base of the bed. And then, he approached me from behind, his cock resting in his hand, gently stroking it as he studied me.

"Push your arse out," he said.

I battled with desire and nerves. It felt strange to be on display. Tyler stalked back and forth behind me, studying me from all angles, his hand stroking back and forth over himself. He stopped behind me, dropping to his knees and running his hands up the inside of my thighs. I was so wet, I was fearful my juices would start flowing down my legs to meet him. He kissed each cheek of my backside, biting just a little into the flesh, catching it between his teeth. I closed my eyes, imagining the red and white marks left behind. When he finally brushed against my wetness, his breathing intensified and he pulled his hand away, one finger drenched in my desire. I twisted my head around as he brought his finger to his mouth, sucking it clean.

"Keep your head forward," he said when he noticed me twisting to see him.

I looked forward again, meeting my reflection in the glass. My eyes were glazed, my cheeks aflame. The nipples of my breasts stuck out with arousal.

Tyler's hands returned to my inner thighs. He ran them up and down the tender flesh until I was almost insane with the desire to turn around, push him to the bed and lower myself onto him, riding him until the pleasure washed over me.

"Bend over," Tyler said.

I turned to look at him again, but Tyler got to his feet, wrapping one arm around my waist and guiding me forward with his other placed on my back. When my hands hit the ground, he put his hands between my thighs again, urging them apart. And then he sat back on the bed, cock in hand and simply watched.

"Play with yourself."

"Tyler," I protested. "I want you, not—"

"Keep one hand on the ground, and put the other on your pussy. Play with yourself." His voice was controlled, but it trembled a little in anticipation.

I lifted a hand to myself.

"Do you feel how wet you are?"

"Yes," I whispered.

He stood, walked until he was behind me and then rested his hand on my hips. "Keep playing with yourself but look at me."

I met his eyes in the reflection of the window. He moved against me, running the hardness of his cock over my wetness.

"What do you want, Lauren?"

"You," I said, breathlessly.

He rested at my entrance. "Both hands on the ground. Steady yourself, because I'm not going to hold back." His fingers tightened their grip on my hips and then forcefully pulled me backwards. I gasped with the sensation as he held me against him.

"I love the way your breasts bounce when I fuck you. Do you see them in the glass? Do you see how beautiful you are? You feel so good wrapped around me like you were made for me. Do you feel how well we fit together?"

I shook my head, panting as I stretched to accommodate his width and length. He was holding nothing back. "You are too hard."

Tyler pushed off and then slammed me back. "Too much?"

"Yes," I panted. "No. I don't know."

He reached forward and guided me back up to a standing position, wrapping my arms up and behind his neck, the length of me exposed to him in the reflection of the window. His hands moved to smother my breasts as I ground my hips into him.

"Look at us," he said.

His head rested on my shoulder, and his hands held me possessively as he swelled inside me. "You belong to me. We belong to each other." He stepped forward enough so I had to as well, and pressed me against the glass. "It would only take a glance upwards for someone to see you pushed to the glass, my cock inside you."

The thought both embarrassed and aroused me. He removed my hands from his neck and run them along my arms, spreading them wide across the glass, applying enough pressure to let me know to keep them there before slipping one hand down to my wetness and another to my nipple. He twisted it between his fingers, and I pressed into the beautiful pain. He stayed inside me, rubbing over my clit as I writhed, stuck between the hardness of the glass and the hardness of his body.

"I want you to come," he growled into my ear. "I want to feel you tense and explode over me, and then I am going to pound you relentlessly until I come." His words only increased my desire. I twisted my head, trying to find his mouth, but he pulled back, using his chest to push me back to the glass.

"No distractions," he said. "I want to feel each and every tremble and quiver of your orgasm."

As if reacting to his command, pressure began to build. It started as a burning sensation and only increased in intensity.

"That's it," he said. "You're about to come. I can feel you gripping onto me. Come, Lauren. Come."

I cried out. My arms sagged against the glass as I gasped for air. I quivered and throbbed as Tyler remained still inside, pushing deeper with each pulse of pleasure until there was nothing left and I wanted to collapse to the floor. Hooking his arm around my waist, he pulled me from the glass, remaining inside me as he guided me to the ground, resting me on my hands and knees. His hand twisted into my hair and he jerked my head back to meet his gaze in the glass. When he first withdrew and plunged back inside, my chest fell to the ground, unable to stand firm against his force. His hand twisted harder in my hair, and the other one hooked over my shoulder, holding me in place as he slammed in and out. He didn't stop. He didn't waver or alter his pace until he cried out my name and spurted inside me powerfully.

13

TYLER

When Lauren wasn't mine, I spent most of my time daydreaming about all the things I wanted to do to her. But once she became mine, a nervousness descended. Suddenly, it mattered what I said, how I acted. All of it would have a direct impact on her happiness. On my happiness. I think that was what got me when she first came to visit. I picked her up from the airport, overwhelmed with the intensity of my feelings when I laid eyes on her, but as soon as we got into the car, I didn't know how to act. I had never really had a serious relationship before. Never had much of a relationship at all.

I did not want to fuck it up.

Ever since a moment in my youth, I had planned every step of my life. My education. My career. My social life. And then Lauren walked into my life, and none of it seemed to matter. No longer did I care what my mental list said I required in a partner. Now there was only one thing scrawled across it: Lauren. My attraction to her was instant and intense. I couldn't even place a finger on anything in particular that drew me to her. It was everything.

Distance didn't help. Time allowed anxiety to imagine all the ways I could fuck this thing I had with Lauren up. Most of them involved Gabe.

I gave up trying to concentrate on the spreadsheet open on my laptop and closed the lid, sliding it back into my bag. I agreed to visit Lauren this time. She hoped it would be better if I wasn't able to be called into work at the beck and call of my father. I agreed but reminded her of the interruptions that occurred at her place last time I had been down. I hoped to avoid them this time.

Almost three weeks had passed since I last saw her. Three weeks where we talked via video calls and sent stupid messages counting down the days until we saw each other again. There were a couple of flying visits for her to do more photography of the casino, but they were fleeting and only left me wanting more. And all that time, in the back of my head was the fact that Gabe lived only minutes away from her.

I lived hours.

I hated the distance between us. I wanted nothing more than to scoop her up and carry her back with me to the city. But even I had to admit that was moving rather quickly. Part of me didn't care though. The moment I first saw her I knew we belonged together. I wanted her to know me. Not as part of my family, not as a cog in the wheel of Thornton Industries, but as me and me alone.

I let out a silent prayer of thanks when the wheels of the plane touched the ground. I never let people know, but flying frightened me. I felt panic at the loss of control, placing my life in someone else's hands. Someone that I usually never got to meet, or even catch a glimpse of. The only hint of them was conveyed through a crackled voice over the intercom, and the usual hesitation in their speech did little to calm me. As soon as the plane stopped, people got to their feet, all scrambling to be the first to collect their luggage from the overhead compartment and filing towards the door. I waited until the line started moving before I gathered myself and stood.

The air hostess who had been attempting to chat me up for most of the flight, smiled at me, pressing a piece of paper into my hand. She winked. "It's a small town. Give me a call if you get bored," she said as I ducked to walk out the door. I let the paper fall from my hand and flutter to the ground in the wind.

The airport was small and there was no air bridge to lead us to the terminal. Instead, we crossed the pavement, guided by flight attendants smiling dutifully in the bitter cold, clothing flapping in the wind.

I cleared my throat, trying to dislodge the nervousness resting there. Why I was so nervous, I couldn't tell you. Usually, I never fumbled for words. I could turn on charm like a switch. It didn't seem to work with Lauren though. I guess it was because I didn't want her to fall for my fake display of charm. I wanted her to fall for me.

The line of people approached the sliding doors to the terminal. Inside I could see the gathered crowd. Most of them leaned against walls, or rested in the seats, eyes glued to their phones, but hidden in one corner, I spotted Lauren. She stood balanced on the tips of her toes, eyes scanning the line of people, bouncing just enough so her breasts wobbled beneath her top. When she saw me her eyes lit up and she smiled brilliantly.

And just like that my nervousness faded. But it was replaced by something else. Desire. After all, it had been over three weeks. I wanted to slide inside her and feel her grip onto me. I wanted to feel the softness of her skin under my hands. I wanted to hear her moan and call out my name.

The few days we had spent together were a tease. Ever since she left, I had spent my normally sleepless nights even more disturbed, unable to get the image of her nakedness from my mind until I would relent and masturbate, only for desire to overwhelm me again not long after, my body unsatisfied with the feeble substitute of imagination, and wanting the real thing.

She held her arm up and waved, stepping out from her hiding place and waiting for me as I walked through the doors. I strode over to her, unaware of anything else, and gathered her in my arms, kissing her passionately until I got to the stage where I was going to have to release her or it would become plain to anyone looking just how pleased to see her I really was.

God, she was beautiful. She had these big eyes that looked at me adoringly. This hair than I wanted to get lost in. This body that seemed to spill out of her clothing in the most alluring way. This mind I wanted to explore. This talent I wanted to display.

"Hi," she said, blinking up at me once I had torn myself away from her mouth.

"Hi," I said back and kissed her again. Gently, this time.

She wore a white shirt and black pants, having come straight from her job at the café to greet me. Her ample arse curved delightfully under the dark material and I wanted to grip onto it, pull her towards me and grind my growing erection into her. The shirt was a little too small for her and the buttons holding the fabric together over her chest strained under the pressure, allowing the swell of her breasts and a flash of black lace to peek through. God, she was sexy. She was to be my undoing if I was getting a hard-on merely from looking at her in such plain clothes. But I couldn't get that mental image of her in my bedroom, bent at the waist, arse jutting into the air, hands pressed to the glass out of my head.

She must have mistaken my eyes roaming over her as disapproval as she apologised. "Sorry," she said, looking down at herself. "I had to come straight from work. I didn't have time to get changed."

I noticed a dusting of flour smeared across her chin and wiped it away with my thumb. "Don't ever apologise for the way you look." I bent down close to her ear. "All I was thinking about was taking them off."

She took my hand in hers, squeezing it gently as she led me from the terminal. "I'm parked just outside. Not too far to walk in this wind. It's terrible. It's been like this for days."

I want to say I listened to every word she said, but if I was being honest with myself I could not stop thinking about her naked and all the things I wanted to do to her. With each step, each word, each smile, it felt as though she was taunting me. My eyes kept getting stuck on her mouth and imagining what it would look like wrapped around my cock. It was almost too much.

When we passed by a door in the wall marked with an exit sign, I pulled her to the side and slipped through. As soon as I had made sure we were alone, I pulled her to me, bringing our lips together and pressing my body as close to her as I could get.

She melted beneath me. Her body gravitated towards mine effortlessly, as though it knew it belonged there, and I took her face between my hands, deepening my kiss.

"I've missed you," I murmured into her mouth.

"Really?" she mumbled back, her breath hot and heavy, her hands feverishly exploring my body, but her mouth curving into a slight smile. "I wouldn't have picked up on that."

"Three weeks is too long."

She nodded against me and her hand dove to graze my erection. "Careful," I hissed, pulling back slightly. "Or you'll start something that you will have to finish unless you want me to walk out of here with everyone knowing just how attracted to you I am."

"I wouldn't mind that," she said, as she hooked her leg around mine, pulling me closer. My hands fell to her backside, cupping the cheeks of her arse as she used the leverage to wrap both legs around my waist. Our movements were urgent and unguarded. I walked forward with her draped around me until she was pressed against the wall, my mouth moving across her jawline until I reached one of the spots I loved the most—the curve of her neck. The way she melted when I kissed her there made both my heart and my cock swell. Her head fell to the side and a moan escaped her lips. I hardened more and thrust against her until the desire grew too much and I lowered her legs to the ground. She looked up at me lazily, the smile on her lips dripping with temptation.

"I think I need to get you to a bedroom before I explode," I said, stroking her cheek.

Lauren adjusted her clothing and reached for the door handle. "Well, what are you waiting for?"

"Give me a minute," I said, trying not to look at her, trying not to think of her until my erection faded. She leaned over, pressing onto her tiptoes and kissed me. "That's really not helping," I said, with no effort to move away. I wanted to get lost in her. Get drunk on her.

She laughed and stepped back. "This might help. Peta made me promise that we'd go over for dinner tonight."

"Tonight?" I said, slightly dismayed. I had planned on spending the entire evening with her in bed, taking my time, slowly enjoying her until I fell into a contented sleep.

As well as Lauren being on my mind at nights when I couldn't sleep, so had my father. There was something going on at work that I couldn't put my finger on. Meetings that I wasn't called to.

Discussions that stopped when I walked into the room. This made my usual insomniac tendencies even worse. The last thing I wanted to do was to have to play nice with her friends.

"She really wants to get to know you."

I pouted, letting my lower lip fall playfully. "But tonight?"

"She's working tomorrow night."

Our reunion was restricted to two measly nights. "I don't want to go," I said. "I want to be grumpy and surly and stay in, watching whatever programme is fascinating you at the moment, and fuck you." I smiled wickedly. "Over and over and over and—"

"Please, Tyler," she joked. "Speak plainly. Otherwise, how will I know how you truly feel?" She laughed again and opened the door wider. "You'll like Peta and Shrek."

"Shrek?"

"Peta's husband."

"Where do you meet all these people with such weird names?" I followed her out the door. "And who on earth would call their kid Shrek?"

Lauren rolled her eyes and threaded her fingers through my free hand. "It's a nickname."

I watched her as she drove us back to her place, the way she ran her tongue over her bottom lip each time she turned a corner, the way her fingers gripped onto the steering wheel, making me wish that I was the one under her hands, the way her breasts flashed through the stretched strip of material.

"Fine," I said as we pulled into her driveway.

She looked at me with surprise. "Fine, what?"

"Fine, I'll go."

She screwed up her face. "It wasn't really a request."

I couldn't help the hint of a smirk from crossing my face. "It wasn't?"

Her nose twisted again and she shook her head. "Nope."

"Well, in that case," I said, opening the door of her small car and reaching into the back to grab my bag. "I will need you to help me relieve some of this built-up pressure I've been feeling over the past few weeks before we go."

Lauren slammed her door shut and unlocked the door to the house. "Is that a request?" She walked inside, holding the door open.

"Nope," I echoed her, throwing my bags onto the couch and immediately turning and taking her in my arms, wrapping my hands around her arse and hoisting her to my waist. She threw her head back in laughter as I walked her down the hallway, and then she started undoing the buttons of my shirt, kissing my chest when each one fell open. By the time we reached the bedroom, my shirt had been tossed to the floor and I lowered her onto the bed, buried my head between her breasts, breathing in her scent, and nipped at the soft flesh with my teeth through the material of her shirt.

The reality was better than the fantasy.

She smiled seductively as I stood to unbuckle my belt and started to undo the buttons of her own shirt, making my movements more urgent. I needed to be free of all clothing. I needed to sink into her and feel her mould around me. I needed her and only her.

"I'm sorry," I said, once I was naked and tugging at her shoes. "But I need to be inside you right this moment. No preamble." Her shoes fell to the floor and she lifted her hips as I pulled her pants down until they joined the puddle of clothes on the floor.

She moved to sit up, but I pushed her back and climbed over top, negotiating her legs further apart with my knees. I pressed against her, feeling her wetness, her readiness, and pushed inside. A low moan escaped as I sunk inside her. This was where I wanted to be. Where I wanted to stay. I bent my head and kissed her softly, moving gently back and forth inside her. The desperate fucking that I thought I longed for, fell to the side and the desire to make love as she looked into my eyes over took me. I wrapped my hand around the back of her neck, holding it firmly as I moved within her. Her eyes rolled back in her head and a dreamy smile passed over her expression. I shifted further up her body, allowing the base of me to rub against her clit as I rocked back and forth. Her eyes opened in surprise then darkened with desire as she squirmed under me, locking her legs around my own.

I would like to say we stayed like that for hours, locked in each other's embrace, twisted in each other's arms, joined at the hips, but it had been three weeks. As Lauren's breathing turned to pants, and her moans grew longer and more desperate, as her walls tensed around my hardness and I felt her impending orgasm, my body responded in time to hers. Our lips met in a messy fumble as we came together in a pile of limbs and lips, sweat and salt.

I rolled off her, content, at least for the time being, and spread across the bed, my head resting on her stomach. Her hands floated down to thread through my hair, running the tip of her nails over my scalp until a shudder ran through me. With my ear pressed to her skin, her heartbeat pounded faintly, and I lifted my hand to trace the scar that ran across the base of her stomach.

She grabbed me. "Don't," she said. And then fearing her tone was too harsh, she brought my fingers to her mouth, brushing her lips across the knuckles. "I don't like to be touched there." She took a deep breath. "It feels wrong somehow."

"Is it from what I think it is?" The scar ran between her hip bones in a jagged line. "What happened?" I whispered when she didn't answer.

"I had a child with Derek." She spoke so low, I could barely make out the words. "She died." Her voice broke and I wrapped my arm around her waist, pulling her tight. Clearing her throat, Lauren tensed under me. "I can't have children," she blurted out suddenly. "Derek wanted more and we tried but it didn't work. I can't get pregnant. I can't have children."

She shifted beneath me, almost pulling her body away from mine. I wrapped my arm tighter around her waist, holding her in place.

"Why?" I asked, my tone neutral.

A sigh escaped her, though I wasn't sure if it was of sadness or frustration. "They don't know. The doctors say there is no medical reason for why I didn't fall pregnant again, and Derek reminded me often enough that his swimmers were working fine."

"I'm sorry." The tension had gone from her tone, and this time her words were coated in tears. "I probably should have told you earlier."

"It doesn't matter." And to me, it really didn't. I came from a blended family. Family was more than just blood. And I had more to do with my stepmother than the woman who had given birth to me.

"But it does," she protested. "I can't give you children. I mean, not that we've discussed it or anything. I don't want to freak you out but I feel like you should—"

I hushed her as her words became desperate. "There are more ways to have a family than by getting pregnant." I lowered my head and pressed a kiss to the line that graced her belly. "To me you are perfect."

A sob fell from her lips. "So you're not annoyed I didn't tell you? There were times I could have mentioned it but for some reason, it is a scary thing to admit to anyone, let alone the man I'm falling in love with."

I twisted my head to look at her. Those large eyes of hers were glistening with tears, her lips still swollen and bruised from my attention. She was everything I had ever wanted and more. "You're falling in love with me?" I couldn't help the smirk that crossed my face.

Wiping away the few tears that had managed to escape, she smiled. "Maybe," she said.

I lowered my head back to her stomach and smiled even though she couldn't see it. "I'll take that."

14

LAUREN

Tyler lifted himself from the bed and stood, stretching into the air. He appeared unaffected by my confession, ready to move onto the next subject. A wave of warmness washed over me as I stared at him bared before me. I was falling for him. Hard.

"Do we have to go?" he asked as a yawn overtook him.

I picked up a pillow and threw it at him. "Yes."

He caught the pillow and climbed back onto the bed, straddling me with his knees, his cock lying heavily on my stomach as he playfully hit me with the pillow.

"But I really don't want to," he whined exaggeratedly. Tossing the pillow away, he pinned my arms to my sides, leaning over so his face was only inches from mine. "I really, really, really want to stay here. With you. In bed." He bent lower until his lips hovered over mine and his breath danced over my face. Despite our recent tangle, my heart beat a little faster and warmth spread between my legs. Tyler's cock twitched on my stomach, and Tyler, having noticed the hitch of my breath, moved further up my body, removing his hands and locking my arms with his knees until the length of him was between my breasts. With eyes trapped on my chest, he pushed my breasts together until they engulfed him. I felt him lengthen and harden.

"Tyler," I warned, even though I didn't want to. "We haven't got time. We have to go."

He pushed forward, his cock straining between my breasts, and he nodded absently.

"Tyler," I warned again.

This time, instead of replying, his hand moved behind him and ran up the seam of my thighs until he brushed against my sex. Pushing a little deeper, his eyes flew to mine when he found wetness there, and he lifted a single brow. "It seems your body is saying something different than your mouth." He pushed a finger inside me, and I gasped, resisting the urge to roll my head back and enjoy the sensation.

"Believe me." My breath came out all in a rush. "My mouth wants to say what my body is, but I promised Peta we wouldn't be late."

Tyler circled my clit, and I bit my lip, again trying to resist the sensation. I squirmed under him, but with my arms locked to my sides, I was left defenceless. Tyler twisted on top of me so he could plunge his finger deeper. All I wanted to do was succumb.

His fingers slid in and out easily and Tyler groaned, "You want me, don't you?"

By now his fingers were tormenting me. "Ah, huh," I moaned. Two fingers slid in and out while his thumb brushed over my hardened nub, sending tingling waves of pleasure throughout my body. His cock hardened to the point where it lifted from between my breasts, and I dipped my chin and opened my mouth, eager to taste him. But Tyler shook his head, tilting his pelvis back and denying me what I wanted.

I squirmed more violently under him, wanting to touch him, to give him the same pleasure he was giving to me, but it was a pointless endeavour. Tyler simply tightened the grip of his thighs, holding me firmly under him as I bucked with anticipation. A tremble started deep within and I clenched around his fingers. Dinner was forgotten. Peta was forgotten. The only thing that existed was Tyler.

His eyes closed when I tensed and a wicked smile crossed his face. "You're just about there, aren't you?" he growled.

I nodded and moaned, no longer having use for words, only sounds. But instead of bringing me to climax, Tyler withdrew his hand, bringing his fingers to his mouth and licking each one clean, before leaning close to my ear. "Well, you're just going to have to wait. We need to go. You promised Peta."

"What?" I said, sitting up and propping myself onto my elbows as he climbed off, the wicked grin still plastered across his expression. "You're just going to leave me like this?"

Tyler walked into the ensuite, his tight butt cheeks taunting me, and turned on the water, raising his voice to be heard over the stream. "You're more than welcome to join me in the shower, but we won't be finishing this until later."

"That's just mean." I lifted myself from the bed and leaned against the bathroom door, arms crossed and mouth pouting. Tyler stepped under the water and it streamed over his body, playfully sliding over every dip and hollow. My desire only intensified. For a moment, I considered calling Peta and telling her we couldn't make it, but I knew she would work the truth out of me, and then there would be no end to her teasing.

Tyler lathered the soap in his hands and then ran them over his body. I followed their trail with my eyes, imagining what would happen if those hands were mine instead of his. They certainly wouldn't skip so quickly. I would move them slowly, over the curve of his shoulders, down the lines of muscles that decorated his back. They would grip onto the tight flesh of his backside and over the fine dark hairs that graced his thighs. Unable to resist the desire welling within, I stepped into the shower and wrapped my arms around his waist, resting my head against his back and kissing the taut flesh. Catching my hands with his own, he peeled them away and backed me into the wall, pushing me against the cold glass. While turning to face me, he held my arms away, stretching them from my sides. His eyes skipped over my body like fire. He leaned forward, dipping his head to take one of my nipples between his teeth, eyes locking with mine as I cried out, pushing myself further towards him. But he pushed me back against the glass.

"Stay," he ordered, releasing me, once again lathering the soap in his hands. He started at my shoulders and worked his way down my body. The roughness of his hands mixed with the soft bubbles of the soap created a delightful friction that only served to increase my desire, but every time I reached for him, or arched my body towards his, he pushed me back, shaking his head, though his eyes remained firmly on my body.

Once he was done, he directed me back under the flow of water and the bubbles washed away. He turned the shower off and dropped to his knees, running his tongue along my wet slit just once, before getting back up and wrapping a towel around his waist. I felt as though the steam in the room had invaded my brain, clouding my thought process and blocking me from thinking clearly.

"We'd better get going," he said with a teasing lilt.

I simply nodded and watched as Tyler dried himself. Once done, he walked from the bathroom and I followed, running the same towel over my body as had been on his. We both dressed, our eyes slipping to each other, fixating on the flashes of flesh hidden under clothing.

* * *

On the drive there, Tyler's hand rested on my thigh, occasionally slipping higher, raising the hem of my dress and brushing against the thin fabric of my underwear until I would gasp, or moan, or some sound of arousal would be elicited from my mouth and he would remove his hand, a satisfied smirk on his lips.

Peta and Shrek were outside when we arrived. Their house was two-storey with an expanse of grass in front. There were very few gardens. Peta hated gardening. The two eldest boys played with a rugby ball on the grass, while Shrek and Peta watched, the baby planted on her hip.

"Welcome!" she called as we stepped out of the car. Shrek's head cocked to the side when he saw Tyler. An expression of confusion quickly passed over his features but he stepped forward and offered his hand.

"Dylan," he said, shaking Tyler's hand. "But people usually call me Shrek."

"So Lauren informs me," Tyler replied, smiling easily. "Tyler Thornton."

"So Lauren informs me." Shrek laughed and started to walk to the house, throwing his arm at the outside chairs on offer. "Make yourself at home. Beer okay? Peta's on the wine if you'd prefer, or we have got something stronger."

"Beer would be good." Instead of taking a seat, Tyler strolled over the grass and picked up the ball, tossing it back to Nicholas who grinned widely.

Peta sighed heavily. "He's gorgeous," she said as she watched Tyler play with the boys.

I laughed. There was no point denying it. Tyler was beautiful.

Shrek appeared again. "For fuck's sake," he cursed quietly. Peta and I looked up at him quizzically as he placed the two beers on the table and handed me a glass of wine. "I think I just grew ovaries."

Tyler spent the first half hour playing with the boys, much to Shrek's disgust, who declared his disdain for Tyler's perfection. Peta, being the organised woman she was, had already sorted dinner and it was heating in the oven, waiting to be served. The boys noisily entertained us during dinner, each of them battling for Tyler's attention, and competing who could tell the grossest story. Tyler politely screwed his face up with disgust when he was supposed to and laughed when the boys indicated he should. Sometimes it was hard to tell what the correct response was.

Once dinner was finished, Shrek moved the boys into the lounge with the TV going and plates of ice-cream on their laps, allowing the adults a chance to talk. Despite Tyler's hesitation at coming, he appeared perfectly at ease, discussing Shrek's part-time painting and wallpapering business, as well as the perils of staffing issues with Peta, who, very deliberately, kept sliding her eyes to mine.

"Has Lauren told you of my suggestion she go into business for herself?" Tyler asked, looking across the table at Peta. His hand found mine under the table, his thumb moving in slow circles over the soft pad of flesh between my thumb and forefinger.

Peta's eyebrows raised. "No. No, she hasn't." Turning her head slowly in my direction, she looked at me accusingly.

I laughed. "It's just something Tyler brought up. I haven't thought that much about it."

"But I think it's a brilliant idea," Tyler said. "She has the talent for it, and if she moved to the city there would be no lack of clients, especially in the hospitality and construction industries. New buildings are going up everywhere. And, of course, she would have Sadie and me at her beck and call."

"Sadie?" Peta asked.

"My assistant," Tyler replied. "Well, I hate calling her that. She is so much more than an assistant. She is also currently studying a degree in marketing."

"Is that so?" Peta lifted her wine glass to her lips and took a sip. "Who knew you had been introduced to all these wonderful people." There was a hint of annoyance in her voice, and I looked at her questioningly. "Would you help me in the kitchen a moment, Lauren? You boys will be able to entertain yourselves for a moment or two, won't you?"

Once inside the enclosed safety of the kitchen, Peta turned to face me. "You're moving to the city?"

I shook my head. "No, no, it was just something Tyler mentioned. I haven't really thought about it."

Peta muttered something under her breath.

"What was that?" I asked, stepping closer to her as she loaded some plates into the dishwasher.

"I said, he's very intense, isn't he?"

"Intense?" I shrugged and gathered the dirty glasses. "I guess he is."

"He is," Peta reiterated. "He's always watching you. Touching you."

"And?" I said, getting slightly annoyed with her tone. "Is there something wrong with that?"

Peta shrugged. "And now he wants you to move in with him?"

"He's never actually said that. He just thinks it would be a good idea for me to go into business for myself and the chance of it working in the city is a lot greater than here."

"And what do you think?" By this stage, Peta had stopped loading the dishwasher and leaned against the kitchen counter, arms crossed and tea towel flung over her shoulder.

"I've told you I haven't really thought about it."

"But you will?"

"Did Tyler say something to annoy you?" I asked, mimicking her stance.

Peta turned back to the bench, adjusting the tea towel over her shoulder. "I've just never seen you look at someone like you look at him. I'm not used to it."

"And how do I look at him?"

"Like the rest of the world disappears."

"Is that a bad thing?""

"Meh," she said.

"Meh?" I repeated. "What do you mean by meh? It's barely even a word. It's a sound."

Peta sighed again. "He's just rather intense, that's all." She walked back towards the dining room.

"You've said that already," I called after her.

"Just look out for her mother," Shrek was saying when we walked back into the room. "She's an interesting one. You should have been there at Lauren's last birthday." Shrek laughed and slapped his thigh, looking over to Peta who was trying to shake her head without shaking her head. "Her parents came down to surprise her after Lauren had told them some lie about Peta making her work on her birthday, and, of course, she wasn't ready to introduce them to—" He stopped abruptly, eyes locking on Peta's with a look of panic.

"They're just very conservative," Peta said.

"Conservative?" Tyler repeated, waiting for the story to continue.

"Her parents were expecting her to still be with Derek, and—" Shrek cleared his throat nervously. "Well, she wasn't. Not that they knew that. But her niece was…" he let his voice fall at the shake of Peta's head.

Tyler nodded slowly and narrowed his eyes in my direction. "I know Lauren was with my brother," he told Shrek, even though his attention was directed towards me. "Was he there that night?"

I cleared my throat. "Yes."

Tyler's hand found my thigh under the table and his fingers gripped into my leg almost painfully. The table fell into silence. Relief only came when Tyler's cell phone started ringing. He glanced down and rolled his eyes.

"I'm so sorry, this is very rude of me, but I need to take this call. Work," he said when I glanced over at him. The grip on my thigh had lessened and he stroked my skin softly before excusing himself.

Shrek let his head fall into his hands as soon as Tyler was gone. "I am so fucking sorry, Ren. I just didn't think. It just sort of fell out and before I knew what was happening I was there."

"It's okay." I reached out to pat his hand. "As Tyler said, he knows I was with his brother. He had to watch it for months."

Shrek let out a whistle of air and shook his head. "Has to be a blow to the old joystick every time he thinks of it though."

"Seriously," I said. "Don't worry about it. It will be fine."

"It's got to be awkward between you sometimes though, right?" he asked.

Peta gently whacked him over the head, hissing, "Just drop it, would you?"

He smiled playfully over at her and blew her a kiss. "Sorry, babe."

"Do not call me babe." Peta scowled. "I hate that word."

"Sorry, love."

She narrowed her eyes. "Peta is fine."

Shrek reached over and mussed up her hair. "Ah, there's my romantic gal."

I excused myself and tried to find Tyler. He had walked into the bathroom and I stopped outside the door and listened.

"No," he said bluntly. "This has nothing to do with her. This has everything to do with you risking every—" The door to the bathroom shut and I was left unable to hear the rest of the conversation. It had to be his father. My heart dropped a little. Would my relationship with Gabe forever follow us?

I returned to the table, interrupting Shrek and Peta in a lip-lock, and sat down heavily.

"Everything okay?" Peta asked once she had separated herself from Shrek.

"Just tired, I think."

Shrek wiggled his eyebrows and reached out for Peta, pulling her back between his legs and wrapping his arms around her waist. "Tyler been working you too hard?"

I rolled my eyes and ignored him. Tyler walked back into the room wearing a stern expression.

"We need to go," he said to me.

"I hope everything is okay?" Peta asked, once again detangling herself from Shrek's embrace.

"Everything's fine," Tyler said gruffly. "There are just a few phone calls I need to make before it gets too late. I'm very sorry. It was a wonderful meal."

"You're more than welcome," Shrek said, holding out his hand and shaking Tyler's. "We'll have to do it again sometime."

Tyler nodded and leaned over to kiss Peta's cheek, thanking her again for the meal. Peta just looked at me questioningly and I tried to avoid her gaze. I was sure she thought our sudden departure was due to the Gabe conversation and not the phone call Tyler received. And if I was being truthful, I was wondering the same thing.

15

LAUREN

"I'll drive." Tyler held his hands out for the keys as we walked to the car.

"You've had more to drink than me," I replied, inserting the key into the driver's door and unlocking the doors.

He took a deep breath and got into the passenger's seat. His leg jiggled impatiently.

"Everything okay?" I asked.

"Fine," he replied, looking out the window. He looked too large in my car, curled up on the passenger's seat, head slightly bent to accommodate the height of the roof. He looked large and annoyed.

"Was it because Shrek brought up Gabe?" I asked quietly.

"No." He shifted in his seat. "I'm just dealing with some stuff at work at the moment."

"Want to talk about it?"

He shook his head, shifting in the seat, adjusting his position. "It's nothing to do with you." The way he said it made my heart shrink. His voice was cold and sharp.

We pulled up the driveway and walked into the house without speaking. As soon as we were inside, Tyler turned and took my face between his hands, crushing his lips onto mine desperately. "I need you," he growled.

The suddenness of his movement surprised me and I pushed back from him.

He took a step forward. "Please?" he begged.

"I thought you had phone calls to make?"

"I lied." He reached for me again, but I stepped out from his grasp. "Lauren," he said, his eyes dark and hungry. "I want you. I need you." He grabbed my shoulders and pulled me to him, once again crushing his mouth against mine with a desperation I hadn't felt before.

"Tyler!" I pushed against him. "We need to talk about this."

"About what?" he asked, frustrated.

"About whatever is going on in that head of yours. You're clearly annoyed about something and fucking me isn't the answer."

Tyler smirked. "It sounds like a pretty decent answer to me."

I narrowed my eyes and he turned away, sighing and running his hands through his hair. "What do you want me to say, Lauren? Do you want me to tell you that the mere mention of his name in connection to yours drives me insane? Because it does. I know you were with him. I know you shared yourself with him in a way I wished had never happened. It tears me apart. I want to smother you. I want to cover you in me until there is nothing of him left. I want to make love to you until you forget he ever existed."

"There is nothing of him left." I stepped in front of him. "I want you, Tyler. I am with you."

He moved forward, his body undeniably close, but his hands remained clenched at his sides. "Prove it. Prove you want me as much as I want you. Prove to me that it would drive you insane if you had to hear about another woman that I had been inside."

As if by instinct, my hand raised as though I were about to slap him, but I stopped with it trembling in the air. "Don't you dare talk about being inside another woman," I hissed, surprising myself with the vehemence in my words.

He caught my hand, his fingers digging into my wrist painfully. "Prove it," he said again, and let go.

Instead of anger, his challenge ignited desire and I pushed until his body collided with the wall and tore at his shirt, not caring when the buttons popped and fell to the ground. My hands on his chest trapped him against the wall and I lifted myself to the tip of my toes so I could press my mouth against his hungrily, desperately. He opened easily and let me devour him, and I grazed my teeth over his bottom lip, sliding my tongue into his mouth. All the while his heart beat dangerously under my hands. The aggression of my desire excited me and I trailed my lips downwards over his jawline, and then back up his neck so I could nip on his earlobe, eliciting a sharp breath of air hissed between his teeth. My mouth fell to his collarbone, his chest, his stomach as I made my way down his body, fumbling with the buttons of his jeans urgently until they fell away. He watched intently as I slid his boxers over his hips and let them fall to the floor. His erection almost pulsated with desire, but, although I longed to, I did not touch. I dropped to my knees, staring up at him so he could see the lust in my eyes. Starting at the base, I ran my tongue slowly along the length of him, watching in amazement as his erection grew even harder. I ran my tongue up and down, over and around, relishing the sounds he uttered. Then, when I thought he couldn't stand the teasing anymore, I took him in my mouth, slowly taking as much of him as I could before I gagged. I reeled back, gasping for air, before taking him again and sucking. Moisture pooled between my thighs. My body trembled as he wound his hands into my hair, pulling it from my scalp in delicious pain.

After taking all of him that I could into my mouth, I froze and lifted my eyes up his body, coming to rest on his steel eyes burning with desire. His hands tightened their grip and he urged me forward. I relaxed my throat and closed my eyes as he fed himself into my mouth until I could take no more. I pushed against his thighs. He spilled from my mouth and I gasped for air once again.

Tyler ran his thumb over my bottom lip roughly. "Open," he said, his voice like gravel.

Obediently I did what he said, the moisture now trickling between my legs. He twisted my hair into a knot at the top of my head and used the leverage to rock me back and forth, my mouth sliding over his hardness. The intensity throbbing between my legs was almost unbearable. I needed to feel him inside. I needed his hardness. I needed him.

As if able to read my mind, Tyler pulled my head back, tugging on my hair until I looked up at him, and then he was on the ground with me, over me, pulling my dress off, tearing at my underwear and lifting my legs to his shoulders. The sound that fell out of his mouth when he entered me was animalistic. It was one of satisfaction, desire, want and need.

He pushed inside so deeply I lost myself. Removing my legs from his shoulders, he allowed himself more access by bending my knees and pinning me down with his hands on the back of my thighs. He grunted with each thrust. Sweat beaded across his skin as he wrenched me across the carpet, my skin on fire with the friction even as his hands tried to hold me in place. It felt as though he was trying to crawl inside, plant himself as deeply as he could. My hair caught sharply under my head and I cried out as it snagged. Tyler withdrew himself, placing his mouth where his cock had just been. His hands moved under my rounded cheeks, tilting my pelvis towards his mouth as he sucked hungrily. There was nothing gentle about the way he touched me. Everything spoke of his need, his desperation. With his mouth on me, the desire to come rose quickly. Sensing my need, Tyler sat up and plunged inside.

Holding himself still, he lifted my legs to his shoulders once again, but this time, his hands wrapped around each foot and pulled them apart widely, pushing into me further. I cried out again as he towered over me, arms wide, shoulders rippling with muscles. He tipped his head back and I marvelled at his body, stretched and exposed. The way his chest rose and fell with each fervent breath. The undulating curves of his muscles. The fine trail of dark hair that highlighted the way down to his cock plunged inside me.

"Play with yourself," he said. I was so close, just on the edge. "I want to feel you come."

I didn't need any further encouragement and barely touched myself before I cried out, overcome by the powerful sensations rippling through my core. I had to close my eyes against the intensity and, when I opened them again, Tyler was staring into my eyes, lips slightly parted, brow damp with sweat and creased with strain.

"I love the way you feel," he whispered darkly. "The way you quiver and tremble." He moved within me and I whimpered, attempting to pull my legs together, unsure if I could handle the steel-like hardness of him, but he held them open firmly. "Don't," he said when he felt my resistance.

Every part of me was done. My limbs had turned to jelly, my insides to a quivering mess.

He moved out and then slammed back with force, causing a grunt of air to escape my mouth. He repeated the action over and over, pulling out slowly, only to slam into me again with enough force that my skin burned against the carpet. The sensation was almost too much. I was tender and sore but the feeling of him so hard inside me created an effect that was hard to deny. The quivering need was mounting again, and Tyler was relentless.

I'm not sure how to describe the sounds that were coming from me. They were uncontrollable. Caught somewhere between desire and pain, they fell out of my mouth with each thrust.

"I want you to come for me again," Tyler said.

I shook my head and mumbled out a no. It wasn't possible. I was done. Tyler pulled my legs further apart, then released them, leaning forward to press a kiss to my neck, and my body responded. Desire mounted. Pleasure trembled.

"I can feel you tensing," he whispered into my ear. "You're close again, aren't you?"

I didn't know if the answer was yes or no. Tyler was everywhere and everything. He filled and surrounded me. His mouth found mine and I was surprised by the ardour with which I could return his kiss. His hands pressed to the carpet either side of my face and I wrapped my arms around his neck, my legs around his hips.

"Fuck, Lauren," he panted. "Why do you do this to me?" He started moving faster, thrusting in and out with urgency.

I dug my nails into his shoulder as I came again. My release triggered his and we cried out together, collapsing back to the floor when our bodies finally surrendered and relaxed.

Tyler rolled off me, his hand resting on his forehead and his chest rising and falling with exertion. He lay still, staring at the ceiling as I crawled over to him, laying my head on his chest until his breathing returned to normal. His hand brushed over my face, pulling away the hair that covered it.

"I don't want this to end," he said, and his voice rumbled in his chest. "I want to wake up to you every morning. I don't like it that you're this far away." One finger twisted in my hair, wrapping the strand around and around. "Move in with me."

Peta's words rattled through my mind.

"Tyler," I admonished gently. "It's too soon."

A line creased his brow. "Why?"

"My whole life is down here."

He ran his fingers down my side and I shivered under his touch. "Not your whole life, I hope."

I didn't reply. Instead, I let silence overwhelm us again, the only sound being the steady thud of his heart. I didn't know what to say. Part of me wanted to leap at the chance to be with him more, but another part was scared of giving that much of myself. Again.

When Derek and I broke up, I realised my whole life revolved around him and with him gone, there was very little of me left. I didn't want that to happen again, and with the way I felt about Tyler, I was worried he would swallow me whole.

Tyler took a deep breath and my head rose and fell with his chest. "You know you don't have to prove anything, don't you?"

I twisted to look at him.

"What I said before." A smirk covered his face. "Before this." His arm wrapped around my shoulder and squeezed me against his hard body. "You don't have to prove anything. I was just caught up in the moment. Desperate for you. I'm the one with the problem. I chased you while you were with him. I'm the one who needs to prove something. I need to prove that it was worth it, worth putting you through all this." His finger traced patterns on my bare shoulder. "I'm sorry for what Dad said. I know it's my fault you have to hear things like that. I promise to make it up to you. I promise that one day this will all be behind us."

I tilted my head and pressed a kiss to his chest. "I hope not all of this will be left behind. There are certain aspects of our current relationship I'm very fond of."

From the corner of the room, Tyler's phone rang from the pocket of his jeans. He stretched across the floor but couldn't reach, so I lifted myself from where I lay sprawled across him.

"Don't worry," he said as he got to his feet. He leaned down and planted a kiss on my nose. "I'm not sure if that aspect will ever dull." He winked. "The need is too strong." By this time he had pulled his cell phone from the pocket of his pants. Glancing down at the screen, he scowled. "I've got to get this."

He moved into the hallway, shrugging his shirt over his head, but leaving the bottom half naked. I leaned back against the wall and watched him. His body moved with agitation as he spoke. He paced the hall, only to stop periodically, no words coming out of his mouth. He glanced at me occasionally and moved further down the hall as the frustration in his voice rose. I wished I could take it all away from him. I wished that for just this one weekend his work, his father, everything that was keeping him from me would disappear.

16

LAUREN

We spent the remainder of our time together naked, twisted in each other's arms, a delirious combination of leisurely love-making, lazy eating and lingered conversation. The time for him to leave came all too soon again. I found my throat tightening as he packed his scattered clothing and collected his toothbrush from the bathroom.

I huddled into his chest when he pulled me close and breathed in his scent. Mint and musk. "I don't want you to go," I said.

"Come with me."

I looked up into his steel-grey eyes. There was no demand there, only a plea. "I can't," I stammered. "I've got shifts this week."

"Quit. Work for yourself. Work for me. Do anything you want, just move to the city. Live with me."

I pulled away as a car rolled into the driveway. I frowned when I noticed the dark station wagon and moved to get a better look. My sister, Morgan, got out of the front seat, pulling a large bag with her.

"What is she doing here?" I whispered even though there was no way she could hear.

"Who?" Tyler joined me to peer out the window.

"My sister. Shit," I cursed.

Tyler raised a single brow. "Not pleased to see her, I take it?"

"Shit," I said again, running my hands through my messy hair. "Shit, shit, shit."

"Am I missing something?" Tyler looked out the window. "She's almost at the door."

How did I tell him that my family still thought I was with Gabe? That I never plucked up the courage to tell them that we broke it off, or that I was now dating his brother.

Morgan banged on the door loudly. "Lauren?" she called out, not giving me the time to answer.

I reached for the handle of the door and froze, looking over my shoulder at Tyler and wincing. "I'm sorry," I said.

Tyler narrowed his eyes. "For what?"

"I haven't told my family about you."

Disappointment hovered across his features for a fraction before he covered it with a tight smile. "No time like the present."

Taking a deep breath, I pulled open the door. "Morgan!" I embraced her. "What are you doing here?"

Morgan stormed past and dumped her bag onto the floor. "It's over," she said. "I'm done."

I glanced over at Tyler. She hadn't noticed him yet. "What's over?"

"My marriage. I've left him."

"What?" Surprise skyrocketed my eyebrows. "But—"

"It's okay if I stay here a few days, isn't it? If I have to look at that pathetic face of his for one minute longer I think I might end up strangling him. Do you know what he said to me?"

Tyler moved and it caught Morgan's eye. Confusion flashed, then curiosity, which was quickly followed by the twitching of the corners of her mouth. "And who do we have here?" A light bulb smile spread across her face and she walked over to Tyler, hand extended.

"Tyler Thornton." He shook her hand firmly.

Morgan looked back at me, her expression a mix between a question and a smirk. "Thornton?" she repeated. "Any relation to the gorgeous Gabe Thornton?"

Tyler cleared his throat. "My brother."

"Oh." The word was littered with intent. "His brother?"

I pulled her away from Tyler and she stumbled after me, a stupid grin on her face. "What happened?" I hissed.

"Who is he?" she hissed back, her eyes still stuck on Tyler. "He's gorgeous. I mean, I thought Gabe was divine and believe me he is, but this guy?" She let out a low whistle. "Is he single?"

I whacked her arm. "Stop it!"

"What?" she said innocently, but still with a coy smile on her face while staring at Tyler. Unsure what to do, Tyler pulled out his phone and started tapping on the screen.

"Tell me what happened?" I said again.

"Don't get your knickers in a twist. He thinks I'm just down visiting for the weekend. I haven't actually done anything yet." Her eyes moved back to Tyler. "But I'll tell you something I would like to do."

"Morgan!" I tugged her arm again to get her attention back, but she sauntered away from me, her focus firmly set on Tyler.

"So tell me, Tyler Thornton, what are you doing here?" She ran her eyes over his body, not ashamed as she blatantly ogled him.

Tyler merely looked over at me.

Morgan spun around, narrowing her eyes. "Where's Gabe?" It was said as an accusation.

"Gabe and I broke up," I said quietly, meeting Tyler's eyes over the top of her head.

"And?" Morgan prodded.

"And now I've got to take Tyler to the airport."

Morgan crossed her arms. "Great. You can fill me in on the way."

Tyler's eyes burned into mine across the room. "Lauren and I are together," he said, his gaze never slipping from mine. "She and Gabe broke up a few months back and now we are together."

Morgan's eyes grew round. "You moved from Gabe to this?" Her thumb jutted in Tyler's direction.

"This?" Tyler and I said at the same time.

Morgan turned to Tyler. "I'm sorry," she said. "I didn't mean to refer to you as an object, but you are, well…" She paused. "Quite delightful."

Tyler smiled at her though his eyes remained hard. "Well, it is delightful to meet Lauren's sister."

I opened the door wide, indicating for Morgan to walk out so we could drive to the airport.

"Where do you find these men?" she whispered as she passed. "And where can I get one?"

During the trip to the airport, Morgan peppered Tyler with questions from the backseat, leaning forward between us so she could engage him in conversation. Tyler kept his answers short, but polite. His hand slid between us to rest on my thigh. When Morgan sat back in the seat, no longer invading the space between us, he slid it between my legs, working his way up until he brushed over the material of my underwear. Morgan continued to chat from the back, complaining about Alistair, updating me on Madison's life.

I told Morgan to stay back when it was time to say goodbye. Tyler had been quiet. Quieter than usual, which was almost impossible. He pulled me to him and planted a kiss onto my scalp, inhaling deeply.

"When will I see you again?"

"I'm not sure." My reply was muffled into his shoulder.

"I hate leaving."

"You're not annoyed with me for letting my family believe I was still with Gabe?"

He kissed my head again. "Yes, I am."

I pulled away, tears immediately welling to my eyes. I blinked rapidly, annoyed with myself. "It wasn't intentional. It was just because—"

"Do you know the worst thing about being annoyed with you?" His voice was low. "All I want to do is be inside you. Claim you. Remind you who you belong to."

"Belong?" Even as the word rubbed against my conscience, it excited me.

Tyler looked around the crowded airport as the intercom buzzed with the final boarding call for his flight. Placing a finger under my chin, he tilted my head upwards, lowering his until our mouths met in a blinding kiss of passion and urgency. "Don't make me wait too long," he said, and then he was gone, the door left swinging in his wake.

I lifted a trembling hand to my mouth, running my finger over my crushed and bruised lips, relishing the relived memory of him.

I was jolted out of the reverie by the door banging against the wall and a gleeful Morgan holding it open.

"Start talking. Now," she demanded.

On the way back to the house I explained, in the briefest way possible, what had occurred between Gabe, Tyler and I. Morgan devoured the information like she would a soap opera, eyes wide and wicked, hands clasped in enthrallment. When we walked back inside the house, she threw herself onto the couch dramatically.

"Well," she said, eyes glittering with the scandal of it. "Your life has certainly got a lot more interesting."

"You could say that," I agreed.

"You could say that?" she mocked. "Have you seen the man you are currently bedding? He is panty-dropping gorgeous, Lauren." She said it as though it was something I was unaware of. It wasn't. "And those eyes! Have you seen those eyes?" She held her hand to her chest, clutching at her heart. "How they burn!" She sat up suddenly. "Are there any more Thornton brothers? Can I have one?"

"Morgan," I admonished.

"What? As I said, I'm done with Alistair. If I have to see the stupid expression that crosses his face as he grunts on top of me one more time, it will be too soon."

I covered my ears with my hands. "Morgan you're my sister," I said loudly, emphasising the fact that I didn't want to hear what she said. "Alistair is my brother-in-law. I do not want to hear what he is like in bed."

"But seriously," Morgan said. "Is there?"

I cautiously removed my hands. "Is there what?"

She rolled her eyes. "Any more brothers?"

"For goodness sake, Morgan!"

Her eyes lit with realisation. "There is, isn't there? Spill. Tell me all the details now. Is he older? Younger? Like Gabe, young, carefree and beautiful, or like Tyler, dark, intense and brooding?" She shuddered. "I don't know which I'm hoping for more."

"Jake is nothing like his brothers. He's not long returned from a stint with the army, though he looks more like a caveman than a soldier."

"Oh," Morgan rubbed her hands together. "A wild one."

"You seriously need to stop this. You're freaking me out. You can't leave Alistair. What about Madison?"

Morgan waved my concerns aside. "I'm not leaving him, drama queen. I'm just taking a break for the weekend. I need a few days off from the monotony of my life. Call Peta, tell her we are hitting the town tonight."

"I've got work tomorrow."

"So?"

"So, I'm not twenty anymore. I need sleep."

Morgan let out a snort. "Nonsense. It's one night and I need this, Lauren. Don't make me get on the phone and tell Mum about your change in relationship status. I'm sure she would be all too pleased to keep you on the phone, lecturing you on the loose morals of your lifestyle."

Frustrated, I groaned and flopped onto the couch beside Morgan after reaching for the phone. "Fine. But you owe me."

Morgan clapped her hands together and let out a small whoop of happiness. "I promise I will return to my normal life after this, but for now, this mama's going to party like it's nineteen ninety-nine!"

I groaned again.

17

LAUREN

Peta wasn't keen when I first called, but I managed to plead, beg and pester her until she agreed. Morgan shuffled through my wardrobe, not having actually thought about bringing clothes for going out, and let out sighs of disappointment as most of my outfits were discarded to the side. She finally settled on a silver dress with a split up the side that I had forgotten I even owned. She selected a black pantsuit with a plunging neckline for me. She scowled when we stood side by side in the mirror.

"Maybe I should go for boobs rather than legs." The reflection of her body twisted in the mirror as Morgan attempted to study herself from all angles. "My legs do look very good in this dress though, and we both know if it comes down to a cleavage competition, you're going to win."

"It's not a competition, Morgan. We are simply heading out for a few quiet drinks."

Morgan shook her head and turned around to catch her reflection over her shoulder. "That is not what tonight is about."

"Yes, it is," I replied firmly.

"Well, it might be for you, but I intend on drinking myself into a state where I no longer care about anything and then dancing the night away with whatever handsome man I can wrap my arms around."

"All the while remembering you have a husband at home."

Morgan rolled her eyes and slipped on a pair of black heels. "As if I could forget."

We picked Peta up on the way and were soon seated on stools at a busy bar, Morgan eagerly surveying the crowd for potential dance partners. She sipped on her drink frequently, the straw bobbing in her glass as she jiggled on the seat.

Peta stifled a yawn. "So what are we doing here?"

"Looking for virile sex gods for me to have an affair with just like my little sister." Morgan patted my knee, her eyes dancing across the writhing crowd of people in the centre of the dance floor. She put her glass onto the bar and spun off her seat. "Wish me luck." She moved towards the dance floor, hips swaying, and arms in the air. "I'm going in!" she called over her shoulder.

"What's up with her?" Peta asked as we watched Morgan get swallowed into the pulsating crowd.

I shook my head. "Don't ask."

Peta toyed with her glass, running her finger around the rim until the faint humming sound floated over the beat of the music. "How was the rest of your time with Tyler?" She looked at me innocently, but I knew the question was anything but.

"Good," I replied. "We didn't get up to much. Just stayed at home."

"He seemed rather pissed when you guys left our place."

"He was," I said, without offering any more information.

Morgan had inserted herself in the middle of a group of young men, hands lifted in the air, knees bent, hips bopping as though she was doing some stilted raise-the-roof dance craze. A familiar smile flashed behind her.

"Shit," I said, trying not to make eye contact.

"You swear a lot more than you used to," Peta informed me, taking another sip of wine.

"It's Stefan."

She scanned the crowd looking for Gabe's flatmate. Catching his eye, she waved.

"What are you doing?" I hissed, pulling her arm back down.

"Being friendly."

"Lauren!" Stefan yelled out my name and broke away from the group to stumble our way. As he wrapped me in a sweaty embrace the crowd parted a little and Gabe came into my sight, standing next to the pool table, head resting on his hands wrapped around the tip of a cue. Morgan spotted him at the same time as I did and lurched towards him, wrapping her arms around his neck from behind.

I spun around, turning my back to them. Peta elbowed me as Stefan grabbed my arm, pulling me off the seat.

"I know someone who will want to see you," he tried to whisper but ended up yelling in my ear, spit flying from his mouth. He leaned in closer as he dragged me across the floor. "He's missed you something wicked. It was pretty low fucking his brother like that."

Stefan deposited me in front of a surprised Gabe who still had Morgan's arms draped over him.

"Look, Lauren. It's Gabe," she said gleefully.

I offered a hesitant smile. "Hi."

"Hi." He smiled back and pushed his hair away from his eyes. It was fully blond again and the length almost brushed over his shoulders like it used to. A shudder of familiarity washed over me as the memory of running my hands through that hair flickered across my mind.

"How are you?" I asked, somewhat awkwardly over Morgan's shoulder as I leaned to embrace him.

"Good," he said, nodding his head. His eyes fell to the floor and then back up to me. They held sadness and regret. He took a swig of beer and turned back to the pool table. "Want to play?" he asked.

I shook my head as Morgan bobbed up and down on her toes. "I will, I will!"

Gabe tilted the cue towards her and she took it, reaching around him to slap his backside, causing him to look up with alarm and amusement. He nodded to some stools against the wall and we sat down next to each other. "Morgan appears to be having a good night."

"She's sure making the most of it."

Over at the pool table, Morgan lined up her ball, swaying as she did so, but still managed to pocket the red. She let out a whoop of excitement.

Gabe folded and unfolded his arms. He looped his hands together and hung them between his legs, only to detangle them again and shove them into the pockets of his jeans. "How are things at the café?" he asked.

"Pretty good."

"Mark still moaning about everyone and everything?"

"I think it's bred into him. He couldn't stop if he tried."

Gabe chuckled. "Whinging bastard."

He got off the stool and shifted it closer to mine as Morgan took a shot at one of the pool balls. She sunk it easily and quickly and turned her attention to the next.

He leaned close so I could hear him over the music but still spoke low enough so no one else could hear. "I'm really sorry about the way I behaved."

"I don't think any apology is necessary."

"But it is. I shouldn't have reacted the way I did. I know I need to grow up, take responsibility for myself instead of drinking my way through life."

"You still taking that course?"

Gabe shook his head. "Nope. I got kicked out when I stopped turning up for a few weeks. It's a bit hazy really. There was a lot of drinking involved. I'm thinking of moving to the city, actually."

"You?" I asked. Gabe hated big city life.

He nodded and took another swig of his beer. "Thinking of approaching Dad on bended knee and asking for a job."

"But you would hate that."

He shrugged, his eyes sliding over to meet mine. "I might not. All I know is that I couldn't give you what you needed. But I'm going to change that."

"Gabe." I said his name as a sigh and he reached over to take my hand, but I pulled away.

"Sorry," he said, eyes fixed on the floor.

Morgan let out another excited whoop, claiming ownership for the win. "Back to the dance floor!" She caught Gabe's hands in her own and tugged him off the seat.

"You're not with her anymore," she said loudly. "Don't look at her like that."

Gabe threw his head back and laughed before looking at her incredulously. "Like what?"

"You know what like," Morgan said, dragging him away.

"Come dance?" Gabe asked with hopeful eyes.

I shook my head, but he wrenched his hands from Morgan long enough to grab one of mine and pull me after him. After a little protesting, I relented and followed them both through the crowd until the group of us formed a circle, Peta reluctantly joining us. Gabe danced beside me, but kept his distance, preferring to use only his eyes in an attempt to sway me. He looked at me darkly, moving his body in a fashion that I was too well acquainted with, his gaze slipping from my eyes, to my lips, to the exposed swell of my breasts. By the time the third song came on and with another glass of wine consumed, I had relaxed enough to start enjoying the music. Morgan was in a world of her own, dancing in the middle of the circle. Alcohol warmed my insides. Music flooded my senses and, before I realised what had happened, I found myself alone on the floor with Gabe dancing dangerously close. His hand snaked around my waist and pulled me to him, but not so close that he actually touched me anywhere other than where his hand rested on the small of my back. Tilting his head forward he spoke loudly into my ear. "You look gorgeous." His hand increased pressure on the small of my back and he pressed against me, his head hovering over my shoulder, his mouth brushing against my ear. "I miss you," he said, his voice smooth. I stepped back but he just held me tighter. "Please don't," he said. "Don't move away. Just give me one night. One night to make you remember how good we were together. How I made you feel." In one smooth movement, he crushed his lips against mine.

I pushed against him violently. "Gabe!"

He held his hands up. "I'm sorry." He took a step forward, hands still raised in an innocent plea. "I shouldn't have done that. I'm sorry." He caught the material of my outfit as I turned. "Don't leave."

I jerked away from him.

"Stay," he begged. "Please stay. I promise I'll keep my hands to myself. I promise I'll behave. Anything. Please, just stay."

I let his words fall behind me as I pushed my way through the crowd and out the door into the cold night. My breath came out as white puffs under the streetlight.

"You okay?" Peta pushed her way through the door.

"I can't," I said. "I can't be around him like that. I want Tyler. I love Tyler."

Peta leaned on the brick wall of the building, resting her backside on her hands. "You love him?"

I turned to look at her. "I do. My heart actually aches when I think of him."

"Are you sure that's love?" she asked.

"If it's not, I don't know what is."

"I'll go get Morgan." Pushing off the wall, she disappeared into the nightclub and returned, dragging a complaining Morgan behind her.

When I called Tyler in the early hours of the morning, he was still up, and I heard the noise of his fingers tapping on the laptop in the background. I told him about our night out. About Morgan and the massive hangover she would have the next day. But when it came to telling him about Gabe the words stuck in my throat. I couldn't tell him over the phone without any way to read his expression. I wasn't there to assure him with my touch, or make promises with my mouth. So I didn't tell him.

* * *

Over the next month, I travelled to the city each week, sometimes staying the night with Tyler, sometimes having to make quick day-trips because of my work at the café. Due to Hamish's increasing demands on Tyler's time, he couldn't make it back to visit me either. The distance ate at us, both wanting to spend more time together, both longing to be wrapped in each other's embrace.

It was Sadie who came up with a solution with a contract she applied for on my behalf. A time-limited contract for six weeks photographing the setup and development of a weekend winery concert from concept to completion. The organisers were taken with the images Sadie supplied, and after a meeting, they hired me. I packed the few things I would need to take with me, provided the neighbour with enough jellymeat to feed a whole litter of cats, and soon I was wrapped in Tyler's arms as he greeted me off the plane. It was to be a trial. A test for living together. Peta couldn't help but be a little annoyed when I handed in my resignation, but she still sighed and hugged me, tears in her eyes when she told me how much she would miss me. I reminded her that it was only for six weeks, but we both knew it was more than that.

18

LAUREN

The thing that struck me most in our first few weeks of living together was Tyler's routine. I had no idea what time he actually rose in the morning as I was sound asleep, but he greeted me with a kiss and smelled faintly of sweat before the shower was turned on. He had the same thing for breakfast every morning. He ordered from the same place for lunch. He often worked late and I wouldn't see him until he rolled into bed, fumbling under the covers until he pressed against my back, spooning me until I woke with his hands exploring my body.

After the seventh day of my new job, I rode the elevator up to the top level, expecting Tyler to still be at work. So I was surprised when I opened the clunky metal door and found Tyler, Jake, Sadie and three other people I didn't recognise, sitting around a large table that hadn't been there previously, glasses swirling with dark liquid and lazily staring at cards in their hands.

"You're home." Tyler pulled out the seat beside him and I flopped into it, letting my bag drop to the floor. My day of intense boredom had drained me of energy. All I did was trail after the event organisers, taking images of them studying marketing brochures and online adverts until the colours started to blur in my mind. Tyler pulled my chair closer to his so I could lean back, my head nestling into the curve of his shoulder. He introduced me to the two men I didn't know. One was a colleague from the office, the other a friend of his and Sadie's from their University days.

"So, how's it going?" Sadie inquired.

"Some days are great."

She laughed. "Not today?"

"Not so much."

"You play?" she nodded to the cards splayed in her hand. "Five hundred."

"We used to play poker," Jake said. "But someone," he glared at Tyler, "kept getting a little too competitive and we got sick of losing money."

"Now we mix it up with pairs to keep it interesting." Sadie glanced at me over her cards.

"It's not my fault if you guys can't remember what has been played." Tyler placed a card on the pile in the centre. "Trumps."

"You don't have any spades?" Sadie threw her cards face down on the table before picking them back up and rearranging them in her hand. "Thought I had that trick."

I glanced at Tyler's cards. "Dad taught me years ago when Mother was away. Dad, Morgan and I spent the entire weekend eating pizza, playing cards, watching telly and listening to all the music Dad wasn't allowed to listen to when Mother was home. Oh, and Dad almost constantly had a beer in his hand. It was like being on vacation."

"What has your mother got against cards?" Jake asked before tossing a card to the centre of the table.

"She thinks they are of the devil."

"Cards?" Jake asked.

I nodded. "Love not the world, neither the things that are in the world."

Jake's eyebrow's furrowed together. "What?"

"It's from the Bible," Tyler's school friend said. Early was his name. I had never heard of someone called Early before and asked about the idea behind it. He explained that his parents had taken a long time to name him, and people used to quote the saying, 'you can call him anything just don't call him late for dinner.' His parents decided to call him Early.

I laughed at his explanation as Tyler rose to get me a glass of wine. "Don't believe a word he says." Tyler shook his head.

"So you're name isn't Early?" I asked.

"His name is Early, alright," Tyler replied for him. "But don't believe anything else. He's got a reputation for exaggeration."

"Hey," Early said, feigning offence. "It's not exaggeration. It's fabrication." He winked and took a sip of his drink.

Tyler was still dressed in a suit, though his jacket and tie had been discarded, his shoes were tossed to the floor, and the top buttons of his shirt were undone. I drained the glass of wine as soon as he placed it in my hand and lifted it back for a refill.

Laughing, Tyler took the glass from me and pulled me to my feet. "Excuse me for a moment," he said. "Quick break? Early, you may as well head downstairs to indulge in that filthy habit of yours. Won't be long."

"I quit!" Early called out.

"Sure you did," Tyler replied as he pulled me into the bedroom and closed the door.

I sat down heavily on the edge of the bed.

"What's the matter?" he asked, crossing to sit beside me.

"You host a cards night?" I asked, not really wanting to bore him with the details of my day.

"It's as close as I get to a social life. Now, tell me, what's the matter?"

I let out a sigh. "It's nothing. It was just one intensely boring day and then Morgan called. Mother hounded her about her time down staying with me until she relented and she now knows that we're together. She went on and on about my reputation and what people will think of me moving from one man to the next." I sat up and mocked her voice. "Do you not care what people think, Lauren? First, you break it off with that lovely fiancé of yours, then you insist on dating a teenager, and now you are embarrassing our family by flaunting your relationship with his brother in my face."

Tyler inched closer and drew back the hair from my shoulder, exposing my neck. "Flaunting it in her face?" he repeated, before placing a kiss right on the spot that he knew made me melt.

I sighed and tilted my head, allowing him better access. "I haven't seen her in months. There has been zero flaunting. I just don't understand her sometimes. She goes on about how I need to settle down, and even though she knows the truth about Derek and what he did, in her mind, I still belong with him."

"You don't belong with him," he said, his voice less playful than it was before.

"Sometimes I just wish she would leave me alone. She has an opinion on everything. Even my photography of the casino. She says it's a sin." I knew I was rambling.

"A sin?" he mumbled. His mouth had found its way across my collarbone and was starting to dip between my breasts.

"Not the photography, the actual casino because of the gambling."

Tyler lifted his head. "Are you done yet?"

I smiled. "Maybe."

"There's something extremely appealing when you get all flustered and annoyed like this."

"There is?"

Tyler kissed my mouth, blocking the words that were about to fall. "Extremely," he said. "But it's time to kiss me now."

Pushing me back onto the bed, he leaned over me and claimed my mouth as his own. His hand slid up the inside of my shirt, running over my flesh until he cupped my breast, massaging the soft flesh through the lace of my bra. My nipple hardened and his fingers toyed with the buttons of my shirt until it fell open, and his mouth dipped to take me. His tongue felt like velvet and the lace felt rough. When he lifted his head the white lace had turned translucent with moisture and Tyler groaned, reaching down to adjust the hardness straining against the material of his pants.

"We need to stop," I said, even as I arched my chest towards his mouth again.

Tyler dipped his head to the other breast. "Ah, huh," he agreed. "But I can't leave you uneven. It would be unfair." He sucked my flesh, eliciting a sharp breath of air that filled my lungs.

"There are people waiting for you to return to the card game."

Tyler rolled away, throwing his arm over his eyes. "But I don't want to. I'm all worked up now. Tell them to leave."

"I can't." I whacked his arm playfully. "It's rude."

"I don't care." Tyler stretched into the air and then pulled himself off the bed. "No, you're right. It's rude getting you to tell them to leave. I will."

"Tyler!" I dove after him, gripping onto the material of his shirt to hold him back. He swung the door open and poked his head into the lounge. "Game's over," he said. "Go home."

I poked my head around the edge of the door. "He's only joking."

"I'm not. Go."

Jake stretched into the air. "Anyone care to retire this to my level? It's not quite at the same stage as this, yet, but at least we can play a few hands of poker without the fear of losing everything to Ty."

Sadie pushed out her chair and stood. "I'm keen."

"Seriously, you guys don't have to leave," I told them.

Sadie winked. "I think Tyler has other ideas."

Tyler smirked. "I do."

My phone started ringing in my bag and I hurriedly did up the buttons of my shirt before running to grab it. I stupidly pressed accept before checking who was calling.

"Hi Dad," I said, rolling my eyes. Tyler shook his head, slicing across his throat—cut the line—as the others gathered their stuff and headed out the door with a wave.

"Your mother is rather upset," Dad began.

"She told you, did she?"

"You know how she is. She's certain that she's losing you. She says you've been dating this man for a while now. We want to know why you didn't tell us earlier."

"We want to know, or she wants to know?"

Tyler came up behind me and wrapped his arms around my waist, his hands massaging my flesh, moving further and further up me until they pressed against my breasts. I gave him a playful, warning look and pulled away.

Dad sighed. "Does it matter?"

"I'm thirty now, Dad, a little past the age where I need to call my parents if I date someone." Tyler leaned against the wall, arms crossed over his chest and a playful pout on his mouth. Once my gaze was directed his way, he uncrossed his arms and began to unbutton his shirt, moving his hips to unheard music and wiggling his brows in a comically sexy way. Even though he was just teasing, a wave of desire shot through me as his shirt fell to the floor. I shook my head and turned away, determined not to be distracted by him, and tuned back into my father's voice.

"But not past the age of keeping your parents informed concerning your life. How did you think we felt after assuming you were still with that young man—" Dad paused, searching for his name.

"Gabe," I said.

"Yes, Gabe," Dad repeated. "And yet your sister informs us you've been with his brother for months. We need to meet him, Lauren. If he's part of your life, he's part of ours too."

I sat down on the couch. Tyler had dropped to all fours, playfully crawling across the ground until he was so close, I had to stop him with my foot pressed against his shoulder.

"I know, Dad," I said, though I was a little unsure of what I was admitting. "And you will get the chance to meet him, I promise." Tyler grabbed my foot and tossed my shoe away, running his hands up my leg.

"When?" Dad asked.

As Tyler's hand ran up the inside of my thigh, I let out a hiss of air. "Shit," I panted down the phone.

"Lauren!" Dad exclaimed. I never swore in front of my parents.

"Sorry, Dad." I widened my eyes and shook my head at Tyler. "That wasn't meant for you." I inwardly cursed as Tyler's attention to the inside of my thigh continued. I placed my foot back on his shoulder and pushed him away. Tyler chuckled silently as he got to his feet, arms held up in surrender, and walked to the bedroom.

Mother's voice sounded in the background and Dad spoke again. "So when are we going to get to meet this man?"

"Soon," I replied.

Dad sighed and repeated my answer to Mother. I could hear her asking for the phone and Dad held it away as he answered but I still heard him. "I'm dealing with it, just like you asked, Clementine. She said soon."

Tyler appeared back out of the bedroom dressed in the grey sweatpants I was such a fan of, and shirtless. Another thing I was a fan of. He flopped down on the couch beside me, lifted his laptop to his lap and placed his glasses over his nose. He was gorgeous all the time but I loved him most like this. Academia and sex. He winked at me before giving his attention to the screen.

"Look, Dad, I've got to go now, okay. But I'll call again soon and arrange for us to get together."

"We care about you, Lauren. We want to know what's going on in your life." His voice was weary.

"I know, Dad."

I sighed deeply when I hung up. Talking to my parents drained me in a way that talking with no one else did. Needing to get out of my work clothes, I lifted myself from the couch and headed towards the bedroom. I needed a hot shower, clean pyjamas and a good TV show.

Tyler caught my wrist as I walked past, the pressure of my skin between his thumb and forefinger once again sending shivers through me. It scared me how easily Tyler turned me on. I was hungry for his touch. My body cried out for him and melted to a liquid when it got what it wanted. I felt vulnerable around him, knowing that I would succumb to his every whim.

"Come back here." Tyler placed his laptop on the ground and sat up a little on the couch, creating more space for me to sit between his legs. His hands wrapped over my shoulders and his thumbs dug into my skin, creating circles as he massaged. The pent up anxiety began to seep from me, allowing me to sag against him as his fingers worked magic on my neck, shoulders and back.

"Would it help if we went down for a visit?" Tyler asked.

Distracted by the movement of his hands, I barely heard what he said but I mumbled some sort of approval.

"Do you want to go this weekend? I've got a few meetings but I'll see if I can get Sadie to reschedule them."

Suddenly aware of what he said, I shook my head. "No," I said quickly.

"You don't want me to meet them?" He sounded a little surprised, and his voice tightened.

"Yes, of course," I said, straightening my back and leaning forward as his hands massaged the lower portion. "I'm just not ready for it yet. I like where we are now. Meeting my parents would only ruin it."

Tyler laughed. "I highly doubt that. Meeting the people that created you would be wonderful."

I looked over my shoulder, smirking and lifting my eyebrows. "I bet you won't say that after you meet them. Dad's great, but Mother…" I let the words trail off, partly because there was no real way to finish the sentence and partly because I just wanted to get lost in what his hands were doing.

"Well, I would like to meet them at some stage," Tyler said.

"Same," I replied.

"You already have."

"Not your mother. What's she like?" The first wife of Hamish Thornton was rarely mentioned. "Does she live nearby?"

Tyler froze for an instant. He was silent, then his hands moved over my back once again, but his voice was robotic. "She lives over on the West Coast."

I twisted around to look at him. "So I will get to meet her soon?"

Tyler's hands kept moving but his voice was dead. "There are some issues we need to work through."

"Issues?"

Tyler nodded, his attention firmly fixed on the knot he had suddenly found in my shoulder. I squirmed as his fingers dug in deeply, enjoying the painful pleasure.

"Issues," he repeated.

"Hers or ours?"

"Mine," Tyler said. The way he said it left no room for questions. I wasn't ready for Tyler to meet my parents so I could understand why he might be hesitant for me to meet his mother. From what Jake had told me, I knew the woman had battled some demons in her life.

19

LAUREN

Six weeks turned into ten. The young couple renting my house down home were happy to continue to do so, although I packed Smudge into a carrier and brought him to the city. Each Friday I met Billie for lunch and I took photography jobs in the city that lined up one after the other until I wondered why I hadn't done it sooner. We printed some business cards and Tyler even discussed building an office on the lower level of the building as a base to work from. They were small jobs, a day here, a week there, but they paid the bills and I enjoyed it far more than making coffee, though I missed the contact with Peta.

Tyler was more than happy to see me stay on, though stress at work had begun to eat away at him. He never discussed it with me, but more and more times he would leave the room to take a phone call and his raised voice would float through the walls.

One night his cell phone rang at three o'clock in the morning, and Tyler's sleep drenched voice answered it quietly as he climbed out of bed, trying not to wake me, closing himself off in the bathroom. He didn't quite close the door fully, so I tiptoed over and watched him through the crack. He paced the polished concrete floor, one hand tugging on the roots of his hair as he listened. He tried to talk on occasion but whoever was on the other end of the line clearly was in no mood for interruptions. Blowing an exasperated stream of air up his face, Tyler turned and caught me peering at him through the crack in the door. He smiled sweetly and sadly. His naked body shone in the light of the moon streaming in through the window. Unaroused, his member hung heavily between his thighs. My gaze travelled over his body unashamedly as he listened, dark eyes locked on mine. I usually wore one of his t-shirts to bed, one that his scent clung to, one that made me dream of him even as he lay beside me, and my nipples hardened against the white material. I opened the door a little more, allowing the light from the window to pool over me and Tyler's eyes dropped to my chest and then slowly roamed over the rest of my body as he replied in short direct answers to the person on the phone. I took a step closer and his cock twitched and began to rise, growing with each step I took towards him. He reached out and brushed a finger over my nipple, watching as it hardened further and beaded beneath the flimsy material. Taking my nipple between his thumb and his finger he rolled it, pinching hard enough for me to draw in my breath sharply. His cock was now fully engorged and I took him in my hand, wrapped my fingers around his hardness, and stroked up and down as his eyes rolled back in his head before fixing back on my body. As he lifted the hem of the t-shirt, I raised my arms over my head and he peeled the material away. His free hand skimmed over my body while the other held his phone to his ear. The voice on the other end was slurred and broken. It sounded like his father, but a drunk Hamish, a messy and broken Hamish.

"I've got to go now," Tyler said. "We'll talk in the morning."

The voice on the other end complained, but Tyler hung up.

"Everything okay?" I asked.

"Nothing you need to worry about." Tyler lowered his head and took my mouth with his, crushing my lips as he kissed me passionately. His cock pushed into the base of my belly, and Tyler dipped until it slipped between my legs and slid along the slickness it found. I ran my hands over his shoulders and chest. Everything about him strained with tension and trembled under my touch.

"I'm worried about you," I whispered into his ear. "You're too tense. You need to relax. Maybe you should have some pot," I suggested, laughing because of his reaction the time he found Jake, Gabe and I stoned in the basement of his parents' house.

Tyler reeled back. "Seriously?" he spat. "Drugs?"

I blinked. "I was only kidding. Though from the way you just reacted, it might not do you any harm."

Tyler turned away from me and strode over to the window, looking out over the lights of the city with the fullness of the moon above them. I followed and wrapped my arms around his waist, my hands falling to the hardness between his legs. But he grabbed my hands and removed them from his body. "Not now," he said dismissively.

Resting my chin on his shoulder, I pressed my body against his but did not touch him in any other way. "Is it because of your mother?" Even though I didn't think it possible, the tension in Tyler's body tightened. "Jake mentioned something," I continued. "He said something about her having a dependency."

"It was years ago."

"What happened?" I asked. I kept my voice as quiet as possible, trying not to break the spell of melancholy that had descended over him. As sad as it was to see, there was something so vulnerable and needy about him in that moment, a sadness that was hard to resist.

"When she and Dad were younger and just starting up the business, they were introduced to a world of high rollers, one that revolved around gambling and drinking, drugs and parties. Both of them indulged on occasion, but when Dad left, Mum's affection for that 'state of oblivion' as she called it, became more of an addiction. It's why we lived with Dad. Mum didn't want to challenge him for custody because she didn't want her dependency getting out. As I grew up, she attended countless rehabilitation facilities but it just never stuck. She would give up for weeks, sometimes even months, but then something would happen she couldn't deal with and the cycle would start all over again. Jake doesn't remember it like I do. Being a couple of years younger, his memories aren't the same. Besides, I shielded him from most of it. He never once saw her in agony, never once held her hair back as she vomited, promising that she would never indulge again, only to find her in a similar state the next day. Drugs weren't her only addiction."

"So what happened? How did she finally beat it?"

"Beat it?" Tyler repeated. "I don't know if she will ever beat it, but Jake tells me she hasn't slipped in years." Tyler sighed and his shoulder blade rose and fell under my cheek. I wrapped my arms around his chest and squeezed tightly.

"Go back to bed," he said, pulling one of my hands to his mouth and kissing the back of it. "I'll be there soon."

I left him flooded in a pool of moonlight and climbed back into bed, my eyelids already drooping as I pulled the sheets to my chin. But even after Tyler slipped out the door, leaving me alone, I couldn't fall asleep. I kept thinking of him so sad and lonely in the moonlight. I was torn by the desire to comfort him and his seeming want to be left alone.

At some stage, I must have fallen asleep because, when I woke a little while later, the moon had shifted its position in the sky, but Tyler's side of the bed was still empty and cold. Pulling a dressing gown over my naked body, I padded across the floor and pulled open the door, but the loft was deserted.

"Tyler?" I called into the dimly lit room, the only light coming from the moon and the city lights. But no reply came. A slice of panic cut through my chest. I ran over to the elevator and pushed the buttons to stop on the second floor, the floor he had dedicated to his gym. Even before the doors opened I could hear weights crashing to the ground.

A single light shone over him. He crouched over a weight bar, no longer naked, but with only his grey pants covering him. Fingers white with chalk wrapped around the metal bar and sweat dripped from his forehead. He flexed, straightening his back, straining the muscles across his chest into position, and then let out a cry as he lifted the weight in one fluid motion and rested it on his shoulders. He took a few deep breaths, dipped, and lifted the weight over his head before lowering it back to his shoulders and then to the ground before repeating it again. I watched him do it over and over. Sweat poured from his body and his muscles trembled with the effort, but the only time he took a break was to add more weight and then he would repeat the process again. He added more and more until he could no longer lift it, although he continued to try, muscles quivering, face red with exertion. Frustrated with his inability to lift the weight, he cursed and let the bar fall to the ground, banging loudly as it bounced. With a heaving chest, he bent over, pressing the palms of his hands to his eyes and letting out a frustrated grunt before picking up a weighted ball and tossing it into the wall.

"Talk to me," I said as I stepped out of the darkened area. "Tell me how to help."

If Tyler was startled, he didn't show it. "It's nothing," he said.

"It's clearly not nothing," I replied.

"Work. It's just work."

"Maybe I can help, even if it's just to listen?"

Tyler shook his head and lifted a towel from where it hung over his squat rack, running it over his forehead. "It's nothing. Dad is just insisting I replace the contractors on this job because he thinks they are not living up to their end of the bargain, but what he doesn't realise is that he's pissed off just about everyone else who is available so I've got no other options left. See?" He looked over at me. "Nothing."

"Why don't I believe you?"

Tyler sighed and smiled slightly, walking over to place a kiss on my forehead. "It's nothing," he said again.

I lightly feathered my fingers over the glistening skin of his chest and he shuddered, a tremble rippling over his muscles. I let my fingers trail over him as I walked, circling until I stood behind him and began to massage the tension from his shoulders. Tyler rolled his head from side to side, moaning deliciously as I worked at his flesh. I kissed his shoulder blade and then ran my tongue over my lips, tasting the salt left there. My hands fluttered down his back until they skimmed under the waistband of his pants, pushing them over his hips and letting them fall to the ground. He was gloriously naked and I clutched his backside, digging my fingers into the firm flesh. Tyler groaned. I circled him again until I was facing him and he watched as I placed kisses over his chest, across his abdomen and pressed them into the crease of his groin. His cock flanked his stomach, but I didn't go near it. I kissed everywhere but, and let the desire flame within me as moans of pleasure and frustration fell from his mouth. Lifting my eyes, I continued to lick, suck and kiss his body as he watched me, eyes scorched with lust. He wound his fingers through my hair sending tingles of excitement through me as it pulled against my scalp. He tried directing my mouth towards his cock, but I shook my head.

I wanted to feel him inside me. I needed him inside me.

Taking his hand, I led him to the rubber matting that covered the cold concrete floor. "Lie down," I instructed.

Tyler lay on his back, his large cock protruding into the air. I knelt over him, one knee either side of his waist, and let my dressing gown fall from my shoulders. Tyler's eyes locked onto my breasts and I took them between my hands, pushing them together as I writhed dangerously close to his hardness. I hovered over him, letting my wetness slide over the tip but not sinking onto him like I wanted. Tyler watched me with burning eyes but he did not touch. He let me tease and tempt him, his eyes caressing me in ways his hands did not. I lowered my hips, taking the tip of his hardness inside me, ever so slowly lowering myself onto him. Tyler moaned with each inch I took, his hands clenched at his side and I knew he was tempted to force me onto him, push me down and drive his cock in fully, but he was enjoying the torture of my slow seduction too much. Just as I was reaching his fullness, I raised my hips again, revelling in the way he felt inside me. I clamped onto his hardness as I toyed with my breasts, encouraged by the burning intensity with which he followed my movements. Unable to keep his hands from me any longer, they gripped my knees, his thumbs stroking my flesh as his eyes locked on where I began to lower myself onto him again. This time I sunk all the way, whimpering as I impaled myself on his fullness. With as little movement as possible, I leaned forward and kissed him, taking his bottom lip between my teeth and applying the perfect amount of pressure until he groaned into my mouth. Tyler's hands skimmed up my thighs, over my stomach, taking my breasts and massaging the flesh until his movements became feverish and frantic, and his hips ground under me, begging for me to move against him, give him the friction he longed for. Instead, I took his hands and tore them from my body, holding them out to the side, locking my grasp around his forearms, pinning him to the ground and lowering my mouth to his chest. He could have broken free at any stage, but he lay beneath me and let me control the movement as I rocked on top of him. I moved my hips back and forth pleasuring myself on his cock. He kept his hands extended when I let go and moved to his chest, using the leverage to rock back and forth, grinding into him. I wanted to ride him until he exploded under me. I wanted to look into his eyes as he filled me. But Tyler had different ideas. In one smooth movement, he lifted me from him and scooted down until his mouth was under me and he pulled me to his face, his tongue plunging into me. I arched back, my breasts jutting into the air and reached behind to take his cock in my hand.

"Turn around," Tyler grunted, releasing the grip he had on my hips.

I did as he requested, turning around and lowering my mouth to his cock as he pulled me back to sit on his face. The sensation of his tongue inside me and my lips wrapped around him sent shivers of pleasure through me, ones that intensified with each lap of his tongue and each thrust of his hips. Euphoria tightened and twisted until it exploded through every cell and I came as he pushed into my mouth and sucked on my clit. Leaving me no time to recover from the pulsing orgasm, he slid out and pushed me onto all fours, taking my hips between his hands and pulling me back onto him forcefully. When he pushed forward, I slumped to the ground, my cheek and chest hitting the rubber matting, but he pulled me up until I was kneeling, and threaded my arms around his neck. His hands roamed over my sensitive flesh, over my nipples and down my stomach until his fingers dove between my thighs.

I tried to pull them away. It was too much, too soon. But Tyler pulled me back, bending so he rested on his knees with me pressed to his lap, his cock hard and firm inside me. He roughly pushed my arms back behind his head, threading my fingers through his hair, and then skimmed his own fingers down my flesh until they dipped between my folds again. I squirmed against him, unsure whether I wanted to push further into him or pull away.

He stopped moving and held me firm, his mouth against my ear. "Open your legs," he said, his fingers slowly rubbing in circles over my hardened clit.

I moaned, shaking my head. "It's too much," I panted.

Tyler moved, withdrawing temporarily to lie flat under me, his back to the floor, me facing his legs. He lifted my backside, pulling my cheeks apart and lowered me onto his cock.

"My god you're tight," he muttered as I sank onto him. He used his grip on my backside to control our motion, rocking me up and down and pushing me forward so he could watch as he slowly slid in and out. The repetitive motion reduced some of the sensitivity and soon I was moaning and rocking myself onto him. Looking over my shoulder, I watched as Tyler let go of my backside, resting his hands behind his head, eyes glued as I rode him. "I love watching you fuck me," he growled. At his words, pressure built inside me again and Tyler grunted each time I rose and fell.

Gripping my hips, he removed himself and tugged me to my feet. He led me to a discarded pool table in the corner of the room and lifted me onto it, pushing me back so I lay across the felt, then, gripping my thighs, he tugged my backside towards the edge. The lip of the table tilted my pelvis upwards, giving him unfettered access and he held my legs wide apart before thrusting into me. Leaning forward, he gripped onto my hips, holding me in place. I began to tremble as the need to come rose violently. Moving his hands to press over my lower abdomen, he pushed deeper and held himself there, watching as waves of pleasure washed over me. Then he leaned over and I dug my nails into his shoulder, the pain and the pleasure combining until he called out my name as he came.

Climbing onto the pool table, Tyler lay beside me, his head resting on my shoulder, breaths dancing over my breasts causing little goose bumps to dot my skin. Walking his fingers over my stomach, he ran a finger over the curve of my waist.

"This is one of my favourite parts," he said as more dots erupted over my skin. He brought my wrist to his mouth and kissed the sensitive flesh of the underside. "And this part right here." He lifted his head and rubbed his thumb over my bottom lip. "And this little part here where a freckle smudges the line between your lip and your skin." His hand fell to my neck. "And this part right here. The part that makes you melt." He rested his head back on my chest and ran his finger in a circle around my belly button. "And also the dimples just above your arse. My thumbs fit into them perfectly when I grip your hips. I think you were made for me."

He said the last part so quietly I barely heard it.

20

LAUREN

The exterior of the casino was completed and in just over five weeks there was to be a test run of the facility. All the investors and friends of the Thorntons were invited to spend a weekend, test the staff and the procedures, dine at the restaurants and gamble at the tables. Jimmy had long since disappeared from the site, and I wandered through the rooms as interior designers argued over which cushions to place on the plump couches that dotted the reception area. I was there when the electricians installed the massive chandelier. There when they interviewed staff to fill the various positions available. There when the chefs started to test their creations for the menu.

I was out on the balcony of one of the suites when Sadie found me. She wandered into the room, fingers running over the smooth bed linen, heels creating dents in the carpet that disappeared seconds later.

I pressed the shutter, capturing an image of her drenched in the late afternoon sun. "What are you doing here?" I asked.

With being Tyler's best friend and, after getting over my initial reservation, Sadie and I had grown close since I had moved to the city. She was a regular visitor to the loft, and with Tyler's long hours at work we often got dinner together, choosing to go to the movies or watch television afterwards. Even though Sadie was possibly the worst cook I had come across, thankfully it didn't fade her affection for reality cooking shows.

She became a sounding board for ideas for my business and even helped me plan the office space that was being constructed on the ground level of Tyler's building. We fell into a relaxed friendship that I didn't think was possible with anyone but Peta. But something was bothering her. She flopped down onto the chair and lifted her feet to cross her ankles over the table. There was a tension in her shoulders and her expression was one that I usually only saw when she was working.

"What?" I asked her.

She looked up, startled. "What?" she said back.

"As lovely as it is to see you, what are you doing here? Have you decided to up our friendship level to stalker?"

"Tyler told me where you'd be." Her feet came down from the table and she leaned forward, legs wide, elbows on her knees and head in her hands.

"I've heard about the most brilliant opportunity for you."

"For me?" I pressed the shutter, taking an image of the perfect line of balconies bathed in the evening sun.

"You've heard of the Haven's Rest hotel chain?"

I nodded and squinted as I pressed the shutter again.

"They are looking for a new marketing campaign for their relaunch after their renovations. I thought you could put a proposal in."

I lowered my camera. "Me?"

"Yes, you."

"I wouldn't have the first clue about marketing. I might be able to take some creative images, but I'd have no idea how to implement them into a campaign, or even how to present it to them."

Sadie sat back up, pushing her long legs out at an awkward angle then slumped back in the chair again. "Okay," she said, looking up at me hesitantly. "Here's the thing. I know how to do all those things."

I sat down opposite, placing the camera on the table between us and narrowed my eyes. "What are you saying?"

Sadie sat straight again and pulled her chair closer to the table. "I'm saying we do it together. You're a brilliant photographer and some of the ideas you come up with are just shy of genius, and I know how to handle presentations and marketing plans and spreadsheets and numbers and I also have a lot of contacts. I think we'd make a brilliant team."

"But what about Tyler?"

Sadie blinked. "I've been wanting to move on for a while now. He knows that. There is only so long I can play second fiddle to Tyler Thornton. I want my own thing. My own passion. Our company could be that."

Chewing on my bottom lip, I tapped my fingers on the glass surface of the table. "You've thought about this?"

A flicker of excitement flashed through Sadie's eyes. "A lot," she said. "I really think this could be something. Haven's Rest could be our first chance to work together. A trial run, so to speak. We could put our heads together and come up with a kickass campaign. I really think this could work." Sadie pushed her chair back and stood up. "Have a think and let me know."

I sat at the table a good while longer, thinking about Sadie's idea. The excitement of having my own business had been building ever since Tyler first mentioned it, but I never dreamed of it as being any more than a one-man-band with small commercial projects, maybe some bigger stuff thrown my way by Tyler and perhaps the odd wedding to keep the funds trickling in, but what Sadie was proposing was on a whole other level. And she would be just the person to start up a company with. She was organised and outspoken, her skills with people and with computers far outdid anything I could even hope to consider. The more I thought about it, the more excited I got, but there was a little voice in the back of my head that worried about what Tyler might think. He and Sadie had been side by side for the majority of his career and I wasn't sure how he would feel about losing her.

When I got back to the loft later that night, Tyler was home and in the kitchen, a jazz tune eerily crisp through the speakers as he sipped on a glass of wine and finely sliced an onion. He had not long got out of the shower and his damp hair hung messily over his eyes, causing my gut to clench when he looked up at me and smiled.

"You're home." He walked the distance between us, wiping his hands on the apron looped around his neck, and grabbed my face, the faint scent of onions lingering on his fingers. His kiss lifted me to the tip of my toes. Despite having lived together for months, his touch still melted me. Sometimes I worried about my desire for him, my need. I never got weary of him reaching for me. I constantly longed to see the desire in his eyes each time he sank into me. He let me go and I came down from heaven to open my eyes and gaze into his.

"How was your day?" he asked.

Beneath the apron his chest was bare, and I ran my fingers up his muscled arms and threaded them together behind his neck. His skin was soft and smooth.

"Interesting," I replied.

Something sizzled on the stove top and Tyler ducked under my embrace, stepping over to stir the pan and toss in the onions. The scent that wafted from the pan was divine.

"Interesting?" Tyler repeated, prompting me to tell him more as I sat down on the stool beside the kitchen island and watched him work. Grabbing the bottle of wine, he pulled another glass from the cupboard and handed it to me. "Tell me everything," he said.

"You are in an awfully good mood," I said. Usually, he came back from work, shoulders tense and mouth set in a firm line. To see him happy and carefree, working in the kitchen was something that hadn't occurred in a while.

"Don't change the subject," he said. "Why was your day so interesting?"

"Sadie came to visit."

Tyler threw me an inquisitive frown as he poured some white wine into the pan. It bubbled and sizzled and splatters jumped over the sides. "She asked if you were at the casino today."

I reached across the bench and popped a caper into my mouth. "She wants to go into business together."

"You two?"

I nodded and picked up another caper. "Haven's Rest is looking for a new marketing campaign for their relaunch and she wants us to come up with something."

Tyler's expression was often hard to read and this time was no exception. He didn't seem startled or surprised at the news, and yet, I could also tell he hadn't heard the idea before now. "I like it," he said, nodding. "It's a good idea. I think you two would work well together."

"But what about you?"

After adding the capers and some prunes, Tyler poured the white wine sauce over sliced chicken and popped it into the oven. "What about me?"

"Sadie is your assistant."

"I've always known I couldn't keep her forever. As much as I value her and would love her to stay on, I've been waiting for the day she comes to me with her resignation. Working for the family business was my passion, not hers. She's picked up valuable skills along the way, but I've always known she wouldn't stay. Even Dad knows it."

"So you think I should?"

Tyler walked around the kitchen island and pulled out the stool beside me. "I think you should talk to her more about it, yes. She's got a good head for business on her shoulders and you have creativity leaking out your little finger. Together you could be quite the powerhouse."

I laughed. "Powerhouse. Not sure about that."

"Why not? A fresh new marketing company could be just the thing this city is waiting for."

"What about the fact that our first proposal would be for Haven's Rest? Aren't they competition?"

"Everyone can be competition in some way or another. Dad has enough fingers in enough pies to create some level of conflict with most people. But this isn't about him, it isn't about Thornton Industries, it isn't even about me. It's about you. You and Sadie. And if it's something you want to do, then you need to explore that option." He leaned over to place a chaste kiss on the tip of my nose. "I'll help in any way I can, you know that, right?"

I smiled cheekily. "With Sadie on board, I doubt I'll need you."

He cocked his head to the side, a smile playing at his lips. "You've got a point there." His voice deepened and lowered, and a tendril of desire lifted its head. "But there are things I'm good at that Sadie isn't." Getting off the stool, he stepped closer, spreading my legs so he could stand between them. My skirt rode up my thighs and Tyler's fingers brushed over the sides.

"I'm not sure," I said breathlessly, caught between teasing him and melting into him. "Sadie could very well be just as good as you, I just haven't explored that side of her yet."

Tyler groaned and ran his tongue up my neck until his mouth pressed against my ear. "I don't know whether to be turned on or jealous at the thought of you with a woman." With a wink, Tyler returned to cooking dinner. "Something arrived at work today."

"Huh?" I was having a hard time concentrating on the words that came out of his mouth because I wanted that mouth on me. And my eyes kept falling to his exposed flesh and the way his muscles flexed when he performed a simple task such as lifting a pot from the cupboard. "Did it?" I mumbled, hoping it was the right response.

Reaching over the counter, Tyler tipped my chin with his finger, pulling my gaze up to meet his. "My eyes are up here." Laughing, he kissed the tip of my nose before reaching to pull an envelope from his laptop bag resting on the counter. He tossed it into my lap and I opened the glossy envelope to pull out an invitation made from thick and creamy paper. I frowned as I read the information.

"Gabe's twenty-second birthday?" I said.

"I think we should go."

"You do?"

I had spent some time in the presence of each of his family members since we got together, but we had never been as a couple in front of all of them at once. I was updated routinely on Billie's life during our Friday lunches. Occasionally, I saw Hamish at Tyler's office and Jake popped up from the third floor for a visit every now and again. But I hadn't seen Gabe since Morgan's drunken night back home.

"I do," Tyler confirmed. "I think it's time we faced my family as a couple. Are you up for it?"

I turned the invitation over in my hands. It didn't look like something that Gabe would have picked out. The thick cream card had a fine black line as a border and the writing was embossed in gold. "It looks as though he's hired out an entire nightclub."

"Apparently he went to visit Dad a few weeks back. I think he's the one that's organised this."

"Gabe visited Hamish?" The memory of Gabe telling me he was going on bended knee to his father flashed through my mind. I never thought he would actually do it though.

"That's what Dad said. So, am I RSVP-ing with a yes or a no? It's your call. I don't want to go if it will make you uncomfortable, but I do think I need to be there, Dad's sort of insisting on it and I would love it if you were by my side."

I looked over at him and smiled. "Let's go."

Tyler looked happy, if not somewhat surprised. "You sure?"

"Absolutely."

But I wasn't.

21

LAUREN

I bought a new dress for Gabe's party. Tyler helped me pick it out. It was dark emerald and hugged my curves from my neck to my hips and then fell in beautiful folds around my legs but left my back bare. A section was cut out of the chest, allowing the round swells of my breast to be exposed.

We decided to drive down for the party rather than fly, and had only a few minutes to get ready at the hotel room before we were expected to arrive. Thanks to Tyler's distraction while helping me get dressed, we were running late.

There was a blackboard outside the single and understated door to the club which read in plain writing: Private Function. A lone bouncer stood at the door, clipboard in hand, ticking off the guests as they arrived. We joined the line, my hand firmly clasped in Tyler's, butterflies floating in my chest. Instead of Tyler's usual suit, he wore a dark shirt and a pair of jeans that hung loosely on his hips. Knowing I could run my hands around his hips and dip them below the waistband of his jeans sent delicious shivers through me.

The door of the club opened, letting the people in the line ahead of us through, and music spilt out onto the street. Tyler's grip increased on my hand. "Mr Thornton." The bouncer, recognising Tyler, waved him towards the door. "And this must be the lovely Lauren." The bouncer leaned close. "The stories I've heard about you, my dear," he whispered creepily and I scooted past him, eager to be in the safety of the club.

We were handed drinks as soon as we made it through the door. They were cloudy and blue and sparkled in the flashing lights and tasted of vodka and sugar. Tyler shuddered and placed his glass back onto a passing tray, but I drank mine, pleased with the sweet taste. Threading our way through the heaving crowd, we leaned against the bar, waiting for the bartender to bring Tyler his whiskey. From a rounded table in the corner of the room, Billie waved. After collecting Tyler's drink we battled through the throng once again to slide beside her. She was dressed simply in an olive green Grecian-styled gown that fell gracefully around her protruding belly. Leaning across the table, she lifted her nose over Tyler's glass and inhaled the scent.

"I would kill for a drink," she said. "Literally kill."

Tyler pushed his glass further away and she scowled. "Do not mess with me, Tyler Thornton or I will knock your fucking head off."

Tyler's eyes widened with amusement. "Feeling good today, are we?"

"Don't start. I've been to the bathroom four fucking times since we arrived an hour ago. Four." She held up four fingers and mouthed the number again.

Tyler's eyes darted around the room, taking in the people of importance, the young crowd already drunk and writhing on the dance floor, and the group gathered around the pool tables.

"Where's Gabe," he yelled across the music to Billie. "And Dad?"

Billie shrugged. "Fucked if I know. They went off to talk to someone together or something. I really don't give a shit."

She was a ray of sunshine.

A hand protruded out of the crowd and waved at us. Soon, the face it belonged to smiled happily as Sadie sat down beside Tyler. "Where's the birthday boy?" she asked.

"Fucked if Billie knows," Tyler replied. Sadie frowned at Tyler's lack of explanation and just shrugged her shoulders. A man who could have been her twin joined us at the table.

"Have you met my brother?" she asked me.

I stuck my hand out. "No, haven't had the pleasure. I'm Lauren."

"Saxton," he replied, shaking my hand heartily. His hair was as long and as streaked with blonde as Sadie's. They both wore it in a messy bun on the top of their heads, but Saxton sported a full beard, making him look like a tamed and more civilised version of Jake.

"Are they twins?" I whispered in Tyler's ear.

He shook his head. "Saxton's a little younger than Sadie. She has a younger sister too, Roan."

It was hard to talk above the volume of the music, so we sat, feet tapping to the beat and sipping on our drinks. I spotted Drew through the crowd and gave him a wave. He waved for me to join them, but I shook my head. I could still feel the tension in Tyler's body each time I touched him. "Later," I mouthed back to Drew but I don't know if he understood. Soon, he was too busy throwing back another bottle of beer to notice anyway.

Two hours after we arrived, we still hadn't spotted Gabe. Then the lights came on, the music faded and Hamish took a microphone to the front of the stage, clearing his throat and tapping it to get everyone's attention. He told stories of Gabe's upbringing that made Tyler roll his eyes. He spoke of their close family bond, of all the things he hoped his boys would accomplish. When he called Gabe to the stage, he threw his arm around his shoulder, and informed the crowd that he had an important announcement to make. Gabe grinned happily next to him. His eyes were glazed and I wondered how many drinks he had already consumed.

"It is with immense pride and honour, that I am able to announce this evening that my son, Gable Thornton, has decided to join the realms of the Thornton Industries."

I slipped my hand onto Tyler's thigh. The threads of his neck strained and the muscle of his jaw bulged as he clenched his teeth.

"Starting next month, my son Gabe will oversee the project for our latest investment, The Range. A new five-star estate, complete with a golf course, on the outskirts of the city."

Clapping erupted and Hamish took his exit from the stage, leaving Gabe to give a garbled acceptance speech, slurred by alcohol.

Sadie leaned over the table. "Did you know about this?" she hissed at Tyler.

He shook his head slowly, not meeting her eye. My hand fell from his thigh as he stood. "I'll be back in a minute."

Sadie met my gaze across the table but I just shrugged. I didn't know if Tyler had prior warning to this announcement, but from his reaction, I guessed he was just as surprised as the rest of us.

Gabe's speech was short and didn't entirely make sense but thunderous applause still drowned out the music as it went back to full volume. Drinks appeared on trays once again and I grabbed one of the cloudy blue ones as it passed. I lost sight of Tyler as he made his way through the people, but I was sure I saw his dark head disappear out one of the doors at the rear of the building. When he didn't return after about half an hour, I decided to follow. I found him standing at the top of the stairs leading down to the fire exit from the building. Hamish was with him. They didn't notice me as I stood in the dark, listening to their strained voices.

"The problem you have is with yourself, not with Gable," Hamish was saying. "He came to me and said he was done fooling around. He was ready to commit to the family business."

"But the Range project?" Tyler said, his voice drawn tight.

"Yes," Hamish said firmly. "It was your choice to start at the bottom of the company and work your way up. I offered to put you in a leadership role the second you graduated, but you refused. Don't blame Gable for not making the same mistake. He is my son. If he's willing to put the time and effort in, I'm willing to give him the chance to prove himself."

"Do you really think now is the time though?"

"Now is the perfect time," Hamish insisted. "Gabe is young and handsome. A playboy. His attendance at parties and his whoring ways will be fodder for the press. The attention he brings might be good for the company."

"Whoring ways?" Tyler growled.

"Don't look at me like that. I wasn't referring to Lauren. She was the first decent girl I've seen him with. Obviously, you thought so too or you wouldn't have felt the need to steal your brother's happiness."

"Steal his happiness?" Tyler half laughed, half coughed. "Since when did you become Gabe's biggest fan? It wasn't that long ago that—"

"Enough," Hamish said gruffly.

I took the opportunity to slip back inside, careful not to let the door shut too loudly. The raised voices of Tyler and his Dad reached through the crack, and as I turned, I bumped straight into Gabe.

"Lauren," he said, startled. A smile broke out over his face and he reached to embrace me.

Avoiding his arms, I leaned over and placed a kiss on his cheek. "Happy Birthday!"

He pressed against me for a fraction longer than needed, his fingers running down the inside of my arm as light as a feather. "It's good to see you," he said. "You look fantastic." His eyes darkened as he looked over me, his tongue running over his bottom lip. Pulling his gaze back to my face, he asked, "Did you hear the news? I've succumbed and joined the ranks of the Thornton Empire."

"So, you did it? You asked Hamish for a job."

He laughed, running his hands through his hair and pushing it back from his face. It was as long as when I first met him again and hung past his shoulders. I missed that hair.

"I never thought I'd see the day, but yes. I sucked up my pride and fell on bended knee before the old man. To be honest, I expected him to stick me on a friend's construction crew somewhere until I proved myself, not to assign me as an overseer."

The door opened and a grave-faced Tyler walked in, surprised to find Gabe in his path.

"Brother." Gabe extended his hand.

The muscles of Tyler's jaw worked back and forth as he took the offered hand and shook it firmly. "Congratulations," he said tightly.

They stood opposite each other, both tense, both unsure until finally Gabe moved past and opened the door to the outside stairs to join his father.

"Everything okay?" I asked Tyler as he strode over to the bar.

"Whiskey," Tyler barked at the bartender. "Double." He threw the drink back in one swoop and asked for another. "Fine and dandy," he said, finally answering my question. "Why wouldn't it be? It's not as though my kid brother has just waltzed into the position I have worked my whole life for." He smiled, but it didn't reach his eyes. Throwing the next drink down his throat, he turned around to find Gabe there once again.

"I hope there are no hard feelings," Gabe said.

"Hard feelings?" Tyler laughed cruelly, his usual cool and calm demeanour slipping. "Why would there be any hard feelings?"

"I just thought..." Gabe let his words fall and looked over at me hopefully, asking me to rescue him from the conversation. My mind went blank. I couldn't think of a single thing to say to relieve the mounting tension. Gabe opened his mouth and then promptly shut it again. Tyler's eyes scanned the crowd over Gabe's head as if determined not to show how much the recent announcement had upset him.

Finally, Gabe spoke. "So?" he said, turning to me. "How was Morgan after that night? She was pretty messy."

Tyler's eyes snapped to mine. "What night?" he asked.

Gabe stepped towards me as panic sliced through my chest.

"Oh, it was months ago," Gabe said. He stood close. Uncomfortably close. His arm pressed against mine and Tyler's eyes shone with displeasure. "Morgan forced Lauren out for a night on the town."

Tyler's heated gaze didn't waver as I dropped mine to the floor. I had never told him of running into Gabe that night. I didn't think it would matter. No, that was a lie. I knew it would matter but I didn't want it to, so I never mentioned it. I was scared of his reaction.

"You saw them that night?" Tyler asked. I knew he wanted me to look at him so he could read the answers in my eyes, but I kept them glued to the ground, not wanting to see the hurt in Tyler's expression.

"Saw them?" Gabe laughed. "Heck, who didn't see Morgan? She was a mess. How was her head the next day?"

Morgan had spent all her time moaning from the couch, complaining that the sun was too bright, my breathing too loud, her head too foggy, but I didn't say any of that. I swallowed, hoping to get rid of the dryness in my mouth and tried to ignore the burn of Tyler's glare.

"Is this true?" Tyler asked.

"Why wouldn't it be?" Gabe replied.

"Because she never told me she ran into you." Tyler turned to me again and I forced myself to look up into eyes blazing with anger. "Were you with Gabe that night?"

"Oh, come on, Ty," Gabe said. "It wasn't as though anything happened. We danced, that's it."

Tyler swallowed and his Adam's apple bobbed up and down. "You danced?"

"Yes." I pleaded with him through my eyes. I never meant to lie. I never wanted to upset him. In fact, the whole reason I never told him was to avoid this very situation.

Tyler tossed his whiskey down his throat, slammed the glass onto the bar and strode away. Gabe reached for me when I went to follow but I tore away, stretching my hand out to clutch onto the material of Tyler's shirt.

"Tyler," I called, the fabric slipping through my fingers. "Tyler!"

Ignoring me, Tyler strode through the people, pushing them out of his way when they didn't move fast enough, down the stairs and out the front entrance and onto the street. He stood below the streetlight, eyes flashing, and chest rising and falling with laboured breaths.

"Why didn't you fucking tell me?" he said when I approached. His voice was calm and cold. A shiver ran across me and I reached out to touch him, but he pulled away. "Answer me," he demanded.

"Because I was afraid you'd react like this."

"Like what?" he bellowed. I wanted to shrink under his searing gaze.

"Tyler, please," I said, reaching for him again. But he jerked away from me like I was poison and ran his hands through his hair. "I can't do this right now." He stormed back towards the door and flung it open, disappearing into the darkness and leaving me standing with the bouncer looking on apologetically.

"You alright, love? Do you need me to call a taxi?"

I shook my head and crossed my arms over my chest, annoyed at the tears that threatened to spill. Ignoring the inquisitive looks of the bouncer, I followed Tyler back inside and found him at the bar, throwing another whiskey down his throat. I was desperate to make him listen, make him understand.

I didn't want Gabe. I wanted him. I needed him. The sheer reaction of him withdrawing from me, jerking away from my touch, created swells of nausea in my gut.

"Another," he said, slamming the glass on the counter.

I tried reaching for him again, craving closeness. "Tyler."

"Don't fucking touch me!" His eyes were wild now. "You know how I feel. You knew what spending time with him would do to me, and yet here we are with me having to learn from my brother that you've been out fucking dancing with him?" He drained the

201

contents of the next glass and demanded another. The bartender looked at me with raised eyebrows.

Tyler's voice faded to a growl. "Did he touch you?"

"Tyler, you know I would never—"

"I know?" Tyler's eyebrows lifted high, mocking me. "I thought I fucking knew. I thought I knew you would tell me if you spent time with him. I thought you would say no to him taking you in his arms and dancing with you. How did you think I'd react? How did you think I'd feel about it? Or were you not thinking at all?"

"Tyler, please." I was desperate for him to hear me. Desperate for him to touch me, make everything okay again. Forgive me. "Nothing happened. I had no idea he would be there. I—"

But Tyler stormed off again, disappearing into the crowd. Half an hour passed before I found him outside, alone under the streetlight again.

"You made me feel like a fucking fool," he said without looking at me. "What am I supposed to think when you didn't tell me? Did something happen?"

"No," I implored. "Nothing happened. How could you even think that?"

Tyler smirked cruelly. "How could I think that?" he leaned in close, his breath brushing over my ear. Shivers ran up my spine but they weren't from his closeness, they were from the tone of his voice, so cold, so empty. "Perhaps it was because you were fucking him when I first met you."

I lifted my gaze to meet his and set my chin. "How dare you." I wanted to say more but the anger seething beneath my skin garbled the words in my head. In the end, I simply turned and left, hailing the taxi that was passing.

"Lauren." His voice was softer now. "Lauren, I shouldn't have said that. I didn't mean it."

I opened the door to the taxi, gave the driver Peta's address and then slammed the door shut, watching Tyler standing alone in a pool of light through eyes blurred with tears.

22

TYLER

There was no excuse. I shouldn't have said what I did, but the words were out of my mouth before I could stop them. They were true words. She was with Gabe when I first met her, but I'm the one who wanted her. I'm the one who chased her, and yet, there I was, blaming her for giving herself to me.

I wanted to follow, but after what I had just said, after the alcohol I had consumed, I would have only added fuel to the fire. So I just stood there, leaning against the streetlight, watching her disappear into the dark night, letting her think I didn't care.

Or, letting her think I cared too much.

I knew she was crying from the way her head fell to her hands as soon as she was alone in the car, and I hated myself for it. But I was annoyed. Annoyed and drunk.

Anger coursed through my veins, masquerading as blood. I was angry at my father for inviting Gabe back into the fold when things were so uncertain. And the fact that he had handed it to him on a silver platter. I had worked my way through the ranks to get where I was. Dad had made sure of it. Nothing less than perfect grades in school and a perfect work ethic was expected of me, and now Gabe sauntered in without any effort. If that wasn't enough, I was furious at him for the way he taunted me. And I was hurt by Lauren's lies. Even though my heart told me otherwise, my head still shouted and screamed, asking why she never told me. Was there something to hide? Just the mere thought of his hands on her was enough to send my head spinning. And he stood so close to her. He pressed against her. And, as he spoke, his eyes fixed on her mouth and her body, as though he knew her intimately and it cut deep knowing that he did. He knew the sound of her whimper. He knew what it felt like to—

I needed to stop thinking before I made myself sick, before I did something stupid. Taking a deep breath, the cold night air played with my emotions, elevating them to dangerous levels, igniting the liquor and boiling it in my veins. I needed to go back inside. I needed to drown those thoughts before they left permanent scars on my mind. Lauren was quickly becoming everything to me. She was the only woman I'd ever met who, if she left, I would follow.

So why didn't I?

Why didn't I call a taxi and follow her? I knew where she would go. I knew she would be at Peta's. So why didn't I follow? Why didn't I wrap her in my arms and whisper sweet apologies into her ear? Why didn't I drown out my worry with kisses instead of whiskey?

The bouncer said something as I passed, but I didn't know what it was. The blood, the alcohol, the anger, whatever it was that pulsed through me, rushed too loudly to hear anything else. Brewing in my head was a storm, a squall and I needed something to calm it. The bartender lifted a questioning eyebrow when I demanded another drink so I added a please and a tight smile.

What I didn't need was to be refused service. Whiskey was to be my saviour.

It burned and I relished the sensation as it slid down my throat, leaving my breath on fire. The beat of the music pulsed in my head. Her smile flashed through my mind. Her mouth, open and panting, head rolled back in ecstasy, hands caressing her neck. But they weren't my hands. They were his. They wrapped around her smooth flesh and moulded it for his pleasure. I leaned on the bar, elbows damp from the spilt drinks and ran my hands through my hair, tugging on the roots until the pain brought distraction.

"Hey, handsome." A bag was placed on the bar, and I lifted my weary eyes to find Molly smiling back at me.

"Hi," I said coldly and pulled my hands from my hair.

"What's up?" She took a sip of wine. "You look like shit."

I laughed half-heartedly. Molly was one of the girls on my roster, as I'd heard Gabe call it. It wasn't anything like that though. I couldn't be bothered dating before Lauren. There wasn't anyone I met that I wanted to spend more time with than absolutely necessary, apart from Sadie, but she didn't count. Molly was a model. A model who liked to be out and about on the town. We had a mutually beneficial relationship. I had a date on my arm to attend the countless social engagements on my calendar, and she got to attend said social engagements and make contacts, get her face seen. It was a win-win situation. We never dated. We were never interested in each other, although there were times when I went to her bed, but I considered them again to be mutually beneficial, fulfilling an itch without the need for any relationship.

"Thanks," I said dryly. I sipped at the whiskey, the effects of throwing the previous one down my throat now burning through my brain. My thoughts had become muggy. The music was too loud. The lights too bright. I needed to slow down.

Molly looked at me expectantly so I added, "You don't," and took another sip, hoping that would satisfy her. Sure, she looked good, but I couldn't think about her now. Lauren filled too much of my mind already. "What are you doing here?"

She shrugged and drained the contents of her wine glass, lifting it into the air to signal a refill to the bartender. "Our families know each other, remember? My parents are here too." She looked around the room. "Somewhere."

The bartender provided a fresh glass of wine, looking at me to ask if I needed a refill. I shook my head.

"Right," I replied, shaking my head again as though the action could clear my muddled thoughts. "I forgot. How are they?"

"You know." She took a sip of wine, her fingers toying with the stem of the glass. "They're the same as always." With two fingers she twisted the base of her glass on the bar, leaving a smudged ring of liquid. "I haven't heard from you in a while. Did you find someone to replace me?" She looked up and attempted to blink at me either seductively or innocently. I had lost the ability to tell the difference.

"I kind of did, actually," I replied. "I'm dating Lauren."

She frowned and the smallest, tightest of lines appeared between her thick, dark and perfectly manicured eyebrows. I had always hated those eyebrows. They were too groomed, too thick and dark.

"Lauren? Don't believe I know her."

"You've met her," I replied without thinking of where the conversation would lead.

"When?"

I swallowed deeply, wanting to curse myself for my stupidity. The night of the charity boxing event was something I didn't need to be reminded of in this moment. "That boxing match we went to." I avoided her gaze and took another sip of whiskey as realisation passed across her face.

"But I thought she was with…" She let her words fall.

"She was," I replied gruffly. I closed my eyes at the thought of Lauren entering that night, cheeks flushed, hand gripped in Gabe's. I didn't know if I was more finely tuned to her than everyone else, but I immediately knew what had happened before they arrived. It was the same look on her face as the first time I met her. The same look I was now deeply acquainted with and preferred to not think of it being on her face from anyone other than myself.

"Oh," Molly said quietly.

She toyed with the stem of her glass again, although this time she held the stem between her finger and thumb and ran them up and down the length slowly, her eyes meeting mine across the bar. She lifted a single brow in a question and took a step closer, but a deep voice sounded behind me.

"Tyler." My blood boiled the instant he said my name.

"What?" I turned around slowly, not giving him the satisfaction of seeing my discomfort.

Gabe tucked his hair behind his ears. I hated that hair. "Is she okay?"

Molly turned and smiled brilliantly, looping her arm through mine. "Gabe, wasn't it?"

Gabe's eyes moved to our joined arms and I untangled myself from Molly, taking a step back and letting the annoyance show clearly in my expression. "She left."

"She left?" Gabe repeated, completely ignoring the woman by my side.

"She left," I repeated firmly.

"How could you let her leave?"

I pulled myself straighter, emphasising the height difference between us. "I don't let Lauren do anything. She's a big girl. She makes decisions all on her own."

"Like the decision to go out with Morgan that night?"

"Yes." I adjusted the stance of my shoulders. "Like that one." I was done sipping whiskey and threw the rest of it into my mouth, slamming the glass on the bar. The bartender was there with a refill before I could ask.

"It was good to see her that night," Gabe continued. He was aware of what his words were doing to me. I didn't blame him. I would have done the same if I was in his position. "She was so happy," he said, smirking. "So relaxed. It was like the old Lauren was back, you know? The one that danced and laughed."

"Speaking of dancing," Molly interrupted. She held out her hand, offering me an excuse to leave the conversation. "Shall we?"

I looked at Molly's offered hand. I looked at Gabe. To take her hand would be to do the very same thing I was annoyed with Lauren for doing. To stay would continue the conversation with Gabe and, I could already tell from his stance, the set of his shoulders, he was looking for an excuse to start something.

So I took Molly's hand, draining the contents of my whiskey glass and let her lead me onto the floor. All I could think while dancing with her was why didn't I do this with Lauren? Why did I let my father's announcement ruin the evening? And why the fuck was I still here when she wasn't?

Gabe watched from the sidelines until a girl with large breasts practically rubbed herself against him and he laughed and led her onto the floor. He was all hands. And as he danced with the girl, he stared at me, taunting me as though he was pretending she was Lauren and I was watching on. He slid his hands down her back and squished the flesh of her arse. The girl simply laughed and threw her head back, pretending to scold him even as she adjusted his hands to gain a better grip. The girl wanted Gabe and he knew it.

Molly tried to distract me, physically pulling my face away from where it was stuck on Gabe and the girl. "Tyler," she said. "Tyler, just ignore him."

I pulled away from her, once again running my hand through my hair. "I can't fucking ignore him," I replied. "He's doing everything he can to aggravate me."

Molly lifted a brow. "He's just dancing."

"He's not," I insisted. Truth was, I didn't know if he was or not. I had lost all reasoning capabilities. All I could think of was Lauren. Flashes of the intimate times we had spent together danced through my mind, mixing with the times I had been witness to Gabe's mouth and hands on her until the image seemed to scream in my head. Before I knew what was happening, I lunged across the dance floor and grabbed Gabe around the throat, pushing him backwards through the crowd of people until I had him pressed against the wall.

"Keep your fucking hands off her!"

Gabe had the audacity to grin. "Off who?" he taunted. "Off Haleigh?" He nodded to where the girl with large breasts watched on in horror, her hand clamped over her mouth.

"Tyler." Sadie's voice was quiet behind me. "Let him go, Tyler."

Even with my hands around his neck and with blood heating his face, Gabe laughed. Well, half laughed, half choked. "Or were you talking about Lauren?"

My fist hovered in the air, wavering before his face.

"Go on," Gabe said. "Hit me. I'm sure Lauren would love to hear all about it."

I let my fist fall and released the pressure around his neck. Gabe didn't suck in a breath of air in relief, his hand didn't go to rub against the redness of his neck. He merely grinned at me. Fucking grinned.

Sadie's hand reached out and rested on my arm. "Come on," she said, gently pulling me away. "Let's get you out of here."

She led me down the stairs, talking softly into her cell phone, requesting a taxi.

"Thanks," I mumbled in her direction.

"You've had too much," she replied.

"I know."

She rubbed my arm, something my grandmother would do, and took a deep breath. "Everything okay?"

I swallowed the lump at the back of my throat. "No."

"It's going to be okay, Ty. She loves you. You can tell simply from the way she looks at you that she is smitten. I would kill for someone to look at me that way."

"Do you really think so? All I can think of is that fact that I stole her away from Gabe. She was happy with him. She was content. She loved him, but it didn't stop me. And if I can do it to him, what's to stop someone from doing it to me?"

"You mean, Gabe stealing her back?"

I nodded, letting my head fall to my hands. The world swayed.

"She wouldn't do that."

"How can you possibly say that, knowing our past?"

"Because I believe it would have never worked out with her and Gabe. He's too young for her. And she adores you, Tyler. I mean it."

I looked at her sceptically.

"She does," she insisted.

"But why?" My voice broke on those words.

"Are you fucking kidding me?" Sadie laughed. "You are Tyler Thornton. Have you ever felt the need to ask yourself that before?"

I shook my head. There was no need. Each woman I had fallen into bed with knew what they were getting. I knew what I was getting. There was nothing other than a mutual fulfilment of need for both.

"But the women I've been with before knew it was nothing serious. I didn't need to offer them anything. With Lauren, I want to offer my life. But why would she want it?"

By this time the taxi had pulled up, and Sadie held the door open. "You're a very blind man at times, you know that?"

"What do you mean?"

"But the women I've been with knew it was nothing serious?" she mocked, repeating my words. "Of course they did, but clearly, what you didn't know, is that most of the women accepted what you offered in the hope of getting more."

"Fuck off," I said.

Sadie pulled the seatbelt across her lap. "It's true. You might not have been able to see it, but I sure did. I had to follow you around with these woman looking at you like you were the last drop of water in the middle of a desert, and you just carried on completely oblivious. It's almost a little comical how naïve you are."

I let the roll of the car slide me over to lean on Sadie's shoulder. "I should go to her."

"No." Sadie adjusted the position of my head on her shoulder. "You shouldn't. Not in this state. Not minutes after you had your hands around Gabe's throat. You're going to have to apologise, you know."

"I know." The taxi fell into silence. "Sadie?" I asked after a while.

"Yes, Tyler?"

"I think I'm falling for her."

"I could have told you that months ago. I don't blame you."

I sat up and the world swayed again. "Don't tell me I have to worry about you too?"

"Well…" Sadie let the word hang before laughing. "She is an awfully attractive woman. There's something very natural and—" Sadie held her hand in the air and scrunched her fingers as though there was something under them, and she was struggling to figure out what it was.

"Fucking beautiful?" I prompted.

She let her hand fall and shrugged. "That will do."

"Sadie?"

"Yes, Tyler?"

"I love her."

Sadie patted my hand. "I know, Ty. I know."

"Sadie?"

I could almost hear the corners of her mouth turning upwards. "Yes, Tyler?"

"Does she love me?"

"She's the only one who can tell you that."

"Sadie?" I asked again.

"Yes, Tyler?"

"I think I'm drunk."

23

LAUREN

When the taxi pulled up at Peta's house, all the lights were off. Stones crunched under my feet as I walked across the driveway and the security light flicked on when I crossed the path to the door. I knocked quietly but no one came. Sending Peta a text, I waited for her to come to the door but she didn't. The night air was cool and I rubbed my hands over my bare arms, willing some warmth back into them. After waiting a few minutes, and after calling her cell phone and Shrek's, I banged loudly on the door. There were footsteps and a crash and a curse before the door was flung open and Shrek stood in his boxers, eyes blurred with sleep.

"Lauren?" he asked, rubbing his eyes as though they deceived him. "What are you doing here? It's like—" He paused to look at his watch. "It's like one o'clock in the morning." He looked at me then, and noticed my bloodshot eyes. Even though my tears had dried on the way over, as soon as Shrek realised I was upset and concern crinkled his expression, my tears came back with a vengeance, falling down my cheeks faster than I could wipe them away.

"Aww, Ren." Shrek embraced me, rubbing my back comfortingly. "Peta!" he called up the stairs. "Peta, it's for you."

"Everything okay?" he asked, pulling me inside. "Are you hurt? Did someone hurt you?"

Peta appeared at the top of the stairs, tying the front of her dressing gown together. "Lauren?" she questioned when she saw me. Stomping down the stairs, she took me in her arms. "What did he do?"

I wanted to protest. I wanted to reel back and demand why she thought it was Tyler who had done something, but instead, I just sobbed into her shoulder as she ran her hand over my hair, waiting for my tears to subside enough so I could talk.

It took a while.

"It was me, not him," I said with hiccups breaking my words.

Peta rolled her eyes and pulled me close again. "Tell me what happened? Was it at Gabe's party? I heard he was having one this weekend."

Pulling away from her, I drew in deep breaths, trying to calm myself. I was annoyed at the emotions leaking out of me. Annoyed that such a small argument could upset me as much as it did. But the thought of losing Tyler was almost more than I could bear.

"I don't think he'll forgive me." I hiccupped.

"Nonsense," Peta admonished. "Now tell me what happened."

So I let it all spill out. I told her how I had never informed him of meeting up with Gabe that night. I told her how I had basically lied to him and how Gabe was the one to tell him. I told her of the hurt in his eyes, the way he shied away from me. I told her what he had said.

Once I was done, Shrek brought through a cup of tea and sat it before me. "I'm not even sure if you drink tea, but I didn't know what else to do."

I pulled the cup close and wrapped my hands around its exterior, hoping the warmth would seep into my skin and remove the coldness in my chest. It didn't. The coldness stayed there, sharp and blunt at the same time, a knife twisting into my heart.

"I know I'm overreacting," I said at Peta's concerned look.

"You're not. You're allowed to react however you feel. There are no rules when it comes to reactions."

"I just didn't want to upset him."

Peta covered one of my hands with her own. "Does he get upset a lot?"

Picking up on the tone of her voice, my eyes flew wide with panic. "No! Nothing like that. He's not an angry man. He is just a little testy when he comes to Gabe. I knew this. I don't blame him. I can imagine being the same and yet, I still never told him about running into Gabe. Dancing with Gabe."

"But he knew the situation when he started chasing you. He knew you were with Gabe. He knew what he was getting into. There was no need for him to say what he did. Everyone has a past."

"I know," I said, my shoulders slumping. "I guess it's just a little more difficult when your girlfriend's past is your little brother."

Shrek rested a hand on my shoulder. "Do you want me to go sort him out?" He flexed his muscles. "I'm sure I could take him on. I may return a little worse for wear, and possibly a little turned on, but I'd do it for you, Ren. Anything for you."

Peta laughed. "Slightly turned on?"

Shrek walked towards the door. "I think that's my cue to leave. But Peta?"

"Yes, dear?" A smile played with her lips.

"You have seen him, right? The guy is gorgeous."

Peta rolled her eyes. "I'm not denying it."

"Really?" Shrek asked as he moved down the hallway. "I feel like you are a little."

Peta laughed. "That man." She sighed deeply and looked across at me as I took a sip of the tea. The fragrant drink was just what I needed in that moment. One thing was sure; I didn't need more wine. "Are you going to be okay, Ren?"

I nodded, not trusting my voice to answer. I needed a good night's sleep. I needed to forget the words Tyler had hurled at me and just sleep.

"You want to talk some more?"

I shook my head as Peta lifted herself from the table. "There's no spare room, sorry. You're going to have to bunk with Henry. Come on."

Henry, the baby of the family, was sleeping in his cot. Peta pulled out an old couch from the wall and let it fall down into a bed. She threw a few blankets in my direction and found a spare pillow. When she left me alone, I thought I would fall asleep immediately. I was wrong. Henry slept with a nightlight and cartoon planes danced across the walls. He had a cold and there was a hitch in his breath. And Tyler wasn't there.

I had forgotten how long it had been since I slept alone. Since moving in with Tyler, each night had been spent with him. He often came to bed late, he almost always rose early, but he was always there, pressed against me, hands wrapped around my waist, chin tucked over my shoulder and whispering sweet nothings in my ear. I felt cold and empty without him. The fear that he had grown tired of me seeped into my brain. Maybe he just wanted out and the way he spoke was his way of telling me.

I squeezed my eyes shut when the tears threatened again. I checked my phone but there were no calls, no texts, nothing to let me know that Tyler was thinking of me.

And then the fears started. What if this was it? What if we were over? Where would I go? I had promised myself after my world fell apart from my reliance on Derek that I would never let a man dominate my life like that again. But here I was, living in Tyler's house, working from his building. Everything about my life depended on him and I had been the one to allow it.

* * *

I woke with a start. Someone was laughing. It took me a while to get my bearings. I was in a strange bedroom, one with sun-soaked light blue curtains and the faintest of planes flying over the walls.

Henry stood in his cot, knees bouncing and grinning at me in such a way I couldn't help but return it.

"Hey, buddy," I said, sitting up. Henry bounced some more and said something that was either supposed to be a word, or maybe just a garbled sound.

Shrek walked in the door and lifted Henry onto his hip. "So sorry. This little guy isn't supposed to be awake yet. I didn't want him to disturb you."

"It's fine." I stretched into the air, before remembering I had stripped down to only my underwear.

"Peta had to open this morning. She had to leave. You want breakfast or are you going to sleep a little longer? I can make sure the boys stay quiet."

"No, no," I said, even though I flopped back onto the bed. "I'll get up. I should probably get going, anyway."

Shrek jiggled Henry who laughed and clapped his chubby hands together. "Did he call?" he asked while pretending to eat Henry's fingers.

I dove for my phone. "No," I said when I checked the notifications. I had one text message but it was from Sadie, not Tyler. "I would have thought by this age I would be past all this."

"All what?"

"Drama," I replied.

Shrek's laughter was muffled by Henry's fingers. "I think it would be a sad life with no drama. And even if a couple did ever reach that stage where there was none, I would say it's because their lives were controlled by their children's dramas instead. You'll see." He let go of Henry's fingers in his mouth. "I'm sorry. I didn't mean to bring up—I mean I know that you can't—Shit. I don't know what to say, Ren."

I rubbed my hands over my face, not caring that I was probably smearing the day old makeup. "Don't worry, Shrek. I know what you mean."

"I've got a big mouth, sorry."

"You've got a perfectly normal mouth. It's fine. Don't ever feel like you have to censor yourself around me."

"Well, come down when you're ready. We have lots on offer for breakfast. All packaged. All processed. All filled with sugar just the way we like it." He disappeared out the door but I heard him muttering to Henry. "You hear that, kid? She said my mouth was normal. Mummy doesn't think my mouth is normal. She thinks it's too big. You just wait until we tell her."

The only thing I had to wear was the dress from the night before. I could have asked Shrek for something of Peta's, but for some reason, the thought of moping around in the emerald green dress appealed to me. As I wrestled the material over my hips, it seemed as though the dress was a lot tighter than it had been the night before. I stood in front of the mirror in the hallway and leaned forward so I could run a wet finger under my eyes, attempting to remove the stains of mascara.

I was a mess. My hair, no longer styled neatly, fell in messy tangled waves around my face. My breasts spilled out of the bodice of the dress in a way that seemed indecent in front of young children. My ankles could barely hold me upright in the high heels and, what I thought was mascara under my eyes, turned out to be smudges of tiredness.

I walked slowly down the stairs, staring at the screen of my phone as if I could magically make Tyler call.

Shrek whistled when I walked in the door. "Well," he said, stroking his chin. "I'm not really sure what to say."

I laughed and plonked myself down at the table. "I don't think there are words."

"There are definitely words," Shrek replied. "I'm just not sure if you'd want to hear them, or even if I should say them."

"Never stopped you before."

"Well how about I start with the polite offer of a shower?"

It surprised me that I hadn't even thought to have one myself. I lifted my shoulders and let them fall. "I don't know if I can be bothered. I'm enjoying feeling miserable. A shower might change that."

"Wallowing." Shrek nodded his head. "I get it. Peta should be back around two. What are your plans? I know she'd love it if you stayed for a few days."

I glanced at my phone again. Nothing. "I'm not sure. I've got a shoot tomorrow, but maybe today, at least."

"We're planning on hitting the playground later on. You keen?"

I looked over my dress and swung my legs out from under me to wiggle my shoes. "Might have to borrow some clothes."

Shrek grinned. "I'm sure I'll have something in my wardrobe that fits."

It was my turn to roll my eyes. Shrek leaned over to Henry. "I think she means Mummy's clothes." Henry laughed and clapped his hands together again, not caring that they were covered in some sticky concoction I could only assume was baby food.

"Other boys still sleeping?"

Shrek stuck Henry's spoon into his mouth and nodded. "We won't have the pleasure of those little rascals for another hour yet. Hopefully." He walked across and opened one of the cupboards in the kitchen. "Help yourself to cereal and the coffee is ready."

There was a knock on the door. Shrek looked at me, eyebrow raised. "You want to get it?"

I shook my head and glanced at my phone. Tyler didn't know where I was. It wouldn't be him. Shrek shrugged and headed for the door, not caring that his shirt was covered in baby food.

I listened as the door swung open.

"Oh, hey," Shrek said.

"Is she here?" Tyler's voice was cold.

Shrek looked through the doorway at me. Unknowingly, I had risen to my feet, glancing with hope at the door. I nodded.

"Sure." Shrek opened the door wider. "Come on in."

24

LAUREN

Tyler looked as though he had barely slept. Like me, he was still dressed in the clothes from the night before. Dark marks bruised the skin beneath his eyes, his hair was dishevelled and messy, but he still looked like heaven.

The relief that crossed his face when his eyes lighted on me was visible. He pulled himself straight. "Come home," he said. His voice had a roughness to it, but whether it was from lack of sleep or worry, I wasn't sure.

I twisted my hands together, aware that they were trembling. He said come home. Those words ripped through my chest, leaving it open and vulnerable and tears threatening. I wanted to run to him. I wanted to wrap my arms around his neck and bury my face in his chest, inhaling his scent, kissing his skin.

I wanted to, but I didn't.

"Tyler," I said and nodded at him.

"Lauren." It was more of a question than a greeting. His gaze held steadily onto mine. Stepping past Shrek, he walked until we stood face to face, eyes pleading with me. "I'm sorry." He didn't say any more, just those two words, but they were enough. His steel-grey eyes searched mine, begging for the forgiveness his words didn't. "Will you come home with me?"

Shrek stood with the jar of baby food in his hand, eyes darting between us as he dipped the spoon in and lifted it to his mouth. Henry cried out from his high chair. "Shh," Shrek scolded. "Daddy's watching a real life soap opera."

Tyler threw a withering glance his way and held out his hand. Sparks flew when our skin touched, but neither of us said a word. I gathered my things, thanking Shrek over and over again, even as he told me I was more than welcome to stay, and followed Tyler back to the car. Tyler held the door open and waited until I was safely inside before shaking Shrek's hand and thanking him for giving me somewhere to stay.

"She's welcome anytime," Shrek replied. "She knows that. She will always have a place to come if she needs it." There was a threat behind Shrek's words that didn't go unnoticed by Tyler. He nodded and shook Shrek's hand again before climbing into the driver's seat.

The first hour of the trip was spent in silence. There were so many things to say, but I didn't know where to start. Tyler's expression was cold. His teeth were clenched together and his fingers were wrapped tightly around the steering wheel. When he turned the music on and let it fill the space, I knew he wasn't ready to talk. I wasn't either. I didn't know what to say and even if I had, I didn't know how to say it. I hated that I had hurt him. I hated that he spoke to me the way he did. I hated what he said. I hated that he couldn't be in the same room as Gabe without something breaking out between them. Between us.

But more than anything, I hated that there was this tension between us. I hated that he hadn't kissed me. He'd barely touched me. My skin was burning for him. I needed reassurance that he wasn't giving.

Six hours seemed like an eternity. I don't know when it flipped over to be an unspoken competition, but I felt like neither of us wanted to be the one to break the silence.

* * *

The groan of the elevator was loud as we rose to the loft and the metal door clanged as Tyler slid it across the rollers. Smudge was there to greet us, an odd occurrence since moving to the city as he spent most of his time catching mice on the lower levels, or lounging in the sun. He smooched against Tyler's legs, more happy to see him than me. Traitor.

We stood in the middle of the room, staring at each other, both hoping the other would be the one to relent and speak first. But words weren't the form of communication Tyler chose. He walked over to stand in front of me and dropped his gaze, reaching out to take the tips of my fingers in his. His fingers toyed with mine, threading them together almost apologetically. His eyes were slow to meet mine and when they did, instead of an apology, they held desire. My heart fluttered in my chest as he lifted the tender underside of my wrist to his mouth and pressed a kiss there. My skin burned under his touch as he trailed kisses up my arm, looking up at me for permission each time he touched my skin, moving further and further up my arm until there was only a breath between our mouths. His lips were soft at first, pushing against mine hesitantly, searching for permission and forgiveness, at the same time as letting me feel the pain and hurt in his touch.

"Tyler," I breathed into his mouth.

At the sound of his name on my lips, he let out a groan that spoke of his turmoil and he crushed his mouth to mine, his hands clasping the side of my face, drawing me further into him until they wound through my hair and tugged at the angle of my mouth on his. Then he lifted me to his waist, my legs locking around him, and walked into the bedroom. He set me down and turned so he could release the back of my dress, letting it fall in an emerald puddle at my feet. Unclasping the hooks of my bra, his fingers brushed over my shoulder as he removed the straps, then tossed it to the floor. Next, he knelt and peeled my underwear over my hips, running his hands over the length of my legs as he guided them to the floor and I stepped out. My shoes were next. Still kneeling, Tyler lifted my feet and removed one then the other.

He was gentle when he led me to the bed and lay me down. Standing for a moment, he just stared before undressing slowly, his eyes never leaving mine as first his shoes, then his shirt and jeans were removed, and finally his boxers. As he stood before me, my heart beat erratically and my eyes traced the lines of his body hungrily. Lust pulsed through my veins.

Climbing over me, Tyler pressed the length of his body along mine as if he couldn't stand for any part of us not to be touching. With lips pressed to my shoulder, he guided himself and slid into me, my breath hitching as his hardness filled me. He pushed his body upwards, causing the base of him to rub over my clit and then he just rocked back and forth so slowly it was torture. With my hands gripping the flesh of his back, my head rolled back and my chest arched upwards, pressing further into him, needing to be as close as possible.

Grabbing my chin between his finger and thumb, he roughly jerked my head down, forcing me to look into his eyes as he continued his slow torture. I whimpered, needing to move, to writhe under him, but he let his weight press my body into the mattress and held my head in place with the grip of his fingers, demanding that I look at him, demanding that my body stay still under his.

He rocked back and forth, watching as the pleasure trembled over my body until it erupted and I came, panting and crying out his name. Only then did he release me. He let go of the grip on my chin, lifted the weight of his body and withdrew to sit on the edge of the bed, his hard cock protruding proudly between his legs, hands left trailing over my stomach.

"Tyler?" I said, sitting up and moving beside him. I reached between his legs and wrapped my hands around his hardness but he took my wrist and pulled my hand away.

"You should have told me," he said finally.

"I know." I dropped my gaze to the floor as Tyler lay back. "You shouldn't have said what you did."

"I know," he replied. "I'm sorry."

"How are we going to move past this? Gabe is always going to be part of your life, more so now with his involvement in the company, and there will always be that knowledge of me being with him."

Tyler didn't reply. The muscles of his jaw worked back and forth as he stared at the ceiling.

"Tell me about your past. Surely you've got some baggage that you could share, even the load a little. It's not fair that I've got an ex-fiancé and, well, and Gabe."

Tyler shook his head. "There isn't anyone really."

"So you had no one before me? I find that hard to believe." I lay back on the bed, mimicking Tyler's position, and stared at the ceiling lined with dark rafters.

"I suppose there was this one girl."

"Just the one?"

Tyler turned to his side, propping his head on his hand with his elbow digging into the mattress. "I didn't really have anyone before you. There were women, women like Molly and Amanda, but they were dates to functions. They had no place in the rest of my life."

"So tell me about this one girl."

Tyler reached over and traced circles around my belly button with his finger. "It was nothing really. I was sixteen and Jake and I were spending the summer holidays with our mother. She lived in this little town. I didn't want to go. But I discovered that living with Mum was a lot different than living with Dad. We had freedom. We roamed the streets and attended all the small town parties we could. I got drunk for the first time, and I got stoned for the first time, all under the supervision of good old Gloria. Anyway, I met this girl at one of the parties. She was a few years older than me, and I thought she was gorgeous. She was my first. I was young and naïve and thought I was in love. She was everything exciting and forbidden. Or so I thought."

"What happened?"

"What do you mean, what happened?"

"How did it end?" I prompted.

Tyler flopped onto his back again. "A few days before I was due to come back home, she changed. I walked over to her house and she refused to let me in. She just stood there, shouting through the closed door for me to go away. I did. And then I went back later on but she still refused to see me. I didn't know what I had done wrong. And, of course, me being the naïve kid that I was, it never occurred to me that there was more going on in her life than just me. Anyway, after refusing to move from her door on the day I was supposed to leave, she finally let me in and told me what was going on. She was pregnant. It wasn't mine, but I didn't know that when the words first came out of her mouth and I literally froze. I was only sixteen. I was in no way ready to be a father. But then I couldn't stand the thought of not being with her. I was prepared to give up everything to be with her, even if it meant raising some other guy's kid." He spoke with a twinkle in his eye, rolling his bottom lip over his teeth almost as if he was daring me to jealousy.

"So what happened to her? Did she go back to the father of the baby?"

Tyler shook his head against the duvet. "Didn't see her again after that. Mum called Dad to come and pick me up because she was worried I was getting too attached. I snuck out late one night and caught a bus all the way back there but when I arrived, Mum was in a state and the things she said about me, about Claudia..." He sighed heavily. "I've barely seen Mum since."

I moved across the bed and lay my head on his chest. "That's a rather sad story."

He shrugged and my head shifted on his chest. "It is what it is."

"When was the last time you saw your Mum?"

Tyler tensed under me. "Clark's funeral."

"And there've been no other girls since?" I asked, sensing the need to change the subject away from his mother.

A smile creased Tyler's face. "Of course there have been women, just none that I've felt a connection to. Not that there weren't plenty who tried."

"Oh really?" I teased.

"Really." He laughed and it rumbled around his chest. "At one stage I was thinking of hiring security just to keep them away."

I rolled my eyes and shoved him playfully. "So with all these women chasing you, what made you want me?" I shifted the tilt of my chin so I could look up at him.

"That's easy," he said and pressed a kiss to my head. "You're smart, you're talented, and you make me laugh as well as drive me insane. And, you're incredibly beautiful. No matter how much I get to know you, I always want to know more."

Tyler silenced any further questions with his mouth, his hands gripping each side of my face. He kissed me until I forgot what we had been talking about, until I forgot the argument we had had, until I forgot we had spent the night apart. He kissed me until everything else melted away and there was nothing but him and me. Nothing else existed.

Suddenly he pulled away and grinned. "Another reason I like you." He pulled his lip between his teeth, trying to smother a smirk.

"Yes?" I prompted.

"You fuck incredibly well."

He kissed me again and I mumbled against his mouth, "Do I now?"

"Yes," he said and his hands slid between us until they found the wetness between my legs. "I like the way you fuck very, very much."

25

LAUREN

In the dim light of the bedroom, our fight the night before seemed trivial. His jealousy of Gabe had no basis, as the way I felt about Gabe paled in comparison to how I felt about Tyler. I was in awe of him.

Tyler's mouth toyed with my nipples as his fingers teased. His hardness pressed into my stomach and I longed for him to be inside me again. But our feverish fumbling was interrupted by Tyler's phone vibrating and starting to ring incessantly. Each time it stopped, only seconds would pass before it started again. Distracted, I lifted my eyes to find where it lay on the floor, brightly lit.

"Just ignore it," Tyler said, his words mumbled by my flesh.

"It's your father," I replied, noticing the capital letters angrily displayed across the screen. It was still ringing.

Tyler's head flopped to my chest and he groaned. Not the sort of groan I was used to hearing in this situation, one of frustration. "I don't want to talk to him." His hands fondled my breasts but the moment was lost to the ringing phone. Sighing exaggeratedly, Tyler dragged himself from the bed and picked up the still ringing phone.

"What?" he demanded. He listened for a moment. His eyebrows shot high and his eyes shifted to mine.

"What?" I mouthed.

Tyler nodded, making affirmative grunts and noises before saying, "We'll be there soon."

"Is everything okay?" I asked as soon as he ended the call.

"Billie's in hospital."

I reached into the bedside cabinet and pulled out a pair of underwear, threading them over my feet and sliding them up my legs. "Is she okay? Is the baby okay?"

"She's in labour. I said we'd go straight there. She's asking for you."

"For me?" A slice of panic cut through me. I didn't want to go to the hospital. I didn't want to sit there and wait, my mind unwillingly stuck on memories of the past.

Dressing quickly, we drove to the hospital on the outskirts of the city. Hamish Thornton stood outside the entrance, phone pressed to his ear, anger emanating from his tone. When he saw us, he quickly ended the call.

"About time," he said.

"We got here as quickly as we could," Tyler replied.

"I called forty minutes ago. Both your brothers are already here." Hamish's eyes moved to me. "Lauren," he said and nodded.

"Hamish," I replied, lifting my chin a little.

We followed him through the hallways of the hospital until we reached a waiting room where Gabe and Jake were sitting. Gabe sat with his head in his hands. He drew his face upwards to look at me with bloodshot eyes. He was hung over.

Just above Jake's left cheekbone, the skin was swollen and shiny and there was a little dried blood beneath his nose.

"What happened to you?" Tyler took a seat opposite his brother, casting a wary glance over at Gabe.

"It's nothing," Jake replied gruffly.

"It looks as though you had the shit kicked out of you."

"I didn't," was all Jake said.

Sitting down next to Tyler, I threaded my arm through his. Gabe followed the movement with his eyes before sitting up, then slouching back in the seat.

"Are you okay?" he asked me.

"Of course," I replied.

"You left awfully early last night."

"It wasn't early." I chose not to elaborate any further.

"It was earlier than when Tyler left. How you feeling today, brother? Worn off some of the anger?"

I turned to look at Tyler. Annoyance burned in his eyes. "Enough," he said to Gabe.

Gabe leaned forward, placed his elbows on his knees and grinned. "Enough what?"

"Enough talking," Tyler growled.

"Really? Enough talking? Are you going to grab me by the throat to stop me?"

"What's he talking about?" I asked Tyler who still glared at Gabe, muscles tensing as though he wanted to leap from his chair and do the very thing Gabe taunted him about.

"And you're okay being here and all?" Gabe asked, turning to me again. There was genuine concern in his eyes this time. He wasn't merely saying it to wind up Tyler.

"I'm fine," I said quietly. I shook my head with the slightest movement, trying to relay to Gabe not to keep talking. Nervously, I flicked a glance at Tyler, but he didn't notice. He was too busy glaring at Gabe.

The door swung open and Hamish walked in, running his hands through his thick grey hair. "She wants to see you."

"Who?" Tyler asked.

"Her," Hamish replied, jerking his head in my direction.

"You mean Lauren?" Gabe said.

"Yes, I fucking mean Lauren," Hamish shouted. He let out a breath of air. "Sorry, it's just rather intense in there."

A nurse poked her head through the door.

Hamish took a seat, his head jerking towards the nurse. "She'll show you the way."

I followed the clipped steps of the nurse down the hall, concentrating on the noises her shoes made on the linoleum rather than the memories that were threatening to rise to the surface. The problem with hospitals was that they all looked the same. Wide corridors, muted colours, sterile simplicity. Flashes of Derek's hand in mine as they wheeled me to the operating theatre bolted through my mind. And the memory of the pressure of the pillow as I hugged it when they injected the epidural into my back almost made me frozen with fear.

The nurse stopped at a door. "She's in here," she said and then walked off, leaving me facing the blue door, standing just out of sight from the glass panel.

Taking a deep breath, I squared my shoulders. I may have lost a child but Billie was just about to bring hers into the world. I needed to concentrate on the joy, not the pain. Plastering a smile on my face, I pushed the door open.

"About fucking time," Billie wailed. She paced the floor, fists balled into the small of her back, feet splayed wide and tummy protruding from a pale green gown.

"We got here as soon as we could." I walked over to embrace her and she clung to me, leaning on me for support.

"I don't want to do this," she whispered in my ear.

I hugged her tighter, well, as tightly as I could with her belly creating distance that couldn't be reduced. "I don't think you have a choice at this point."

Billie laughed but it was unsettled, unhinged, and she let go of me to resume her pacing back and forth over the patch of linoleum in front of the window. "It's not supposed to happen like this." Her usually perfectly groomed hair was plastered to the sides of her face. Smears of mascara stained the skin under her eyes. "I was booked in for a C-section in two weeks. I wasn't supposed to go into labour. I wasn't planning on doing it this way. The 'natural' way." She put air quotes around the word before crying out and clutching her lower back again. She grimaced and started panting with short, sharp breaths.

"Should I get Hamish?"

"No!" she shouted. "No," she said again, this time more quietly. "He's useless. Just sort of stands there with this look on his face like he'd prefer to be anywhere but here."

"I'm sure he's excited."

"Yeah." Billie rolled her eyes. "Really excited for his fifth son."

"I'm sure that—"

But Billie was panting again. "Shut up," she said. "Just shut up, okay?"

I held my hands up in surrender. The room was large, larger than the one I had been in, but the curtains were almost identical. Some hideous striped pattern in blue, orange and green. I ran my fingers over the material and squeezed my eyes shut as the memory flooded through my mind of the knife running along my stomach.

I never felt pain, the epidural made sure of that, but I still felt the slice of the blade, the invasion as they pulled her from my body.

"Hold my hand," Billie demanded, bringing my attention back to the present. She clutched on hard. The knuckles of her fingers turned white as she crushed my bones together. "Oh god," she panted. "I think you're going to have to go and get Hamish."

I was glad to leave the confined space of that room. I didn't feel like I could breathe in there. It was too hot, too stuffy. Gulping in deep breaths of what I considered to be fresh air, even though I knew there was no difference between it and what had been in the room, I started down the corridor. Hamish was already storming towards me, coffee in hand. He didn't speak as he brushed past and entered the room.

I wandered back down to the waiting room and flopped in the chair beside Tyler. He lifted his arm, and I settled back into the curve it created. I was shattered. I had gotten very little sleep the night before, and with the tension of the drive back to the city and the intensity of what happened afterwards, my body was left drained. I tilted my head onto his shoulder and decided to close my eyes for just a moment.

When I woke, my head was in Tyler's lap and he was brushing the hair away from my face. I sat up, startled that I had fallen asleep and looked around the room. Jake was sitting with his ankle hooked over his knee, glaring at it as though it were responsible for all the pain in the world. Gabe was sleeping with his head bent at an awkward angle, hair hanging over his eyes.

"Any news?" I asked.

Tyler shook his head and rested his hand on my shoulder to guide my head back to his lap. "Go back to sleep," he said. "I'll wake you if anything happens."

Needing little encouragement, I nestled back, tucking my hands under my cheek. But I couldn't fall back to sleep. Suddenly the hospital seemed too loud. The swinging doors clanged as they shut. The wheels of the hospital beds squeaked and groaned as they were rolled down the corridors. Even the television hanging in the corner of the room seemed too loud, even though I could barely make out the words spoken.

Tyler ran his hand over my hair again, pushing it behind my ear. The repetitive moment was soothing. Leaning down, he pressed a kiss to my cheek and whispered in my ear. "I love you, Lauren Green. I don't care who you dated in the past, even if I have to see him every day. The only thing I care about is that you are with me now and that you will choose to be with me in the future."

Words not fulfilling the emotions I felt, I reached up and pulled his face close, relishing in the wave of desire and contentment that flowed through me when his lips pressed to mine.

"I love you too, Tyler Thornton."

"For fuck's sake." Gabe, now awake, got to his feet and paced the floor, running his hands through his hair like his father had done earlier. "Get a room," he hissed.

Rather than rising to the jibe, Tyler simply laughed. "You want a coffee?" he asked. I nodded and he collected orders. As soon as he left, Gabe slumped to the vacant chair beside me.

"Are you okay?"

I lifted my eyebrows questioningly. "I'm not the one pushing a baby out."

Gabe shook his head. "Don't," he said. "I don't need the visual." He turned, twisting his body towards mine and hooked one knee over the side of the chair. "I meant, are you okay with all this?" He made a circle with his hand, encompassing the entire hospital, and my stomach.

I shifted uncomfortably. "I'm fine," I said tersely.

"You sure?" he asked, concerned.

"Quite sure." I held my stance straight, determined not to let my true feelings show, but at Gabe's soft eyes, I melted a little and put my hand on his knee. "Thanks for asking though."

Gabe swallowed. His eyes locked on my hand. I took it away just as Tyler walked through the swinging doors, four cups of coffee perfectly balanced in his hands. Gabe flew from the seat, flashing Tyler a mischievous smile and took one of the cups.

"Cheers," he said, lifting it in salute. Tyler scowled.

It was the small hours of the morning before Hamish finally returned to give us the news. A healthy baby boy was born. Oliver Clark Thornton. Gabe's eyes welled with tears. The three brothers rose to hug their father and clap him on the back, and then we all followed Hamish back down the corridor to meet the newest member of the Thornton family.

All traces of Billie's previous frustration at her condition had vanished. She held the baby in her arms, smiling down like there was no better sight in the world. My heart constricted. My throat swelled and I found it difficult to swallow the thick saliva. Behind Tyler's back, Gabe's hand enclosed around mine and he gave me a reassuring smile. I clutched onto the familiar warmth, grateful for the distraction, needing the reassurance and comfort.

Tyler was the first to hold Ollie. Collecting my camera from my bag, I began to take pictures. Billie's smile and look of utter adoration as she gazed at her baby. Hamish's tears of joy as he held Ollie's hand in his. Jake, so big, so wild and untamed, brought to a puddle of goo at the sight of his brother. The chubby and wrinkled fingers of Ollie gripping Tyler's finger. A slight spill of milk down Gabe's chest and the look of horror on his face at its discovery.

In that moment there was nothing more beautiful than the Thornton Brothers.

26

LAUREN

I received daily updates from Billie. Motherhood wasn't what she had expected. She had expected a baby who slept through the night, fed easily and smiled unendingly. What she got was a baby that refused to sleep more than two hours before demanding to be fed again, and then would latch on, only to fall asleep after sating himself. She hated changing diapers. She hated being woken all hours of the night. She hated the mess, the lack of routine, and the disappearance of Hamish who was suddenly busier at work than he had ever been.

But despite everything she hated, she was also in love. I received photo after photo of what she insisted were smiles, even though the midwife had told her they were merely wind. And Ollie was certainly a Thornton. In one photo she sent, I swore he had a single eyebrow raised, a trait of his older brothers.

And as the family fell in love with Ollie, Tyler was drowned in work. The grand opening of the casino was less than a week away, and I had barely seen him. He spent all his time organising everything that would be needed for the event. On the guest list were some family and friends, investors and also media. It was to be a test of the facility. The invitations had been sent months ago, inviting the guests to spend twenty-four hours at the casino to wine, dine, gamble and dance their way through the night.

Sadie had been busy too, but not busy enough to forget our venture. She had managed to get us an appointment to tour one of the recently renovated hotels in a few weeks. And, after touring the building, we were to come up with a marketing campaign. I was completely over my head, but Sadie assured me that with both of us working at it, we would come up with something spectacular. I was a little less certain.

The day before the grand opening wasn't a busy one. Well, not for me. I had no photo shoots booked and I had checked in on Billie the day before. Tyler had left for work so early that it was still pitch black when I watched his headlights fade down the road. I crawled back under the covers that smelled of him, and closed my eyes, determined to make the most of the opportunity to sleep in. So I was very surprised when Tyler shook me awake a few hours later.

"What are you doing back home?" I asked groggily as I stretched into the air.

"We're leaving in an hour. Do you think you can be ready?"

"Leaving to go where?"

"It's a surprise."

"A surprise?" I stretched into the air again, a yawn overtaking me even though it was almost lunchtime.

Tyler patted my leg under the covers. "Come on. Throw some clothes into a bag, and then come join me in the shower." He winked and then began walking to the bathroom, tossing each item of clothing aside as he walked until he was naked just before he disappeared behind the door. I decided that packing could wait.

Emerging from the shower pleasured and satisfied, I threw some clothes into a bag, Tyler informing me that I would need an outfit for the casino opening as well.

A car waited for us outside the loft and drove us to the casino. I looked over at Tyler suspiciously, unsure why we arrived a day early for the opening. A smartly dressed man opened the car door when it rolled to a stop.

"Mr Thornton," he greeted. Then he looked at me and grinned.

"Jimmy?" I said, barely believing that this man in front of me was the same boy who picked me up from the airport all those months ago.

Jimmy stood proudly in his uniform. "You like?" He twirled so I could get the full effect. "Mr Thornton thought I might be better suited to this job and helped me get it. I've got to watch the language though."

I looked at Tyler who just shrugged. "He seemed like a good kid. A good kid that was pretty useless at construction." Taking my hand, Tyler led me into the lobby of the casino. The staff behind the front desk smiled and greeted Tyler by name. Jimmy carried our bags and took us up in the elevator to the top level of the building. The honeymoon suite.

"What's going on?" I asked Tyler as Jimmy opened the door to the magnificent room. I had seen it all before. I had taken photos of the entire building process, after all, but somehow, seeing it as a guest made it different. The luxury of the room became more personal.

Just like in Tyler's loft, one side of the walls were lined with glass overlooking the city. I walked around the room, running my fingers over the elegant bedding and removing my shoes to sink my toes into the plush carpet. The glass sliding doors led out to a balcony, complete with an infinity pool where the water appeared to flow right over the edge of the building.

Tyler walked up behind me and wrapped his arms around my waist, resting his head on my shoulder. "Tonight," he said, "it's only us. We have the full run of the place, apart from the actual casino. We can eat at any of the restaurants, go to the gym, take a wander around the shops, check out the show, or stay here all night and order room service. The choice is yours."

I spun in his arms so I was facing him and looped my hands around his neck. "What about work?"

"I've done all I can do. The rest it up to fate."

"So I really get you all to myself?"

Tyler dipped his knees so our mouths were at the same level and casually brushed his lips over mine. "I am at your disposal. Do with me as you will." As if fate had an ironic sense of humour, his phone started to ring at that very moment. I looked at him, a smirk on my lips.

Tyler ignored the call and then turned his phone off. "I told Sadie I'd check in with her and clear any messages at eight. Other than that, the world can wait." His arms tightened around me and his mouth found mine again, soft yet urgent. "So," he murmured, "What is your wish?"

I contemplated for a while, screwing my face up, twisting my mouth at awkward angles until Tyler rolled his eyes.

"If you're having a difficult time deciding, I'm sure I could think of a few things to keep you entertained." His mouth lowered to my neck, running along the tender flesh before burrowing between the swell of my breasts.

I moaned, letting my head fall back. "I've got it," I said, feigning distraction.

Tyler grinned. "And what do you want to do first?" His eyes were dark and scorched with desire. His hardness pressed against me as his mouth continued to explore my curves.

"Eat," I exclaimed, detangling myself from Tyler's embrace. "I'm starving." I walked over and grabbed my bag, lifting it to the bed to unzip it.

Tyler groaned into his hands. "I'm all worked up now."

I pouted playfully. "Poor Tyler." I held an outfit against my body. It was a long flowing dress that had a bare back and a split right down the middle of my waist that exposed the inside swell of my breasts. "Should I wear this?"

Tyler sat on the couch and nodded, adjusting himself where he strained against his pants. "I think you should."

I pulled my clothes from the bag and hung them in the closet. Tyler watched my every move, his head cocked to the side. Knowing his eyes were on me, I undressed slowly, unbuttoning my shirt and letting it fall off my shoulders, wiggling out of my jeans and sliding them over my hips. Dressed only in black lace and high heels with my hair flowing down my back, I leaned down to slip on my high heels. Tyler stood and stalked towards me, his eyes roaming my body, stopping only inches from me, looking into my eyes.

"You are gorgeous, do you know that?" His finger skimmed over my nipple which tightened in response.

"Now, now, Tyler Thornton," I said, playfully stepping away from him. "Let's not get ahead of ourselves." I turned, feeling the burn of his gaze on my backside. "First we will have lunch, then we can have a look through the shops." I bent over to remove an imaginary speck of fluff from the floor, and Tyler's hands cupped my rounded cheeks, brushing over the flesh softly, causing a pulse of pleasure to tremble through me. He pulled me back against him.

"And then," I said, somewhat breathlessly, "we can perhaps have a drink at the bar, then dinner, then go to that show you mentioned, and maybe finish it all off with a swim. What do you say?"

"I say, when do I get to be inside you?" His finger ran down the seam of my underwear.

I moaned, grinding back into him. "There'll be plenty of time for that later," I said, though my actions denied my words. I turned around, taking his face between my hands and kissing him until my legs turned to liquid.

"And what about now?" Tyler's hands roamed over my bare skin and dipped under the band of my underwear. His fingers toyed with me, pleasuring, teasing. "I want to taste you," he whispered into my ear.

I reached between us and undid his buttons, dipping my hand under his waistband and finding his hardness. Wrapping my fingers around him, I tugged him free, melting a little at the steel-like hardness of him. I began to stroke up and down as his fingers pleasured me. When our movements grew more intense, I removed my hand, pulling away and turning to the closet.

"All in good time," I teased.

Over my shoulder, I watched as Tyler let out a low exhale. My eyes fell to where he was exposed. Wincing, he tucked himself back in place and winked. "As you wish, Lauren Greer."

Tyler must have instructed the staff only to be visible when needed. We were left alone during lunch, a waiter only appearing to take our orders, bring the food to the table and then clear it away once we were done. Afterwards, we ran along the empty corridors of the hotel, laughing like teenagers, opening every door we found and poking our heads inside the various rooms. On occasion, Tyler would push me inside one of the rooms, pressing me against the wall, or pushing me to a bed to tangle his hands in my hair, his mouth on my lips. I gave a fashion show for Tyler of all the dresses from the shop, but he insisted the one I already wore was his favourite. We held hands through the concert, a single performer and a piano that transported me to another world, and finally, we sat down to dinner in the deserted restaurant. Rather than selecting from the menu, the chef took the opportunity to cook every meal available and we picked from the smorgasbord on offer. By the time eight o'clock rolled around and Tyler excused himself from our room to call Sadie, I was happy, content and looking forward to an evening spent with Tyler. Alone. We had teased each other for most of the afternoon, finding secluded areas to have feverish moments of pleasure, our hands exploring each other's bodies beneath our clothing, our mouths trailing along each other's flesh, but we hadn't done more than that. The build-up had left me aching, but when Tyler walked back into the room, his jaw was clenched.

"Everything okay?" I asked, running my hands over his broad shoulders, attempting to relieve some of the tension he held there.

He smiled tightly and kissed the tip of my nose. "Nothing a few moments with you can't wash away. You ready for that swim?"

Someone had already been out onto the balcony. Candles shielded by glass flickered on the edge of the water, gas heaters burned overhead and a tray of nibbles and a bottle of champagne had been left on the table. Having already changed into a bikini, I dropped the towel from around my waist and stepped into the warm water. Sinking down to my shoulders, I swam across the clear water until I reached the edge of the pool and looked out over the lights of the city. The water swirled as Tyler surrounded my body, embracing me from behind.

"It's so beautiful, isn't it?" he said quietly.

"You know, I had never really thought of the city as beautiful until I moved here. All I thought about was the traffic and the people and the bustle and hurry. I didn't think about the lights at night, or the moon shining overhead."

Light and buoyant in the water, I twisted around and wrapped my legs around Tyler's waist, my arms around his neck. Our skin shimmered from the glow of the underwater lights and the slight breeze brought bumps to the exposed parts of my skin. Tyler pulled me closer until my chest pressed against his, and slowly shifted until his mouth met mine. The kiss was soft and tender and teasing. He toyed with my lips, gently biting before his mouth moved to my neck and his hands found their way to untie the loops of my bikini top.

"Tyler," I said, becoming self-conscious at the thought of someone walking in on us.

"No one is here."

My bikini top floated away and Tyler pressed me to him, his hands wandering down to cup my backside, his chest crushing against my breasts. Soon, my bikini bottom joined the floating top and I was naked, wrapped around Tyler as he ravished me with his mouth. Hooking my legs tighter around his waist, I felt his hardness pushing into me. After hours of teasing and pleasure without release, Tyler was burning. He lifted me slightly out of the water as his mouth found my breasts, nibbling and swirling his tongue until I moaned with desire. Lifting me further so I was sitting on the tiles that surrounded the edge, he pushed my legs apart, exposing my vulnerability, before lowering his mouth and tasting me. His licks were gentle. His tongue toyed with my clit, flicking back and forth before sucking against it, causing surges of desire to flame through my entire body. His fingers joined the assault, plunging deep inside me as his mouth remained latched.

Climbing out of the water, Tyler pulled me to my feet, his hand wrapping in my hair before tugging me to my knees.

"Open," he said, and I trembled in response to his command. He used his grip on my hair to guide my mouth to his cock. He was gentle at first, sliding in and out of my mouth, allowing me to twirl my tongue over his tip and up and down the ridges of his cock, then his movements became more intense and he used the leverage of his hands to pull me forward, taking more of him into my mouth. Moisture pooled between my legs and he removed himself long enough to reach down and rub circles over my clit, causing me to moan once again.

I tilted forward, leaning heavily on him for support. He lifted his fingers and dove them into my mouth before removing them, covering my mouth with his own, the taste of me mingling between us.

It sometimes frightened me how much I wanted to please him. I think I would have done almost anything he asked. And I would have enjoyed it. But that still didn't stop me from being nervous as he brought me to my feet and led me over to the waist-height glass barrier that framed the balcony. I looked out over the city, the breeze causing my nipples to tighten even more. Only darkness shielded us from the people milling the streets below, but even then, with the lights behind us, I knew that if anyone glanced across from the other buildings surrounding us, they would see me naked, pressed against the barrier. Tyler stood behind me, parted the cheeks of my backside and ran the tip of his cock along the crease before plunging into my wetness.

"Does it excite you knowing that someone could see?" he asked. I clenched around him, his words igniting a desire within me I hadn't known. Did I really get excited at the thought of being caught?

Tyler twisted his hand through my hair, jerking my head back. "Do you like knowing that if there was someone watching in that building opposite us they would see you bent over the edge? Do you think they would know I am fucking you right now as they watched?"

Unable to answer, I moaned. Tyler withdrew and then plunged back inside forcefully, causing me to grunt with the roughness of the movement.

"Because it excites me," Tyler continued. "I want everyone to know that you are mine." His hands moved to fondle my breasts. "I want everyone to know that it is my hands that get to touch these. My mouth that gets to tease your nipples." Pushing my back, Tyler bent me over the railing, causing me to grip onto the edge of the glass as the drop to the ground fell below.

I was excited. I was terrified. I had never felt so alive.

Tyler fucked me from behind until my body began to turn numb with cold from the crisp night breeze and the railing left an indentation across my belly. Then, leading me over to the deck chair that lay under the gas heater, his mouth trailed over every inch of my body as the heat warmed my skin. He brought me to the brink so many times, only to direct his attention elsewhere until I was delirious with the need to come. I thrust against him, urging him further into me as he lay between my legs.

My need for him was almost too much.

Tyler lifted himself onto his elbows as he slid in and out. "Play with yourself," he instructed. "I want to feel you come around me. I want to feel you clench as you orgasm."

Needing no extra encouragement, my fingers toyed until the explosion I longed for ripped through my body, sending pulses of desire to the very tips of my fingers and toes and leaving me breathless. Tyler stayed still inside me, eyes locked on me as I writhed beneath him. Then, with a final push, he called out my name and I felt him convulse as his release came.

27

LAUREN

After waking to a fully cooked breakfast delivered to our room, I dressed reluctantly, wishing my night with an undistracted Tyler could last forever. As soon as he woke—well, not exactly as soon as he woke, there may have been an extra round of play in there somewhere—Tyler's phone began to ring. And this time he didn't turn it off. The rest of the guests would be arriving not long after lunch, and Tyler was determined for the event to run smoothly. Already the hotel was filling with more staff on last-minute errands to make sure everything was ready for the opening night.

By the time we walked downstairs, ready to greet the guests as they entered the foyer, all the tension that had drained away from Tyler was back. He clasped the hand of every person that came through the doors and smiled, but his smile was too tight, his grasp too hard. No one else seemed to notice as they arrived in their finery, exclaiming over the exquisite beauty of the casino. Tyler had really done an exceptional job. And even though I had seen it all before, I appreciated it in a new light as I watched the guests look around for the first time. They noticed the chandelier dangling as a masterpiece in the foyer. They noticed each piece of artwork that adorned the walls. Each lavish shot of material, each extravagant decoration.

Most of the guests had already arrived by the time the rest of the Thornton family did. Billie had her ear pressed to the phone, already checking on Ollie's babysitter. Both Gabe and Jake were dressed for the occasion and looked very stylish and handsome in their black tuxedos. When the three brothers stood side by side, it almost took my breath away.

But I was surprised by the last people to walk through the door. It was my family.

Tyler leaned down and whispered in my ear. "Surprise. I invited them. I hope you don't mind. I just thought it would be nice to meet your family, and I figured now was as good of a time as any."

"I—I—" I fumbled, struggling to find the right words. "I'm not sure this was a good idea."

Already, Mother was looking around the foyer with a scowl on her face. But when she turned to see Tyler, she broke into a smile.

"Why Tyler," she said. "There you are. I finally get to meet you!" She glared at me accusingly as she embraced him. Dad shook his hand and Morgan winked at me as she returned Tyler's hug.

"Wow." Alistair turned in a slow circle. "This place is amazing. You've done a fantastic job here."

"Thank you." Tyler stepped forward and shook his hand. "It's a pleasure to finally meet Lauren's family. It's been too long."

"It's nice that someone thought to invite us," my mother replied.

"How—Why—" I couldn't get my words to make sense.

Truth be told, I was a little disappointed they were here. Disappointed and annoyed. Of course, I wanted Tyler to meet my family, but I wanted him to meet them when I was ready. Not here.

Not now. Not with my mother's aversion to gambling, alcohol and enjoyment of life in general.

"Just head over to the front desk and Cathy will sort your accommodation." Tyler pointed in the direction. "I've arranged for us all to have dinner together at eight."

"Eight?" my mother exclaimed. "I will be near on ready for bed at that time."

"Nonsense," my father scolded her. "Eight will be fine, thank you, Tyler."

Mother rolled her eyes and sighed, but kept her mouth closed after Dad's warning.

"Did I not do the right thing?" Tyler asked once they were out of earshot. "I thought it would be good for everyone to meet each other at dinner."

"And by everyone, you mean?"

"Dad, Billie, Jake, Gabe, your parents, Morgan and Alistair."

I covered my face with my hands. "What have you done?"

Tyler laughed. "You're being overly dramatic. You'll see. Tonight will go off without a hitch."

I shook my head. "It's so obvious that you don't know my mother."

"She can't be that bad."

"You just wait."

"But I thought you were worried that you hadn't seen your parents in a while. I definitely remember a comment you made about your mother being displeased that she hadn't seen you in months."

"Yes, I was worried," I replied in a hushed voice. "But that didn't mean I actually wanted to see her. When did you even ask them?"

Tyler shrugged. "I called your mother a few weeks ago. We've kept in contact since."

"You what?" His actions reminded me of Derek. My ex-fiancé had a relationship with my mother that was hard to break. Even after we had broken up, he still kept in contact with her. Or she with him. I still wasn't sure which.

* * *

Eight o'clock rolled around all too soon. Tyler had been distracted by the various guests and media interviews from magazines showcasing the newly built casino. I followed him, hoping I nodded and smiled in all the right places, while my mind was distracted by all the possibilities of what could go wrong at dinner.

I'm not sure how it happened, but I found myself seated between Tyler and Gabe while the rest of our families looked at us from around the circular table. The room hummed with conversation. Tyler rested his hand on my thigh under the table. He meant it as reassuring, but the way his fingers gripped into my flesh spoke of the pressure he was under. He needed this night to go well. He had been involved in other projects, but this was the first he was fully responsible for.

"So," Mother said, looking over to Billie after the introductions had been completed. "You've just had a baby?"

Billie's smile filled the room. "Oliver. He's gorgeous. Isn't he gorgeous, Hamish?"

Hamish grunted in response and took a sip of his drink. Already his eyes were slightly glazed and I wondered how many he had consumed before he even got to the table. Hamish was usually rather reserved in his public drinking but tonight was different. Maybe it was the pressure of fatherhood getting to him. Maybe it was because it was Tyler's project and not his.

"How old?" Mother asked.

"Almost three weeks. He's beginning to smile and I'm almost certain that one of the noises he makes is 'mum'."

"Three weeks?" I noted a hint of disapproval in mother's tone. "And who is looking after the wee fella tonight? Is he here?" She looked around the room as though someone would suddenly appear holding Oliver in their arms.

"Oh no!" Billie exclaimed. "This is my first night out since his birth and after being trapped at home I was nearly going insane."

"You poor woman," Mother drawled, her tone proving she thought nothing of the sort.

"He's at home with a sitter," Billie continued, lifting her glass into the air. "Hence." She took a large sip.

"But who will feed him?" Mother appeared genuinely concerned, and completely oblivious that the baby could drink from a bottle.

Billie waved her concern aside. "The sitter has plenty of formula. Don't you worry, he will be well looked after."

Mother lifted her glass of water to her mouth, muttering under her breath. "If you can call feeding a baby with formula well looked after."

I tried to kick her under the table, but I couldn't reach and collided with Gabe instead.

His eyes flew to mine, eyebrows raised playfully. "If you want to play footsie, Lauren, all you need to do is ask."

Dad muttered a warning, "Clementine," under his breath, while Tyler threw daggered looks at Gabe.

But Mother wasn't done yet. "Forgive my ignorance, but this family is rather confusing. Who exactly is the father of your son?"

The colour crept up Billie's cheeks and she leaned closer to Hamish, looping her arm through his. "Why, this handsome devil, right here."

"The father?" Mother exclaimed. "So this child, this Oliver is a brother to these other young men around the table?"

"A twenty-two year age gap between the two youngest isn't all that bad, is it?" Gabe joked and Hamish threw him a withering glare, narrowing his eyes as he took another sip from his glass.

"Are you comfortable with the father of your son being so much older than you?"

"Mother!" I exclaimed.

"What?" She looked at me, eyebrows raised. "I was only asking the question. She doesn't have to answer if she doesn't want to. I was wondering if it had occurred to her how old the father will be by the time the child is a teenager. Men aren't the most helpful at parenting at the best of times, let alone when they're elderly." She leaned towards Hamish. "Sorry, no offence but you are considerably older than your wife. You two are married, aren't you?"

"My god," Gabe whispered in my ear. "This is like watching a really bad television show that for some reason you just can't turn off."

"Yes," Billie said, a lot quieter now. "Yes, we are."

The table descended into an awkward silence. Thankfully, the entrées came and we busied ourselves with eating and making flattering remarks about the food.

Once we were finished, and the silence became louder without the distraction of food, Tyler cleared his throat. "So Alistair, what are you working on these days? Lauren told me about the app you developed. Anything else in the pipelines?"

Alistair looked up, surprised that someone had spoken to him. More often than not, he was a head down, look at the ground sort of person that didn't engage in conversation. Whether that was because of Morgan's dominance or his personality, I wasn't sure.

"I'm actually on the job hunt at the moment. In between things."

"Really?" Tyler leaned forward, resting his elbows on the table. "What sort of skill sets do you have? Maybe we could find a position for him within the company?" Tyler turned to his father who scoffed.

"Like now is the time to be hiring more people."

"You hired Gabe," Tyler said.

"He's my son," Hamish replied gruffly.

"So is Jake, and yet I don't see you offering him any positions."

"Don't drag me into this." Jake held up his hands, tilting his chair back from the table.

"Where do you currently work?" Dad asked. He was sitting next to Jake and I had seen him giving the long-haired man curious glances. Dad had never been considered a small man, but sitting beside Jake, he seemed shrivelled and wrinkled. Old.

Jake flicked a glance Tyler's way before answering. "I guess you could say I'm in the same boat as Alistair. I served in the army for the last six years though."

Dad looked impressed, giving Jake a nod of approval. Being in the army deserved respect in Dad's opinion. He had tried to get in when he was younger but was turned down after the medical.

"In the army with hair like that?" Mother asked, her voice rising to a high pitch.

Jake tossed the tail of his hair over his shoulder as if to rub it in Mother's face. "There were times I needed to blend in. And believe it or not, this look," he gestured to his hair and beard, "did the trick."

A fork hovered in front of Mother's mouth. "It won't help your chances of gaining employment back here though."

Hamish laughed and slapped his thigh. "I think I like you." He raised his glass in Mother's direction, saluting her, then drained the contents.

"Maybe you should slow down?" Tyler said, noting the way his father heavily clunked the glass onto the table.

"So," Mother said exaggeratedly, looking over to Tyler as though it were her conversation topics that relieved the tension rather than created it. "How did you meet my daughter?" Pushing her plate away, she rested her chin on her hands, gazing adoringly at Tyler. I had never seen her quite like this before. She was clearly no fan of the rest of the Thornton men, but Tyler seemed to have woven a spell around her. For some reason it made me swell with pride at the same time as finding it annoying.

Gabe laughed. "How did they meet? Are you serious?"

"Of course I'm serious, young man," she scolded, refusing to use his name. "Why wouldn't I be?"

Gabe sat back in his chair and cupped his hands behind his head, using his infuriatingly charming grin to his advantage. "They met when I took Lauren to meet my family. You remember I dated her first, don't you?"

Mother rolled her eyes, his grin clearly lost on her. "How could I forget? For a while there I was so desperate for her to get back together with Derek. He was so much..." she paused, searching for the right word, "so much better suited to Lauren."

"Because?" Gabe prompted.

"I think we should change the subject," I interjected. "What did everyone order for dessert?" It was a feeble effort and no one took the bait.

"Because you are barely more than a child." My mother didn't miss a beat, talking across me to answer Gabe's question.

"So the cheating bastard was a better option?"

"There is no need for language like that, young man."

Tyler rose to his feet. "I propose a toast," he declared, startling the rest of the guests around the table. "To my father who taught me that it was hard work that would accomplish my dreams." Tyler's gaze bore into his father, who shifted uncomfortably under the glare.

We all lifted our glasses, echoing, "To Hamish," as Tyler tossed the contents of his glass down his throat and signalled the waiter for another.

"Make that two," Hamish added.

"Is everything okay?" I leaned in closer to Tyler so no one else could hear my question.

"Fine," Tyler replied forcefully even though there was very little that could be defined as 'fine' about the evening. "Though I would appreciate it if Gabe stopped looking at you the way he is."

I snuck a glance Gabe's way but he was deep in conversation with Jake. "What way?"

"Like he's dying of starvation and you're the only food left on the planet."

"Don't be silly," I dismissed. His jealousy of Gabe was starting to grate. Gabe was his brother. We should be able to have a meal together without the green-eyed monster rearing its head. He had promised me he would.

"Don't encourage him," Tyler warned, even though I had done nothing other than glance in Gabe's direction.

I flashed him a warning glare. "Don't."

Tyler shook his head as though trying to relieve himself from the thoughts plaguing him and smiled tightly. "Sorry. There's just a lot going on tonight."

"And you dragged my mother into the middle of it."

"I've already apologised for that. I thought you would like it. I was trying to be nice." His words were tight and terse.

Gabe bumped my leg with his, attempting to get my attention. "Did you ever go back to that beach to take more photos?" I furrowed my brows, trying to remember which beach he was referring to. "You know," he continued, "the one we went to that afternoon? I went surfing and you took those photos?"

The memory popped to the front of my mind. Gabe and his flatmates, as well as Haleigh and another girl whose name I couldn't remember, were all there. Gabe had only brought it up to annoy Tyler.

"No," I replied sharply. "I haven't been back. But it was a beautiful place," I added, attempting to reduce the sharpness of my tone.

Gabe nodded, hands behind his head once again. "A bit like that old house. Do you remember going there? We had that picnic on the floor and—"

"I think that's enough." Tyler's voice was little more than a growl.

"What's enough? I'm just reminiscing with an old friend. Or can you not handle thinking about the men who came before you?"

Morgan laughed out loud. "That makes it sound as if you've been through hundreds, L."

"L," Billie repeated. "I forgot that people used to call you that."

"You knew Lauren when she was younger?" Dad asked.

"Oh yes," Billie replied. "We went to high school together, didn't we L?"

"So you're the same age as my daughter?" Mother's eyebrows shot skywards.

"Yes," Billie said. "Though I know I look a lot younger." She winked in my direction.

"And yet you're married to Lauren's boyfriend's father?"

"I think we've established that fact, Mother." My voice was cold and flat. The night was draining me quickly. I couldn't wait to get out of here and lock myself in the bedroom, away from all these people and wait for the night to be over.

"Well, I must say this is a rather confusing family you've chosen to involve yourself with, Lauren. And where is the older boys' mother? Is she no longer with us?"

Covering my face with my hands, I shook my head, wishing I could sink below the table and hide.

Tyler cleared his throat again. His voice was more relaxed this time though. His vocal chords had been recently bathed in whiskey. "Jake and I have a different mother from Gabe. They were married to our father before Billie was. They aren't here."

"You're onto your third wife?" Again, Mother's voice rose to a pitch of incredulousness.

I looked to Morgan for help, wishing she would stuff a bread roll in Mother's mouth, something, anything just to shut her up, but Morgan was staring gleefully at the people around the table, sitting in rapture as the drama unfolded around her. At least I never had to ask what was on Morgan's mind. It was always very clearly displayed in her expressions. She was enjoying this. No doubt about it.

"So," Gabe spoke the word with a long exhale of air. "Have you been back in the boxing ring since you've been home?" he asked Jake.

Jake scratched his chin. "Not exactly."

"You're a boxer?" Dad asked, once again turning to Jake.

"All my boys are. It's in their blood."

"Like you gave us a choice," Tyler muttered.

"Teaches them discipline and commitment."

"Teaches them how to beat the shit out of their girlfriend's arrogant ex, that's what it does." Gabe winked at me. "Speaking of Derek, have you seen any more of him since Christmas?"

The muscles of Tyler's jaw worked back and forth as he lifted yet another whiskey glass to his mouth. At the rate he was going, he was competing with his father for who could consume the most alcohol.

Gabe slapped the table. "That was a great night." He frowned. "Sort of. It did give me a sense of satisfaction when my fist hit his chin."

"You never told me any of this," Mother said, looking over at me with annoyance.

"There's a lot of things she's never told you," Morgan replied, hiding her grin behind a glass of wine.

"Well, I still have a soft spot for Derek. You two were together for such a long time, seemed a pity to throw it all away."

"He was a—"

I put my hand on Gabe's thigh to silence him. He covered it with his own and I attempted to tug away from him, but he held firm and leaned in close. "That night was the first time I told you I loved you."

I closed my eyes, willing the nightmare to end. For the past few months, I had felt like I was in a perfect Tyler-shaped bubble. He was my life. I was his. Sure, there were other things, my new venture with Sadie, his work, but generally, our lives had been wrapped up in each other with the outside world only occasionally rearing its head. Now I felt as though someone had popped that bubble and the rest of the world was pouring in and trying to drown me.

"Leave her alone," Tyler warned, keeping his voice low so as not to draw attention from the rest of the table.

"And I suppose you're going to make me?" Gabe's grip around my fingers intensified.

"Well, I don't care what you say about the man," Mother continued. "I'm certain that if Lauren wasn't barren they would still be together."

The whole room descended into silence. Well, it didn't, but it felt like it. The chatter of conversation around the room faded to nothing and all eyes turned to me. My heart thudded in my chest and my mouth went dry.

28

LAUREN

"Excuse me?" Tyler's voice rumbled deeply. "What did you just say?"

By now it had occurred to Mother that she had taken things a step too far, but being the stubborn woman that she was, she merely lifted her chin. "I'm only speaking the truth."

"Don't you ever speak about Lauren that way again," Tyler growled.

I sat at the table, staring down at the empty plate in front of me, unable to lift my eyes to the people around the table. It was all too much. The glares. The looks of surprise. Pushing my chair back from the table, I rose slowly and walked away, leaving the discomfort behind me.

Tyler followed, reaching out to grab my arm. "Lauren."

I pulled away. "I just need a minute," I replied without looking back.

Mother's words had cut deep. The word knocked against my brain, leaving a sharp stab of pain in its wake. Barren. Empty. Broken. Everything came rushing back, but instead of sadness, it was anger that welled. Walking out of the restaurant, I passed through the lobby and into the bar. The bartender didn't flinch when I ordered straight tequila and threw it back, the liquid burning like fire as I forced it down my throat.

"Another?" the bartender offered, holding the bottle over the small glass and tilting both it and his eyebrows.

I shuddered, nodded my head and swallowed painfully when the burning sensation hit my throat again.

"Rough night?" he asked. I nodded and he filled the glass once again before placing the bottle on the counter. "I'll just leave this here."

"Lauren?" Gabe's voice sounded behind me and I let my shoulders slump.

"What?" I said coldly.

"Are you okay?"

I laughed and swallowed the contents of another glass, letting the fog settle in my mind and numb the pain a little. "I'm fucking fine," I replied. "I just want to be left alone for a while."

Ignoring my comment, Gabe pulled out the chair and sat beside me, turning so he could face me even though I kept my eyes stuck on the rows of bottles in front of the mirrored wall. "Tyler ripped into your Mother. To say he was pissed was an understatement."

"He shouldn't have invited them without asking me."

"What?" Gabe asked, confused. "He invited them without checking whether you wanted them here?"

I sighed heavily and nodded.

"I would have never done that."

Rolling my eyes, I couldn't help but grin at him. The first tendrils of tequila were beginning to work. "Of course you wouldn't."

"It's hard being this perfect." Gabe's eyes twinkled as he reached out and put his hand over mine.

Staring at my hand trapped under his, I tugged it away. "Don't, Gabe. I can't handle much more right now. I either want to go to sleep or drink myself into oblivion."

"Being a seasoned veteran of both options, I would recommend the first if you actually want to feel better, but the second option if you don't want to feel at all."

Shaking my head in amusement, I tilted the bottle towards him.

"Why not?" he said, reaching over the counter to grab an empty glass.

Tossing the drink back, Gabe slammed the glass onto the counter, shaking his head and letting out a whoop after a long low breath. "The burn." He shook his head again before settling himself and shifting his chair closer. "So," he said, letting the word hang between us. "Are you happy with him?"

My shoulders slumped again. "Gabe, I told you I didn't want to do this. Not here. Not now."

"I'm changing my life for you," he replied, his voice low and torn.

"Don't," I said bluntly. The tequila had taken effect and bravado lifted my chest. "I love Tyler. I want Tyler. I choose Tyler."

Even as the words came out of my mouth, I regretted seeing the hurt in Gabe's eyes. He swallowed, his Adam's apple bobbing up and down, and dropped his gaze. "I need you to know that I still love you. Don't you miss me at all?"

I melted a little at the tenderness in his words. Gabe had never been afraid to make himself vulnerable. It was a highly attractive quality he possessed. "Of course I do. You meant—you still mean a lot to me. I care for you." I reached out to tuck a stray strand of his hair behind his ear. It was instinctive. It was meant as comfort, not affection.

It was stupid.

"I truly—" My words were cut off by Gabe's lips crushing against mine, his hands sliding around my waist, running up my back and into my hair. I was frozen in shock, my lips responding before my brain could demand they stop. And then he was gone, torn away from me by a pair of strong hands and desperate eyes.

"Get the fuck off her!" Tyler roared.

All eyes in the bar turned as Tyler's fist swung through the air and connected with a surprised Gabe, knocking him to the ground.

But Gabe was quick to get to his feet. "I loved her first," he yelled at Tyler.

A flash of a camera illuminated them. Tyler's fist swung through the air again, but Gabe was prepared this time. He ducked out of the way and returned a punch of his own, landing squarely on Tyler's cheekbone. The hit only enraged Tyler more and he ran towards Gabe, looping his arms around his waist and tackling him to the floor.

Regaining my wits, I ran over, trying to pull them apart as people watched on in shock. A crowd had gathered around the brawling brothers, but they didn't help to separate them. My interference went unnoticed as Tyler took control of Gabe and sat on top of him, letting punches fly into Gabe's face. He was deaf to my voice. Blind to my actions. Blood splattered when he connected with Gabe's nose, but he didn't stop. Running from the room, I flew into the restaurant, yelling for Jake who immediately ran to the bar where the bartender was yelling at them to stop. They were lost, both intent on inflicting as much pain as possible. I flinched when Tyler's fist split Gabe's lip open.

The crowd had grown and our families were close on our heels. I wanted to yell at them. Scream at the crowd, our families, at Gabe and at Tyler.

Just as Jake got to them and managed to tear them apart with the help of the bartender, the cameras started flashing in earnest, the eyes of media lit with excitement as they snapped photo after photo of the brawling brothers.

Gabe's chest heaved with exertion and Tyler's wild eyes darted around the room until they rested on me. He wiped his hand across his mouth, clearing away the smudge of blood that I wasn't sure belonged to him or to Gabe. I stepped forward, reaching out to him.

"You kissed him!" Tyler spat.

I froze at the venom in his tone. "I—I didn't. He kissed me."

"Don't fucking lie to me again."

Tears stung as I looked into Tyler's eyes, so cold, so filled with anger.

"I—" But he turned and strode away, leaving my words lost in a strangled whisper. "Tyler!" I called out, but he ignored my plea. "Tyler wait. Please wait."

He stopped, eyes blazing and chin jutting into the air. "Do you still love him?" he demanded of me.

"No," I said desperately, ignoring the people surrounding us.

"Then why don't I believe you?" Tyler said coldly. "You kissed him. I saw you, Lauren. Don't try denying it. You fucking kissed him. Have you been lying to me all this time? Did you ever really love me?"

His words cut. "Love you?" I repeated. "I love you more than I've ever loved anyone!" Tears fell freely down my cheeks but I didn't bother to wipe them away. There was no point. They would only be replaced by others.

Seeing the way his words hurt me, Tyler took a step forward. His hand reached out, but he stopped himself before he touched me, coldness pressing over his features once more. "You've lied to me before."

Panic danced across my chest, welling up and tightening until I felt like I could barely breathe. "I love you. Only you, Tyler. Gabe kissed me. You've got to believe me. Ask Gabe, if you don't."

He fell silent as puzzlement danced over his face. His words pounded through my head, *'you've lied to me before,'* but I didn't know what to say in response to them. What he said was true. I had lied. But there was a part of me that wanted to argue, to say it wasn't a lie, per se, more an avoidance of the truth, but semantics weren't going to help me.

Tyler ran his hands through his hair and let out a low breath of air. I stepped closer and lifted my hand to rest it against his chest, but he caught me and held it away. The grip of his fingers dug into my wrist.

"I can't do this," he said, his words broken and strained. "I can't do this here, now. I need space. I need to think, clear my head."

He strode away once again and desperation filled me. "Tyler, please! Don't leave me. Don't—"

"What do you take me for?" Tyler yelled. "Someone you can just walk all over and screw when it suits?" His shoulders heaved with heavy breathing. "Makes me wonder if I should believe anything that comes from your lips."

"Tyler please, you've got it all wrong." All other words failed me.

"Lauren!" he roared. Never had my name sounded so cold on his lips. Our eyes locked. He stared at me coldly, no warmth or flicker of love beating under the surface. Nothing.

"This was a mistake from the beginning. I should have never tried to take you away from Gabe. You lied to him and now you're lying to me."

I fell to my knees. The ground sank beneath me, leaving me in a state of vertigo, but a switch had flipped within Tyler.

He was no longer mine.

Walking over to reception, I heard him ask for another room. His voice, his actions, everything was muted in the background of my mind. By the time I looked up again, Tyler was gone. And no matter how much I wanted to, I couldn't bring him back.

I was still on the floor, hands covering my face, tears falling onto the lavish rug and joining the streaks of light that fell from the chandelier. A hand pressed to my shoulder and for a brief second, hope flooded through my veins.

He had come back.

But it wasn't grey eyes and dark hair that looked down on me. It was blue and blond.

Gabe crouched, wrapping his arms around my shoulders and shielding me from prying eyes. "It's okay," he said. His words were soft and gentle. He pulled my head to his chest, running his hand over the length of my hair. "Shh," he hushed. "I'll talk to him. I'll explain what happened. It was all me."

It was only then I realised I was still crying. And I was doing it rather loudly, on my knees in the middle of the foyer, under the light of the chandelier.

"Come on." Gabe tugged me upwards. "Let's get you out of here." I let him drag me to my feet and pull me towards the elevator. "What level?" he asked once we were inside and staring at the numbers.

"I'm fine," I replied.

"What level?" he asked again.

"Top." We lurched into motion and I leaned back against the cold elevator walls. "You shouldn't be here." I looked over at Gabe. "I shouldn't be here. If Tyler saw us together..." I didn't finish. The thought both saddened and annoyed me. Was I wrong to think that Tyler should trust me?

"I'm just making sure you get to your room okay."

"But if he saw, if he thought—"

"Fuck Tyler," Gabe said abruptly. "He doesn't deserve you, Lauren. To talk to you like that." Gabe shook his head and took a deep breath. He stepped closer, wanting to comfort, wanting to reassure but I backed myself into the wall and covered my face.

"I shouldn't have—"

"You didn't do anything wrong."

Suddenly feeling cold, I wrapped my arms around my chest, essentially hugging myself. "You'll talk to him?" My throat tightened. "I love him. And now I've lost him."

"He doesn't deserve you if this was all it took to put him off." Gabe crossed the space between us. "You know that I will always—"

"Please don't." I drew in a ragged breath. "I just can't." I dissolved into tears again.

Gabe wrapped his arms around me, but I remained limp under his embrace. Everything within me wanted to search for Tyler and explain. Beg. Anything and everything to make him look at me the way he did last night instead of with the coldness of his eyes as he glared at me on my knees in the foyer.

As if reading my thoughts, Gabe murmured against my hair. "You don't owe him anything. Not an explanation or an apology, nothing."

It would have been easy to find reassurance in Gabe's arms. There was a familiarity about him that was comforting. But it wasn't Gabe's arms that I wanted. When the doors slid open silently, I pulled myself away, asking him to stay, asking to be left alone. I felt as though I couldn't breathe with either of them around. The mere proximity of them clouded my brain.

"Is there anything I can do?" he asked.

"Talk to Tyler. Make him understand it wasn't me."

"Of course," Gabe replied. "Consider it done. But you will call me if you need anything?" He looked up with such hopeful eyes, I nodded, knowing that I wouldn't call. No matter what I needed, Gabe would not be the number I would reach for.

"You'll call if you need me?" he repeated.

I nodded again and my eyes locked on him, swimming with tears as the doors to the elevator slid shut and I was left in the hallway. Alone.

29

LAUREN

The hallways that had seemed so empty but filled with promise when I ran along them with Tyler, were now dark and long. I walked quickly to my room and hurriedly shut the door behind me. Leaning on it heavily, I dissolved into tears, letting myself slip until I was a puddle on the floor. The underwater lights of the pool shimmered on the deck and the lights of the city twinkled in the distance, but I didn't care about any of it. Tyler's cold eyes burned into my brain.

I didn't even know how to start sorting through my scattered thoughts. Tyler was mad at me because he thought I had kissed Gabe. But why was he unwilling to listen to me? Why was he so eager to believe I would do that to him? He sounded so cold. So desolate. So definite.

My phone pinged each time a message came through but none of them were from Tyler so I turned it off.

About an hour passed before the sound of people stumbling down the halls crept under the crack of the door. I sat still slumped against it, listening and hoping that one of them would be Tyler.

But they all brushed past my doorway, couples laughing, murmuring words of affection as I sat alone on the floor.

Reaching for my discarded phone, I turned it on. There were still no messages from Tyler. I pressed on his contact and began to tap out a message only to delete it when words failed me. After a wave of imagined brilliance, I tapped out another only to delete it when I read it back and realised how desperate it sounded. Staring at the numbers of the clock, I pressed the palms of my hands to my eyes. I needed to think. I needed to breathe. And trapped here where everything reminded me of him didn't help. I needed comfort. I needed familiarity. And despite my hesitation, there was really only one place that I could get that now, even though my brain was screaming at me to reconsider. Taking a deep breath, I dialled the number.

"Lauren?" A voice burdened with sleep answered. "Lauren, are you alright? I couldn't find you after the—" she stopped talking and gave me the chance to let out one sob-ridden word.

"Mum."

That was the thing about my mother. Despite her harsh words and unrelenting stances on her opinions, if you needed her, she was always there. I just didn't normally need her.

"Where are you, Lauren? I am coming to get you."

"I want to go home." I could barely get the words out.

"Wake up." I imagined Mother shaking a confused Dad awake. "Wake up, we're leaving." Her attention came back to me. "Pack your bags, Lauren. We'll be ready in ten minutes down in the lobby."

"Mum, I need—"

"Hush," she demanded. "We can talk about this on the way home. For now, you just get your stuff. I'll call your sister."

* * *

A dazed Morgan sat in a chair in the lobby, head resting against her hand, the temptation of closing her eyes winning over before waking herself back up every time her head slipped off her hand.

"What's going on?" she asked when I sat down beside her. "Mum wouldn't tell me anything, just that we were going home. Are you coming too?"

Sadie walked through the lobby, stopping when she saw me, a frown crossing her face. "What's going on?"

She hadn't been witness to the incident in the bar, though I was surprised to find that Tyler hadn't gone running to her. Tears welled in my eyes again. I pushed them back but I still couldn't muster a smile.

"Might be best to ask Tyler that."

"Tyler?" Sadie sat down. "What's he done?" Her tone was playful but when she looked into my eyes, she sighed and rested her hand on my thigh. "Do I need to talk to him?"

I shook my head, unable to speak.

"The beautiful bastard yelled at her in front of all these people, basically accusing her of cheating," Morgan said, stifling a yawn.

"Cheating?" Sadie repeated, her frown deepening.

"There was a fight too."

"A fight?" It seemed all Sadie was capable of at this time was repeating words.

"Tyler and Gabe, after he found Gabe and Lauren kissing." The sleep had now left Morgan's eyes and they were awake with gossip instead.

"I didn't kiss him," I added wearily. "He kissed me."

Sadie's eyes grew round. "Gabe kissed you?"

I nodded.

"And Tyler saw?"

I nodded again.

"Shit," she muttered.

"Shit," I repeated.

"Shit," Morgan agreed.

"Language, girls!" Mother scolded, catching the tail end of our conversation.

"I'll find him," Sadie promised. "We'll get this sorted. Don't leave. Not yet."

"He doesn't want to talk to me. I've already tried," I replied. "And to be perfectly honest, it's like the air around here is too thick with Thornton cologne for me to think, to breathe."

"But Tyler wouldn't want—"

"It isn't about what Tyler wants," I said with little emotion in my voice. "It's about what I need. And what I need right now is to get as far away from here as I can."

Sadie pulled me close, patting my shoulder. "I get it. I'll talk to him. I'll explain."

"You shouldn't need to," I replied.

* * *

The car trip home was oddly quiet. Mother didn't lecture me and the rest of my family fell asleep. I was crammed into the back seat with Morgan and Alistair, my head pressed against the glass, staring at the night sky.

My perfect Tyler-shaped bubble had popped but now I was in another kind. One that felt cold and foggy and distanced me from the rest of the world. It made me turn off my phone rather than staring at it constantly, waiting for that one name to appear.

When we finally reached my parents' house, I ignored all the concerned stares and questions regarding my welfare and crawled fully dressed into bed, pulling the covers over my head and drowning myself in darkness.

* * *

Mother shook me awake after what seemed like a second later. "Lauren," she said in the sharp way only Mother could. "Lauren you've got to come see this."

When I made my way into the lounge, the face of the morning news anchor was frozen on the TV screen and red bannered words stood out boldly. THORNTON INDUSTRIES OWNER CRASHES MERCEDES INTO GLASS FRONT OF HIS OWN CASINO.

"What's going on?" I asked.

Dad pressed the remote and the news anchor's face blurred back into motion.

"And finally, we bring to you a rather odd story that unfolded overnight. Police responded to calls after Hamish Thornton, the owner of Thornton Industries, crashed his own car through the lavish glass front of the casino owned by his company. To make matters worse, it was during the opening night of the casino with many important guests and media invited along to the auspicious event."

Images of the shattered glass flashed across the screen, and sure enough, there was Hamish's vehicle planted squarely in the entrance of the lobby. The images switched into motion to reveal a stumbling and drunk Hamish emerging from the vehicle and batting off the people that were attempting to help him. They then switched to him resisting the help of the police and eventually them escorting him away in handcuffs.

The news anchor appeared back on screen. "Photos have also emerged of two of Mr Thornton's sons allegedly in a fist fight earlier on in the evening. Thankfully, no one sustained any serious injuries from either incident." Turning in her chair, the news anchor directed her attention away from the camera and towards the waiting weatherman. "Well, Dan, it sounds as though the evening didn't all go according to plan for the Thornton family."

"One would think not, Hilary," the weatherman replied. "This company better reign in the members of its namesake before they become a 'thorn' in its side."

Dad paused the screen on the news anchor's face mid-smirk and eye roll.

"Seems like that family you are so fond of has got themselves into a spot of bother," Mother said, her brows lifting high in an expression that only meant one thing.

I told you so.

About the Author

Sabre Rose writes about love and lust. Flawed people in messy relationships. Happiness and heartbreak. Loyalty and betrayal.

With stories as unpredictable as they are steamy and intense, Sabre draws you into the lives of her characters and their complicated families.

The ideas floating around her head range from delightful to dark, so sign up to her newsletter at
www.subscribepage.com/sabrerose
to keep up to date with her latest news and releases.

Social Media:
www.facebook.com/sabreroseauthor
www.twitter.com/sabreroseauthor

Website:
www.sabreroseauthor.com

Email:
sabreroseauthor@gmail.com

Other books in the Series

Touched (Thornton Brothers 1)

Tempted (Thornton Brothers 2)

Torn (Thornton Brothers 4)

Printed in Great Britain
by Amazon